YOUR MOVE

Enjoy!

Michelle

YOUR MOVE

A NOVEL

MICHELLE YOUNG

Rock Forest Publishing

Cover Design by Michelle Young
Cover Photograph © Pixabay.com
Author Photograph © Youngs Photography

ISBN-13: 978-1-7750983-2-4

Your Move / Michelle Young. – 1st ed.
Rock Forest Publishing

ALSO BY MICHELLE YOUNG

Salt & Light
Without Fear

For Sarah

"Don't judge yourself by what others did to you."

-C. KENNEDY

PROLOGUE

You don't see me lurking around the corner. I'm not in the shadows. I'm in plain sight, always one step behind you.

You're so busy trying to keep up with the charade of who you're pretending to be for everyone else, that you've stopped looking for me. You've become too self-absorbed to notice I'm still here.

You've probably forgotten all about me after all these years. But I've always been right here, watching you.

You've got a pleasant and simple life now. You've even managed to become quite successful.

I bet you're pretty pleased with yourself. I bet you think you're quite clever to have escaped your old life, but you didn't do a great job, did you? I found you and if I can find you, think about what that means—what I can do.

I've been watching you for a while, waiting to make my move. I know you stopped sleeping with one eye open a long time ago. You're growing more comfortable and confident. I know you've been letting your guard down. It means that when I make my move, you'll lose.

Now is the perfect time to play a little game. Time to pick at that scab you've been working so hard to heal. I know you hoped it wouldn't leave a scar but I can't let you heal, not when you've caused me so much pain.

I know the real you. I know you're full of scars.

Your soul doesn't lie. On the outside, you hide it well. But they don't know you as well as I do. They don't know your deepest scars, the old ones that won't heal. I want to press my fingers inside them and let them bleed for all the hurt you made me suffer. You can pretend to be perfect on the outside, but I know the evil you hide inside. I've seen it.

You might think you've won, but now it's my turn. Don't worry—I'll let you know when the game begins.

PART ONE

1

MONDAY, SEPTEMBER 15TH

CLAIRE

I park in my usual spot closest to the door and step out. I'm always the first one to arrive. Careful to avoid a small puddle on the ground, I sidestep, my tight skirt making it difficult to make such a simple movement. My running shoes clash with my outfit, but I don't care. There's no one else here to see my fashion mishap. Besides, I can't stand to be in heels for longer than is absolutely necessary. Wearing running shoes is my way of silently protesting the acceptable office attire.

The cold mist in the air won't affect my hair too much, unlike most women in the office. Mine, bleach blonde and pin straight, will only mold into a soft wave by the end of the day. I make my way towards the doors of the building and breathe in the coolness of the air. With the beginning of classes a few weeks ago, the traditional initiations and welcome parties have already taken place. I look around and notice the leaves have begun to change colour, making piles on the ground that remind me of my ever-growing workload.

I step into the elevator. The heavy steel door clangs loudly in front of me as I swipe at the apps on my phone.

Uncomfortable in the dim, confined space, I wait impatiently to get up to my floor. I'm still adjusting to the life of routine, but I'm surprised by how much I enjoy it. It's comforting to know what to expect. No room for surprises.

Stepping off the elevator, I turn on the lights as I walk towards my office at the end of the hall. All the other offices are still dark. I'm alone. Being the only one at the office used to unnerve me, but now, I find it comforting. Somehow, being alone feels safer than being surrounded by other people.

As I slump down into my cheap, peeling leather chair, I change out of my running shoes. I wince in pain as I squeeze my feet into the tight, pointy ends of my high heels and focus on a file left on my desk from last week. I sigh as I remember all too well what I need to do today. As a senior communications officer at the University of New Brunswick, I'm working on a social media campaign to market the new programs that will be offered for the winter session.

The promotional group never gives us much notice before announcing any big changes. Most of the departments on campus usually forget that we exist for the better part of the year but, when they need something done, we're suddenly their favourite people in the world.

My director, Phil MacEwan, assigned me to coordinate all our media accounts. I'm to organize a short three-minute video featuring new students attending the university.

He hinted that I should feature the multicultural students to promote the university's progressive diversity. So far, out of hundreds of pictures, I've picked six undergraduate and two graduate students to appear in the video.

My team and I are working on the final touches and will be ready for filming the video in the next few weeks. We're on a tight deadline and can't afford any distractions, so I've delegated my less pressing assignments to my assistant, Sandra. Sandra is a bright, hyper-focused student finishing up her Masters of Arts in photography. She's smarter than half of the people in the office. If there's a problem with a campaign, she'll find it. Where I'm appreciated for my efficiency, clients find Sandra's shy demeanor and personal touches endearing. Physically, we are complete opposites. She's short and carries a little extra weight around the waist. Her red, bob hairstyle, dyed of course, is a contrast to my straight, blonde hair. Sandra also has tiny, piercing green eyes and creamy white skin.

We clicked right away during the interview. Well, as much as I can click with anyone. I knew she wouldn't compete with me professionally, as she will be applying for a different job once her studies are over. She doesn't seem to mind my coldness and doesn't ask too many personal questions, which is perfectly fine by me. She's a hard worker and always stays late, or at least, as late as I do.

I have high standards and Sandra never disappoints. She's saved my ass numerous times on different projects, never hesitating to come to an off-campus client meeting with the important documents I'd printed, but left in the printer at the office.

She knows my schedule better than I do sometimes. She keeps me sane and looking my best in front of high profile clients. If a meeting runs late, she makes sure my next client is taken care of and kept happy until I get back. I'll definitely miss her when she leaves for another job—she'll be hard to replace.

Around ten o'clock, I get up from my desk and pull down on my pencil skirt to adjust where it's been riding up while I sat. I straighten my red silk shirt, careful not to reveal too much cleavage, but also trying to avoid looking like a nun. I grab a handful of bulging manila files and make my way to the conference room.

I feel the tendons in my neck stiffen as I walk on my four-inch heels. God damn it, how I hate those things! Power shoes—that's what my mother calls them. In my opinion, they are just an inch short of an ankle fracture. I'd rather be wearing running shoes any day. At least with those, I can walk without measuring every step. If attacked, I'd even be able to run ahead of anyone who might come after me. Now that's real power. But in this office, I have to follow the dress code. So for now, I'm the Leaning Tower of Pisa—trying my best not to fall on my face.

I rub a hand at the base of my neck where it meets my back and massage my shoulders. I should really schedule a massage soon, I remind myself—the pain is getting worse. The lack of sleep seems to have done me in this time. I'm only managing to clock three hours of sleep a night. My insomnia returned a few months ago as it always does at this time of year.

Only this time, running hasn't cured it.

I'm starting to feel more than just exhausted. It's as though my brain is deteriorating and I can't carry on a conversation as easily as I'm usually able to.

As embarrassing as it is, Sandra has caught me one too many times staring at nothing and asked if I was feeling alright. It's not her fault that she doesn't know. I've never told anyone about my sleep issues or about my other life—the one before my high school graduation.

For me, the past blurs into two sections of time: before graduation and after. I try not to think about the time before. That's where most of my problems started. It's where the insomnia takes me to in the darkest hours of the night. I thought that making a new life would be the best way to move on. Pretend it never happened, pretend I was happy, and if I believed it enough then maybe one day, I would be. I work hard to make it seem like I have it all together, but every September the demons come back.

2

CLAIRE

I find my seat at the front of the room and settle into a mesh office chair at the large mahogany table. I pull myself as close as possible to the table, so I can hide my legs snugly underneath it.

I've always felt uncomfortable in skirts—I hate them.

That and the constant need to cross your legs for fear of showing a little too much. By hiding my long legs under the table, I only need to worry about the top half of my body. I don't want to feel on display or worry about who's seeing what view and what that makes them think about when they go to bed at night. That's why I'm always careful to make sure I'm not sending any signals I don't want to send. I'm a professional and this is my business attire—nothing more.

I try not to focus too hard on the new rolls at my waist. I panicked when I saw them there for the first time last week. My insomnia has dramatically decreased my effectiveness at losing weight. I've given myself two weeks to return to my usual 135 pounds. Not that I care too much about the weight gain. I'm more upset about the loss of strength and speed. I worry that the extra weight is making me lazy. It will take extra care and dedicated runs every night to get back on track, but I can do it—I've done it before.

My red silk blouse is still smooth from ironing this morning. I've been gifted with a decent sized bust and beautiful hair, which I like to keep long and over the shoulder.

Since I graduated from high school, I've been getting highlights and bleaching my hair a lighter blond shade, which seems to compliment my chestnut brown eyes better than my natural dirty blond colour. I have darker roots that always seem to come out only a few weeks after my colouring session—a waste of time and money, if you ask me. I've never bothered to dye my eyebrows; they can stay brown for all I care. I find the darker brows give dimension to my oval face.

I don't wear much jewelry either—I find it unnecessary and too much maintenance. The only jewelry I allow myself is a dainty, gold circle karma necklace which falls just below my collarbone— simple, minimalist. I don't ever bother with earrings as I wear my hair straight and down most of the time in the hopes of reducing the contrasts between my straight nose and the roundness of my high cheekbones. I don't smile often so you'd never know that I have perfect white teeth. I usually stick to a closed-mouth, tight-lipped and slightly-lopsided smile. A wide smile is just not something I allow myself to do anymore.

I believe that in order to smile a genuine smile, like when your face gets all squished and you get wrinkles by your eyes, you need to let your guard down. And if your guard is down, then you're vulnerable. You are allowing yourself to become a victim. I wouldn't want to make the mistake of someone else thinking I was being friendly or inviting. That's why I mostly keep to myself.

I don't own very many things. This tends to surprise people when they find out what I do for a living. True, I make a decent salary and I live alone, but I have no need for spending money.

Money has never been the attraction to my job, nor does it have much impact on the way I live. The safety net I get from having money does, however, help to ease my anxiety a little.

I comfort myself by simply knowing it's there when I need it and that I can use it whenever I want—to run away, to disappear if I ever need to. Having many possessions has never been a priority. The less I have, the quicker I can move away.

***

I look across the large conference room at all the happy smiles and feel annoyed. Sandra who's usually sporting a big smirk on her face, is looking rather grim this morning. Her eyes are downcast and I can't help but wonder if anything's wrong. I quickly shake it off, not wanting to get distracted.

The meeting goes on as normal. There is talk of next steps and who's in charge of what. Sandra takes notes for me, so all that's left is for me to list off responsibilities, mixed with recent accomplishments, so people don't feel overwhelmed or discouraged—not that I care. I'm good at organizing things. I find it necessary.

Time is money, but mostly, I don't like wasting time, not when life doesn't offer a charging station for more of it. I have a no-bullshit approach that people find refreshing. Sure, some find it intimidating, but I get things done and that goes a long way.

I was hired to get a job done and solve problems, not to make people happy. A lot of my work is front facing. I'm often face to face with clients and coworkers, which I don't enjoy very much, but there's also a lot of behind the scenes action with research, analysis and planning. That's what I like most about my job. I prefer dealing with facts, not wishy-washy statements.

It's known around the office that I'm not easily impressed and that I have a knack for grilling people on their ideas to uncover the holes. Sandra and I are both detail-oriented people.

We make a good team.

My director is nearing retirement—he's closing in on sixty-five years old. His face is as pale as his buttercream dress shirt. Phil's wife, Helen, most likely tried to revive his outfit by forcing him to wear a gaudy, bright blue and gold checkered tie. If you look closely enough, you can pretend that it compliments his small, close-set, blue eyes. I can imagine she tried her best to make him look good but failed miserably as the tie completely clashes with his thirty-year-old worn-out grey suit. Phil is a proud man but has no sense of style. He's had the same hairstyle since I started working here over a decade ago. His thinning grey hair is forever slightly combed to the right, similar to a cowlick, but on purpose.

He's leaning with both forearms flat on the table, his knuckle hair as overgrown and crooked as his ear and nose hairs. He's looking at me over the thin, gold frame of his bifocal glasses. I imagine they are the same age as his suit. Phil is quiet and reserved and typically gets me to do all his dirty work for him. Things like hiring and firing or anything he doesn't feel like doing, really. His way of justifying this is that he claims I'm better at it than he is. He's not wrong, but I know it's also because he's a people-pleaser and weak in character. He has a hard time making decisions.

I've been working for the university since completing my four-year undergraduate degree. At the beginning of every year, our office hosts a press conference and launches a "Welcome New Students" campaign, which costs the university an atrocious amount of money.

So much money goes into creating this campaign that I'm convinced a good percentage of each student's tuition goes directly towards funding it.

I'm usually extremely content to be behind the scenes at these press conferences. I much prefer my place be in the back, hiding behind the curtain—unseen. But since I've been working here ten years now, Phil thought it might be important to put a face to the name and for people to finally see who leads the communications department at the university.

Phil hadn't cared how often I'd objected to his request to appear in front of the camera to give a speech or even that I'd threatened to call in sick that day. There was no going around it. He countered that if he had to drag me out of my apartment and drive me to work himself, he would do it. This was confidence I'd never seen in him before. It was so out of character. I didn't want to risk him following through on his threat. I believed him, and rather than being forced to do it, I made myself believe it was my idea.

My little speech only lasted about three minutes. I had a lump in my throat the entire time. All my confident persona had evaporated and was replaced by sheer fear. It was humiliating for me. I felt like it dragged on for hours before the camera returned to Phil and I quickly got to escape back to my preferred place behind the media backdrop. Once the conference was over, I begged Phil never to force me into that position again.

He wasn't pleased, and he even threatened that if I wanted to become Director of Communications after he retired, I had better find a way to get comfortable being seen by the public and fast.

Phil didn't understand that my fear of going in front of the camera had nothing to do with stage fright. It was about preserving my anonymity. For me, it was about survival.

***

As the minutes fly by, the morning meeting is nearing a close for the day. I don't always pay attention to the rest of the team's responsibilities in these meetings and often find myself losing focus. My mind usually wonders through the dark corners of my past. I've talked to Phil repeatedly about cancelling meetings altogether, arguing that they are a thing of the past and that we'd be better off working that extra hour, as most meetings end up in chit chat. He believes it's good for morale and team building. Something he says I should learn more about.

I don't see the point of worrying about everyone else's tasks and to-do lists when I've got enough of my own. Some pressing ones at that. Taking Phil's cue, I nod at him across the table and launch into my next course of action for the upcoming video project. I begin by addressing my newest team member in charge of scheduling the videos segments.

"Devon, I'll need you to call the videographers back and tell them that Tuesday afternoon works to film Prisha's part of the video. It shouldn't take more than ten minutes to get that take. We only truly need thirty seconds of usable footage. Can I count on you to be available to oversee that everything goes smoothly?" I expect more than question. She nods nervously, not yet used to my style of management.

After I quickly assign the remainder of the tasks to the rest of my team, the meeting is done, and we all go back to our respective offices. My office is the last one down the hall.

I have a slight panel window in my thick, wooden door, a feature which I appreciate as it allows me to see who's on the other side.

Having no window behind me makes it impossible for opposing offices to look in while I work into the evenings, which is perfect for me. I barely sit down at my desk when I hear a soft knock on the door.

"Excuse me, Claire." Sandra speaks tentatively, her green, almond-shaped eyes looking anywhere but directly at me. Dread comes over me. Great, this is something personal.

I suppress my impatience and remind myself to be sympathetic. Sandra is uncomfortable, which is making me uncomfortable. I'm not in the mood to pry it out of her. I'm too busy for an emotional exchange. If she wants to share something with me, she'd better do it quickly so I can get back to work. Rifling through paperwork in one of the manila folders, my response is a bit curt, as though I've only got two seconds for her.

"What is it, Sandra?" I demand with an exasperated tone, never once making eye contact with her. My body language lets her know this conversation is neither wanted, nor purposeful to the task at hand, and that she is wasting my time. Not because I'm truly that busy, but because I need to keep up the hard-ass-boss persona so she will stay on her toes, never let her guard down, and never assume that we're friends—because we're not, and I need her to respect me.

I realize I've been biting the dead skin off my lips again, which reminds me that I haven't had any water since earlier this morning. I snap back to focus, needing to keep my mask on. While Sandra's here, I break my rule and look up to see her wide eyes filling with tears.

She is clutching her own stack of folders tightly to her chest, her fingers littered with costume jewelry rings, leaving green stains on her porcelain white fingers when the rings shift, the tarnish strangely matching her eyes. My first instinct is concern, but I brush it off hurriedly before she notices.

There was a time when I was younger when all I wanted was to make friends and be likable, but not anymore. I need to stay focused and not let my old self show. I stand up quickly, not bothering to adjust my skirt and I motion for her to sit down as I shut the door behind her.

"What's wrong?" I ask both annoyed and curious, still standing behind her, my hand on the door knob, before quickly adding, "This is not the place for an emotional breakdown." She twists at the waist to face me, but I stare at the top of her head as she swallows back heavy sobs, her short, red bob shaking uncontrollably. Ah crap, she's crying. I swear softly under my breath as I worry I was too hard on her. I grab a tissue from my desk and hand it to her. She takes this as an open invitation to spill her guts in my office.

"It's Matt," she blurts out, a little too loudly. I glance at her and notice saliva making a disgusting web-like string connecting her top teeth and her bottom lip. "I'm sorry," she adds, stuttering through the rest of her story, mouth wet with spit, which she wipes off with the back of her hand. "We're having a big fight and...," she finally blurts out.

She's making a scene.

I catch Devon and our intern Sophie walking by and eying me suspiciously, like I've got something to do with the state Sandra's in.

Seeing where this is going and not wanting my best assistant to mistake me for one of her peers or her psychologist, I decide I've allowed this scene to unravel for a few minutes too long.

I cut her off mid-sentence, "Look, why don't you go wash up in the bathroom. Don't speak to anyone on your way there and feel free to take the rest of the day off." I pause a moment. "I'll see you tomorrow when you're feeling better."

I open the door, a universal sign and invitation for her to leave, and start moving back to my desk. She nods her understanding and after another minute, she dabs the used tissue under her eyes and gathers her strength. She stands up and runs a hand through her hair as she quietly thanks me and turns to go.

I watch Sandra leave as the door shuts softly behind her, her eyes down. I see her grab her pink fall coat off the hanger by her desk, tears streaming down her face, and I feel my frustration growing. I should have anticipated this when I made a personal rule to only hire women.

This is all my fault—I brought this onto myself. Why do women always have to be so damn emotional? Why do they all seem to think I'm their best friend? I do everything I possibly can to avoid these annoying meltdowns at the office, but with all of these women around, it's difficult to go one week without one of them breaking down and crying. I may have to consider hiring a few men to tip back the scales on the emotional front and balance things out.

I know sometimes hormones come into play, making it hard to control our emotions, but crying over a man, especially one that treats you well, makes no sense to me. Women give men too much power over their emotions.

I used to be just like Sandra, but never again. I learned that difficult lesson a long time ago. Women are confusing. I don't like women, but I hate men. If men ignore us, we like them. If they dote on us, we find them lame. If they are kind, we don't find them attractive. If they treat us badly, usually we don't learn our lesson and we go back for more.

I haven't had a boyfriend since before graduating from high school and I never will again. Don't get me wrong, I used to like men—a lot. I just can't trust them anymore.

I'm not suggesting I've "turned into" a lesbian, as my parents fear, being the traditional Anglican Christian folks that they are. No, I'm just declaring it's just me and that's fine. No one to answer to, no one touching my things, and no one close enough to hurt me. I keep everyone at arm's length—never letting them see the real me. This is the only way I can retain what little distance I've managed to acquire since graduation. Rebecca, my oldest friend from high school, is really the only friend I still have from before graduation and even she doesn't know the real story about that day.

***

I decide to take a break for lunch and head down to the Student Centre which houses the university's cafeteria. The grey cement walls close in on me as I make my way down three narrow flights of stairs.

A deafening hubbub is coming through the open, double metal doors of the cafeteria where a gate separates the vendor booths and the tables. Hundreds of students are eating an assortment of different foods.

Clusters of loud students are chatting at some tables while in a nearby chair, a lonely student, nose-deep inside a textbook, is already getting ready for exams, even though reading week isn't coming up for a few months.

Without meaning to, my nose wrinkles in judgement. Over-achiever much?

September is too early in the term to be worrying about exams. It is supposed to be the best month of all, besides the end of term, that is. The first month of the semester should be all about the parties, making fun of your professors, trying to mingle, and making new friends. It should be about having fun, making mistakes, and getting lost while navigating through all the buildings trying to find your class.

Unfortunately, the month that held magical properties and that used to bring butterflies of excitement in my stomach, has been tarnished and replaced with a strong sense of fear and nausea. It's become one of the months I hate the most, one associated with a great sense of loss. A month darker than even the coldest, gloomiest day in January.

3

CLAIRE

Standing at the counter, I'm having a hard time choosing what I want to eat for lunch. I settle on a shiny, bright green, Granny Smith apple, a pack of overpriced celery, and carrot sticks with ranch dip.

I make a mental note to grab some groceries soon or this new habit of buying lunch is going to cost me a small fortune. It's a good thing lunch is the only meal I buy, as I always make sure to bring dinner with me.

As I reach to grab my leather wallet from under my arm, my index finger catches in the gold chain of my necklace, which breaks off my neck. I feel a sharp pinch at the back of my neck as the delicate chain makes a soft clang on the tiled floor.

"Crap!" I murmur quietly to myself as I frantically search the ground to find out where it landed before someone steps on it.

I spot it a few feet away where it must have flown through the air. Quickly, I bend down to grab the chain from the floor to inspect it and realize to my disappointment that it's broken. I sigh as I put it in the zipper pocket of my wallet, next to my coins. *That's not good*, I think as I hand over a ten-dollar bill and get no change back. A broken necklace is one of the only bad omens I believe to actually bring on bad luck.

Suddenly paranoid, the noise of the crowd too loud, I make my way hastily back up the stairs.

I feel my breathing quickening as I rush back to my office and lean on the closed door in an attempt to calm myself. I'll be hunkered down in my office for the rest of the afternoon, speaking to as few people as possible, hoping the day passes by quickly with no more hiccups. I grab my stress ball and calmly squeeze it ten times per hand to force my heartbeat to return to normal. I don't believe in good luck. But bad luck? I've had enough first-hand experience to know that it definitely exists. And that for some reason, it enjoys picking on me.

***

After lunch, I get up to use the bathroom and when I return, I'm surprised to find Rebecca sitting in my office in the same chair Sandra vacated a few hours ago.

"Hey!" I exclaim, surprise on my face. "What are you doing here?" I add with a smile as I shut the door behind me.

"Hi! I was meeting a client on campus and thought I'd swing over to see you quickly before heading back to the office," she explains. "I tried to call, but you know how spotty reception can be in these cement buildings!" She waves a hand with annoyance.

I know all too well what she means. We work solely with landlines on campus for that very reason.

"So, where's your perky assistant today?" she asks, and I tell her briefly that I let her leave early for personal reasons. We talk for a few minutes before she grabs her large tote bag to dig through it for her red lipstick and applies it while talking about her client meeting. After a while, I glance at the clock and tell her I should really get back to work.

"Do you have any plans tonight? We should grab dinner," she offers.

"Sorry, I've got plans with some other ladies tonight, but I'll send you some dates when I'm free and we can plan something, OK?" I suggest.

"Sounds good." She nods as she stands and wraps her coat around her slender frame before waving at me, "Well, I better be off or the wolves will hunt me down."

This is how she refers to her bosses at the law firm.

"Talk soon!" I wave as I watch her walk down the hall.

***

By early evening, I'm on my third green tea of the day and I've answered a few more emails when my stomach begins to gurgle hungrily. I find dinner in my bag and immediately dig into the crispy, romaine lettuce salad, tossed with flaky, pink tuna, chopped fresh celery, carrots, sliced cucumber and roasted pumpkin seeds.

This morning I opted for an apple cider vinegar and oil-based vinaigrette over my favourite, creamy, French dressing. It's a small step, but over time, I'll begin to notice the results.

Although I feel calmer now, I've kept my office door closed all afternoon. For one, I want the privacy, but also so the smell of the fish doesn't reach my intern, Sophie, down the hall. She has severe fish allergies—or so she claims. I eat fish at least three times a week at the office and she's never once complained about being bothered. I don't care for liars, so I tend not to be sympathetic to their demands.

When you work long hours as I do, you need to plan your meals ahead of time so as not to fall off track of your training routine.

Lunch is usually a grey area for my meal planning, as I never know if I'll be stepping into a meeting or meeting with a client off-campus for marketing services or new promotional material. I often end up buying my lunch, but make a large breakfast at home and bring left-overs for dinner at work.

I'm enjoying my salad when my desk phone rings, the shrill noise piercing the peaceful silence. I wince at the sound, snapping out of the focused attention on my computer screen. I reach for the offending object and I suddenly realize that I've had my legs crossed making my upper body slouch at an awkward angle.

I was so focused on editing this media campaign that I didn't even realize I had been slowly inching closer to the computer. Damn it. That will guarantee a tension headache tonight. I quickly swallow my last bite before answering the call on the third ring. As I pick up the receiver, I swivel in my chair to toss my crumpled-up paper napkin into the trash bin behind my desk, not bothering to check the caller ID before I speak into the phone.

"Claire Martel" I answer, doing my best to sound calm and collected, pretending I didn't just scarf down my salad. I really hate when you can hear people eating on the other end of the phone. I find it so rude. Unfortunately, with my busy schedule and demanding deadlines, I've also picked up this nasty habit. Why waste the opportunity to answer a call and deal with it right away? Better that than having it go to voicemail and cause a lengthy phone tag situation that's just unnecessary and annoying to everyone.

After a few seconds of silence, I press the phone to my ear and listen harder but hear nothing. I wait a few seconds for the caller to introduce themselves, but they don't.

"Hello? Is anyone there?" I ask in the plastic receiver, my voice feigning polite annoyance.

Still no answer.

Irritated, I turn back towards my computer screen, phone pressed to my ear and start scanning my emails. I lazily gaze at the receiver for a number, but the display reads "Private number".

I frown and decide it's just a wrong number. Just as I'm about the hang up, I hear heavy breathing and a muffled sound in the background.

Is that a woman's voice?

I press my palm on my other ear trying to make out what I'm hearing. Is she yelling something? I'm about to speak, when the call cuts out and all I can hear is the long beep of the dead dial tone.

4

CLAIRE

"What the hell?" I ask out loud in my empty office. "That was strange." I frown as I stare at the receiver, bewildered.

I decide that the call was most likely a pocket dial and the caller probably has no idea they've even called me. They might realize their mistake this evening and follow-up later on. I shake off the strange event and mark the time and date of the call in my notebook. I decide to get up and check down the hall to see who is still in the office, but the hallways are empty—I'm alone.

When people see my closed office door, they know not to disturb me. I guess that also means skipping the goodbye when they head home for the night.

I usually prefer to avoid all the gossip and pointless chatter that often happens before people end their work day and start packing it in to go home to their loved ones. But tonight, with the cold, wet, fall evening and the strange call, I wouldn't have minded the company of a few colleagues.

Shutting my office door gives me privacy, but it also creates a barrier, stopping me from creating new relationships. I don't make friends easily. I don't mix well with most people because I tend not to trust others. But who can you really trust anyway?

Probably no one.

The people closest to us have the potential to cause us the greatest pain.

They know our personality, our habits and our favourite hang-out spots. We let our guard down when we're around them and don't see them as a threat, but very often, those closest to us are the most dangerous people of all.

My arms are covered in tiny goose bumps and I suddenly realize that I'm cold. As it's the end of the work day, the building manager usually tries to save on heating costs and turns the temperature down by several degrees after four o'clock.

I try to see outside through my narrow door's panel window, but it's dark and all I see is an unfocused reflection of myself. I check the time. It's only five o'clock. Why does fall always have to be so dark and gloomy? It's so miserable to get to work in the dark and leave work at the end of the day in the cold blackness as well, never seeing the sun, but for a quick glimpse at lunch time.

Thankfully, I have plans with the girls tonight. It was a nice surprise to see Rebecca today, even briefly. She's my oldest friend, one of the only ones I can truly trust and enjoy spending time with. I need to make a note to send her some dates to get together. I wish I could have stayed in and hung out with her tonight. She's so easy going. I need to pump myself up before I go meet the girls. They are the only few women I was able to stand during my undergrad.

I normally don't enjoy social outings during weeknights as I'm usually content to go back to my apartment, go for a run, have a glass of wine and fall into my bed until morning. But it's been several months since I last saw the girls, so it might be good to go.

Plus, I need to keep up appearances of being a normal thirty-two-year-old with a social life. Not that I care what everyone else thinks—just him.

I pick at the dry skin on my lip as I contemplate the last time I saw them, the argument I'd had with Val. Her audacity in talking down to me, happily pointing out where my life fell short, acting oh-so-perfect with her little life so put together.

If only she knew the truth.

The worst is when she gets all vindictive and sure of herself and just lays it on me, never caring about my feelings. Even if I pretend I don't care, it cuts right through me. Inside, I'm still who I used to be, after all.

Val's poisonous words seep from her own insecurities. I know this, but it doesn't make it any easier. I usually try to keep my face unchanged so that no matter how deep she digs, she will not be able to touch me.

Val is used to telling others what to do all day. She's bossy by nature, being an elementary school teacher. But when the time comes for her to sit back and learn something, her mind just shuts down, her own arrogance blocking anything new from reaching her. She has confidence that is really unwise.

No one knows everything. If someone can teach you something, I believe you should gladly take that new knowledge and run with it. It doesn't matter if you use it or not, just keep learning. Always keep improving yourself. That's what I think anyway.

But not Val. She is certain that she's already perfect. That all she's missing is the perfect man. Well, she can tie herself down to one man for the rest of her life and pop out a dozen kids if she wants, destroy her career, and get on the Parent-Teacher Association of her kids' elementary school, for all I care.

OK, so I'm not her biggest fan, that's obvious. We tolerate each other in public.

I'm careful to keep my opinions about her life choices to myself—well, most of the time anyway. I know she senses my disapproval of her choices as she is constantly trying to justify them to me. She believes she's figured out the secret to life. That the secret to happiness is to be with someone else. And she will not hesitate to point out how I'm wrong to want to remain alone forever.

Part of me thinks she pities me. She thinks being alone is the worst thing in the world—a curse leading directly to unhappiness. Val's jumped from boyfriend to boyfriend for as long as I've known her. A serial-romantic, is what I call her. She's never stayed single for more than a month between boyfriends and is always "in love" with whomever she's with at the time. So when she gets on her soap box to tell me about how she's figured out the secret to a fulfilled life and found the love of her life, forgive me if I don't buy her act and space out mid-conversation. I just know how she operates and that next time I see her, she'll be all about some new guy. She's spent most of her twenties looking for "the one"—whatever that means.

I believe you should complete yourself, and not be completed by someone else. It's better to know who you are, your likes and dislikes, before beginning a new relationship. It's too easy to get confused and molded into someone different, just to make your partner happy.

It's a dicey game to play when your own happiness depends on how your relationship is going or how your partner views you. I wouldn't put that kind of pressure on anyone when I don't even really know yet what makes me happy.

**

Doing my best to remain productive and ignore the earlier strange phone call, I write my to-do list for tomorrow and shut down my computer for the night. I grab my forest green pea coat before heading to the outdoor parking lot. As I slip my arms in the coat's sleeves, I realize the red and green outfit faux-pas and curse under my breath "Great, I look like a damn Christmas tree today. Why am I only noticing this now?"

As soon as I realize I've divulged this out loud, I immediately feel both embarrassed and grateful to be alone in the office. This would have been a major set-back in the persona I'm trying to uphold here.

I really do need to get more sleep. I'm not at my best right now.

Walking down the narrow hall, I look into the other open offices on my way by and notice Devon's desk lamp is still on but her coat, shoes, and purse are gone. She must have forgotten it. I hesitantly walk in, feeling frustrated by her carelessness and shut off the lamp.

I make a mental note to discuss this with her in the morning. I feel like I'm constantly having to double-check her reports lately. She works fast to impress me, but her work is sloppy. I might need to let her go, but it won't be that hard to do as she's still well within her three-month probation period.

Hurrying to the elevator doors with my black Coach purse, keys in hand, I begin to go through my day's check list. I really need to get a run in to clear my head before going out tonight. My legs are stiff from lack of exercise, not that I won't place the blame on those damn heels.

As I reach the third floor of the building, I realize I've been so distracted by the earlier phone call that I've forgotten my running shoes upstairs under my desk and my scarf on the back of my chair.

I exhale, annoyed by my own forgetfulness and press the button to bring me back up to the office on the tenth floor. I walk hurriedly back down the same hallway I've just come from and near my office, I do a double-take.

Devon's desk light is on.

5

CLAIRE

Standing in Devon's office doorway confused, I stare at the light as my feet refuse to move, my body physically holding me back. I quickly do a mental check. Did I shut it off correctly before? Maybe the switch didn't latch on properly? It's a simple on/off switch.

Any idiot could get it right.

I wasn't gone that long—a few minutes at most. I frown slightly, my dark brows inching closer to the middle of my forehead, feeling the back of my neck grow cold. There has to be a reasonable explanation for this.

My hand automatically reaches for my necklace, only to find my neck bare. Right, I broke my chain. Then my brain starts to spin. First the anonymous call, now this defective light switch.

Can it be a coincidence?

I glance behind my shoulder and decide to do a quick walk around the office to check the conference room and the other offices before I grab my scarf and shoes.

As far as I can see, I'm still the only one in the office. I decide that Devon was almost certainly in the washroom before and returned to her desk while I was in the elevator to grab something she'd forgotten, just as I did and most likely forgot her light was on again.

Although that seems unlikely.

What else could explain this strange occurrence?

My mind races a mile a minute thinking of many not so innocent scenarios, paranoia enveloping me, like the scarf tightening around my neck. Trying to calm my mind, I think of more mundane options.

Maybe someone from the cleaning crew came in to empty her trash bin and turned it on. I quickly rule that out as I see no sign of a cleaner around. Feeling my earlier headache coming on stronger now, I decide that it's well past time I go home and clear my head.

When I reach the ground floor, the elevator pings and the doors open. My heart is beating fast in my chest as I half-expect to see a guy with a black ski mask coming at me with an axe, but no one is waiting for me.

I force a laugh and shake my head at my silliness.

I push through the circular swivel doors and breathe in the scent of the wet pavement, the cold air, and a faint earthworm smell. The rain has covered the asphalt making it shiny, the puddles reflecting the parking lot lights. I feel my shoulders relax when I spot my car in the parking lot.

My white 2016 Acura TLX sedan is waiting for me, music blaring and heater on. OK, maybe having money does have its perks—like automatic starters and sweet rims, for instance. As usual, mine is one of the last cars left in the Hazen Hall parking lot. This is one of those rare instances where being alone isn't ideal. I never feel safe at night anymore.

Cursing to myself that I never took the time to change into my running shoes, I do a quick scan of the nearby street and the other possible hiding spots around the building. Then I run as fast as I can manage in my stupid high heeled shoes, clicking the unlock button about five times before I reach the handle.

Although, I'm certain no one saw my weak attempt at a sprint in heels, I still hope I made it look effortless.

I yank open my door and sink into the black, leather interior. I take a peak in the back seat and immediately lock the doors. Not lingering much longer, I switch my phone to Bluetooth and pick a playlist with country music before I put the car in drive and speed off towards home, making sure to drive fast through all the deepest puddles as I go.

What can I say? Sometimes in moments of stress, I prefer to be reckless. Who doesn't like to have a little fun sometimes?

When we feel challenged or scared, our *fight or flight* reflexes kicks in. In past situations, my response to fear has always been flight, but as part of my new personality, I'm trying to change my response to fight. Whenever opposed or terrified, I try to shrug it off and act tougher than I really feel.

It works in business—usually.

However, it doesn't always work in every aspect of my life. For now, I'm choosing to act as though the fear slowly taking up residence in my mind doesn't bother me and I speed quickly away from what scared me at the office. So maybe my reflex is still flight?

At least it's faster in the car than on foot.

I try so hard to hide my true feelings and my fears. I don't usually act out in public. So on this dark, wet night, I can allow a little bit of leeway. I mean come on, a deep pot hole filled to the brim with water is like a dare just waiting to be taken.

No one else ever sees this side of me. Well, not anymore.

Now the fun is mine alone.

***

The drive to my apartment takes me just ten minutes in traffic. The car is only a safety measure, not a necessity. Crown Street isn't far from my office, which is extremely convenient for me as I don't like to waste time and want to capitalize on my evenings doing what I enjoy the most—running.

I love my apartment because of its location in a quiet residential area with lovely views of the St. John River, but also because the price is very reasonable. For a two-bedroom suite, I'm only paying $1,600 a month. There are brand new, stainless steel appliances, and granite counters in the kitchen. The kitchen backs onto the master bedroom and hosts a large island, big enough to fit four stools. The island spills into the living room where there is a cozy fireplace and large picture windows with the original brick arches.

Because of the dark oak hardwood floors, I've been in the habit of immediately removing my shoes at the door. I carry them to my bedroom and toss them haphazardly onto the large hand-woven beige area rug I purchased to fit under my king size bed. A lot of people don't approve that I live alone and have a king size bed, but why not? With my insomnia, I want to be as comfortable as I can be—it works for me.

I still remember the quizzical look the property manager gave me when I was searching for apartments. I was very picky about location and which floor it would be on, not wanting any windows to be accessible from the ground. Of course, I never shared this with her, but I was willing to pay extra to have fewest other apartments on the same floor. She wasn't used to showing two-bedroom apartments to single women who didn't have plans of turning one of the bedrooms into an office to work from home.

I saw six apartments that day, but this one stood out to me, being on Crown Street so high above the ground floor. Rebecca had come with me to look for an apartment and insisted I take this one on the seventh floor to bring me good luck. Figuring I could use all the good luck I could get, I signed the papers that day. The property manager was glad to have me off her to-do list, and I was excited to have a place of my own.

Growing up in an old-story-and-a-half house near the beach, I feel the modern apartment is a nice change. Although I live in the city now, my heart still belongs to the beach. I don't own very many personalized pieces, but I figured if I was going to be living here, I may as well make it as comfortable as possible. It had taken me awhile to find just the right pieces, but I'd managed to find furniture that resembled my childhood home, with a twist.

I would have preferred a bedroom with no window, but of course, that would go against regulations, so I've resolved to dark, heavy wool black-out curtains to cover the fantastic view from the bedroom. Most people consider it a shame, but I feel it's a necessity.

I walk directly to my three door closet to pick out a pair of faded, ripped, skinny jeans and a sequined, black, sleeveless shirt I've picked out for tonight. I lay them on the wicker chair in the corner of the room.

I grab my favourite black Adidas running tights that keep me warm during rainy fall days. Over a white T-shirt, I slip on my full zip pullover jacket, the one with the three stripes on the left arm. I put my day running shoes back in the closet and pick-out this year's 'best shoe', the Asics GT-2000 5, in bright pink. They are so comfortable and great for a long run. I wish I could wear them to the office, but I doubt Phil would approve.

Why do men get to decide a woman's dress code anyway? That never made sense to me.

As I tie my shoes, I think that these Asics would certainly make it easier to chase around after Sandra and Devon for their files in the long, narrow hallways whenever I need them to do something. I laugh darkly. Like I need better footwear to catch up to them. They don't get anywhere very fast.

I grab my phone and my keys and leave the apartment to start my run.

I feel no desire to wear earphones, because I always want to hear the noise around me. I prefer to be constantly aware of my surroundings, especially with cars weaving closely around me. The only thing they would see are the stripes on my jacket reflecting the street light.

As soon as my feet hit the wet pavement, I feel the tension in my neck dissipating and my headache fleeing. Running is the only thing from my past that has always remained loyal to me—a true friend. When I run, I don't have to pretend to be anyone else—I'm just me.

I curve to the right to run past the park edging on the bay. It's so peaceful here at night in contrast to the daytime when the place is packed with tourists and people having lunch and taking long walks by the water.

I don't love running at night as it's not the safest, but it does have its perks, one being tranquility. I have three different routes I alternate between, but I never do them in the same order.

It may seem very strange to some. If they only knew everything I do on a daily basis to keep myself safe.

Call it what you will, paranoia or anxiety, it's this very mindset that's kept me hidden and safe on my own for all these years.

I like routine at work, but not for my runs, not when I'm alone.

***

At six p.m., I start to make my way back.

I run all the way up to Crown Street and then walk the rest of the way, to catch my breath, and relax my muscles. The idea of a shower sounds pretty good right about now.

While the elevator takes me up to my floor, I reach for my keys, but they slip out of my hand and fall with a loud clang to the metal floor of the elevator. My hand is slippery with sweat. The sound makes me cringe and all the peace I'd felt on the run evaporates. The familiar kink in my neck is making its presence known once more.

As soon as I retrieve my keys, a bead of sweat falls from the crown of my hair, down the bridge of my nose, and onto the floor of the metal elevator, moving at an agonizingly slow pace.

When its doors finally open, I walk to my suite, Apartment 704. As soon as I open the door, I know something is wrong. I feel the hair on the back of my neck rise up.

To someone else, everything would seem fine as nothing obvious has been tampered with and nothing is missing. Everything is exactly as I left it a little over an hour ago, but I'm not fooled. I can sense it in my gut.

Someone has been in here. I just know it—I can feel it.

They've left a faint, lingering smell behind—an odor that reminds me of wetness and grass, like the dew in the morning.

I think I can even detect a whiff of Ralph Lauren Polo fragrance. Dread overcomes me as I realize I recognize that smell, my mind racing in a panic.

Someone's definitely been in here. Someone might still be hiding in here.

I tighten the hold on my phone, the dial set to 911 just in case, as I quietly scan the open floor plan. My mind is going crazy with different scenarios as my heart pounds loudly, making it hard to hear my own thoughts.

I want to run away, but I don't. I know exactly who was here, who might still be here, and what they might want to do if they've come all this way and snuck into my apartment.

I have no time to think about what all this means. That after all this time, I've been discovered. That I've been followed and that I'm no longer safe.

I cling to my keys, my only weapon, for protection and start slowly making my way through the apartment. At first glance, the kitchen and living spaces seem to be intact. Nothing seems different here.

My eyes dart around the room frantically as I try to see if anyone is hiding somewhere.

I peek behind the couch and under the bed. The heavy curtains are still drawn as I'd left them earlier, but I check behind them too. My purse is still flopped on the kitchen island next to my salad container soaking in the sink, untouched.

I'm alone.

Whoever it is that was in here earlier isn't here now. They weren't interested in my purse, so what did they want? Their goal wasn't to surprise me, it was to send me a message.

As I stand in the apartment, I go through all the possible reasons someone might want to break in. What were they looking for? I realize quickly that I don't even need to ask what they were looking for. I already know exactly why they were here.

I know what they want.

Me. They want me.

6

CLAIRE

I slowly approach my bedroom and my breath catches in my throat. My sequined top and jeans aren't where I left them an hour ago on the wicker chair. Instead, they've been rearranged on my bed.

My clothes are laid out on the duvet in a casual manner, in a way that looks as though I'm lying down on it for a nap, or dead even—lifeless.

A warning?

Perhaps.

My suspicions from earlier are now confirmed. My necklace breaking had been a sign of bad luck coming my way. A cold shudder runs down my spine and my sweaty forehead dries up instantly.

I should leave this place immediately.

My fight or flight instincts are on high alert. My privacy and my safe haven have been invaded. I need to find a secure spot and then call the police, but what would I say to them? That someone has moved my clothes but stolen nothing? Who would believe me anyway?

No, I'm not going to involve the police. Not yet. Not when I have so much to lose and when they might ask questions I don't want to answer. Not when I need to stay under the radar. The last thing I need is for my secret to be exposed.

I glance at the clock. Crap, it's already 7 p.m.

I'm supposed to meet the girls at a bar in town in half an hour.

I try to remain calm and shake off the creepiness of what I've just discovered. A familiar, unsettling feeling in my gut returns. I decide that now, especially now, I need to remain in character. I need him to think he hasn't gotten to me, that I'm not afraid of him. I must keep my commitment to the girls. It will be better if others see me tonight and I do my best to act normal, or at least the normal that they expect of me. I can't let others see me acting differently and asking questions.

As I rush around the apartment and enter my tiny three-piece bathroom, I am hit once again with a wave of panic. There's that smell again. I feel a lump in my throat, my whiney-teenage-self entering my mind.

I don't want to do this anymore. Make it stop.

The shower curtain is pulled across the tub, another sign that someone's been tampering with my things. I know someone else was here because I never leave the shower curtain draped across the tub. No one else would have paid any attention to a shower curtain, except for me.

I hesitate for a couple of seconds as a motivating mantra echoes in my mind. *Just do it! Do it now!*

I yank at the fabric quickly and unhinge one of the plastic rings from the top by pulling too hard in my haste. One of the corners of the curtain falls and brushes my forearm, making me jump and take a step backwards quickly, my shoulder colliding with the open door.

I release a breath when I notice that the bathtub is empty.

There are only my bottles of shampoo and conditioner left to scare me. Relief floods over me and then shame. When did I become so paranoid? Maybe I'm the one who needs a psychologist, not Sandra. What if I'm imagining things?

I scan the apartment one more time before I lock the bathroom door behind me and turn on the hot water. As the steam rolls in, I remove my wet running gear and untie my hair from its ponytail. I step into the white shower/bathtub combo and pull the curtain across, making sure to leave a crack for protection—as though the thin fabric can be a shield from the exterior world. A makeshift security attempt, just in case someone manages to unlock the door and scare me. I stand under the warm jet of water as it slowly washes away my sweat and fear, or so I hope. I start to doubt and replay the day's events in my mind.

Had I left the shower curtain closed?

No, of course not.

I never, ever, leave it closed before I exit the bathroom. I usually draw the curtain after each shower, to let the water drip and to allow it to dry, but only while I do my hair and make-up. I always push it wide open before I leave the bathroom.

Ever since I was little, I've been afraid of closed shower curtains. Afraid to even be in the room with the door closed until I'd pulled back the fabric to make sure I was indeed alone. I've always thought it would be the perfect hiding spot for someone who might want to hurt me.

I think back to this morning after my shower, but I'm sure I left it open, as usual, on my way out.

It's just one of those daily habits I don't spend too much time thinking about, one that I do automatically, every day, without fail.

It's a habit I developed in order to feel safe, to know that I'm the only one in the apartment. Something I developed over time as a woman living alone in the big city.

Every night, I do a walk-through of my small apartment. I check every window and door latch to make sure there is no one in the bathroom, but now, I'm at a loss. Why would someone draw the curtain? To scare me? As a way to let me know they are watching?

Well, message received.

It takes me a while to slow down my breathing. What does this all mean?

I continue analyzing today's events as I blow dry my long hair, not worrying about drying it completely. Especially in this wet weather, it would just be a waste of time, not to mention the hundreds of split ends it would give me. I decide to leave it a little damp. My hair is so straight that it doesn't matter if the blow dryer dries it or if the wind does. I guess I should feel grateful that it almost never gets frizzy—something I often take for granted.

As I brush the long tresses and reapply a little make-up, my mind drifts to Emma, one of the other girls I'll be seeing tonight. Unlike me, Emma has to spend an hour straightening her bleached blond hair with a hot iron. As soon as the humidity hits, or a couple of drops of water fall on her head, it's game over and her curls come back. I've always been a little jealous of her gorgeous waves. No matter how much product I've tried, I can't seem to get my hair to resemble anything like that. Ironically, Emma just wants hers straight.

Isn't that typical of people? Always wanting what we don't have. Then, even when we get what we want, it only makes us want more. The desire for possession.

It's a sad way to live. We're never truly happy with what we have, that's the problem. We'll always be searching, always unhappy.

7

CLAIRE

Once I'm dressed and ready, I hop in my car and make the quick drive around the bay to King's Corner Center. Jess picked which bar we'd be meeting at this time. Conveniently, it's just around the corner from where she works, only a two-minute walk for her. The bar is so close to my apartment, I could have walked too, but with what I've just been through, I don't want to risk it.

Jess works as a senior clerk at one of the main police stations in town. She's been there for almost as long as I've worked at the university. She has an arts degree like me and has been working at the station so long, she should be in management by this point, but she seems to enjoy filing and organizing piles of paperwork. She's now in charge of analyzing important case files and advising her manager on a course of action. She's well respected in her office and a minority amongst the male cops and inspectors. They seem to value her and treat her well in order to keep her around. As far as I'm aware, she's only interviewed once for a position outside the station since the beginning of her career. When her manager found out, he gave her a raise and an extra week of vacation to entice her to stay.

It seems to have worked because she's been there ever since.

I think she gives too much of herself to that place. Her job has become everything to her. Like Jess, I believe in hard work and am willing to put in the long hours, but work isn't my life.

Though I worked late tonight, I still managed to go for a run and clean-up before meeting the girls. Jess is most likely working until the very last minute before meeting us at the bar. I can imagine her now, deep into one fascinating case file or another. At least she enjoys what she does, whereas I tolerate my work.

I appreciate Jess and her straight-forward approach. She gets things done when she says she will. She's never late to our outings and she's more understanding than most, maybe because of her work and the things she's read. She knows much about the psychology of the criminal mind, but she is professional and never speaks of her work with us. She keeps everything in confidence. Jess is one of the few people I would trust with a secret other than Rebecca.

It must be depressing to read about horrible events all day long, but Jess seems able to compartmentalize it away. She's tougher than some, like Val or Emma. But underneath that tough exterior, Jess is still just a regular girl who enjoys talking about men and sex.

I find Richard's, the dingy bar that Jess picked, located on Water Street. Apparently, it's an up and coming spot where all the cool, young kids hang out. I'm confused as to why Jess picked this particular spot for our get-together tonight seeing as we're mainly in our thirties.

I parallel park and sit in the car for a few minutes, gathering my thoughts. Not keen on being the first one to arrive to these get-togethers. Preferring to join in once the conversation has already started so that I don't need to come up with an ice-breaker.

I'm also nervous about running into Val.

I know she'll be there tonight and that she'll still be mad at me for what I called her the last time we met up. But I don't want to apologize. I hate apologizing, even when I'm wrong. I guess I'm not very good at admitting I'm wrong. Unfortunately, that's something I wasn't able to change when I made alterations to everything else in my life.

I wait a few more minutes, biding my time, when I notice Jess walking on the sidewalk a little ways from the bar, hand in hand with someone, a man. He's tall and skinny. That's all I can deduce from my shadowed parking spot. The street light above my car is burnt out, but I'm only realizing this now. Usually I would not have chosen this spot—too obscure. My mind is somewhere else tonight. I didn't pay attention when I pulled into this spot, only content to have found a spot near the bar.

Mondays are half-price pint night, as the illuminated folded wooden chalk-board sign at the entrance advertises. That explains why the place is so packed.

I see Jess kiss the man and rush into the bar, turning only once to wave goodbye to him, a grin so wide, I can see it from my hiding spot.

I check the time—7:40 p.m. Jess is late. Jess is never late. Who is this new guy who's got her changing her habits already? In my opinion, those relationships are based on too many compromises and too many adjustments to work properly. When people change who they are and what they believe in for someone else, they won't ever be happy.

I should know. I do it every day.

I will have to get to the bottom of this and have a heart-to-heart with Jess.

I already disapprove of this new man, even though I have no idea who he is or what he looks like. He's bad news and unworthy of my friend's time.

I'll have to be careful how I bring this up with her. I'm not very tactful when it comes to having difficult conversations with people I've grown to like. I have so few people close enough to consider my friends, so small a group to manage, but yet, I always seem to upset one of them.

Officially late now, I leave my stakeout spot, lock the car and cross the street to the bar.

Richard's is so packed, people are spilling over to the sidewalk. The deal on pints has attracted many students. Good for Richard, I guess.

I walk through a thick cloud of smoke and push my way to the first door of the double door entrance with difficultly. I reach out and find the door handle, but the cold fall wind creates a sucking effect between the two doors.

For a moment, all I hear is the whoosh of air, and then comes the blast of the overhead heater pouring scorching heat on the top of my scalp, seemingly burning away any remaining moisture from my skin, making my face tight. The wind tunnel pressure forces me to quickly step through the second door, to a safer, more neutral climate.

I am immediately hit with amped up music, trance-like, which had been almost completely muted in the wind tunnel. Sweat, mixed with fried food and stale beer is what I smell when I pass through the threshold.

The smell takes me back to my adolescent days, back to that place so long ago, when I was someone else.

I shiver despite the heat and do my best to shake off the flashback.

The entryway is packed with young students wasting their weekend pay cheques on bad food and alcohol. A threesome is doing a round of tequila shots on my right, near the bar. It's not their first round tonight, I presume.

A fraternity is shouting loudly at whatever sports game is playing on wide televisions suspended overhead. There are three female bartenders behind the counter, all wearing short black skirts barely longer than their work aprons, high heels, and faces plastered with dark eyeliner and contouring.

One of the bartenders is punching her orders in the computer behind the bar, chewing gum, mouth open, while another is leaning over the counter flirting with some of the frat boys. The third bartender is pouring ice and making several drinks all going on the same tray. I make my way over to her. She seems to be the most focused on her job, paying attention to the orders—the least likely to waste my time.

She glances up for a split second and sees me in her peripheral vision, her radar working, acknowledging me. She lifts her chin asking what I want without uttering a word. She hasn't stopped mixing the drinks in front of her confirming I've picked a good one.

No messing around, I order a Pinot noir. I prefer red wine now over beer, a more refined choice for a professional of my status. A more appropriate choice at staff Christmas parties, even if the sulphites almost always give me headaches.

For a split second, my mouth waters at the thought of a tall cold draught, but I immediately shake it off.

It doesn't fit the sophisticated profile I'm trying to portray. I need to remind myself often of who I am now. Who I decided to become.

While I wait for my wine, I lean on the counter, scanning the room for the girls. I spot them at a smaller round table near the front door by a window. I must have just missed them when I walked in distracted by the boys' yelling. I wonder if they saw me waiting in my car earlier.

I'm losing my touch.

Being in the bar is making me return to my old ways—I'm becoming more trusting, unaware, and stupid. I hear the soft ping of glass hitting the wooden bar and find my tall dark wine glass, all 8 ounces of it, waiting for me.

I hadn't realized how much I wanted a drink tonight until I scoop it up gently, careful not to spill a drop—it fits almost perfectly in my palm. Like with a perfect mug of tea, the cozy feeling I get makes me want to curl up on a couch with a good book and forget all the strange moments of the day. I drop some bills on the sticky counter and slowly make my way over to join the girls.

The bar is so loud all around me, the music blaring in the overhead speakers, the TV roaring as it plays the latest major sporting events. I see the girls huddled closely together practically sitting up on their legs, trying to lean in closer to the center of the table, presumably, to hear each other better.

The bar has many lights but they must have them on a dimmer as the room is dark. The mahogany floors and overhead beams don't reflect the poor lighting very well.

The girls haven't made an effort to grab me a chair, most likely thinking I'm a no show given how late I am.

I don't blame them since I usually am.

They seem to be having an intense conversation. I have the irrational thought that they are talking about me.

8

CLAIRE

Val is the first one to spot me. Her face is partly hidden by a large bohemian wool scarf wrapped around her neck, her brown hair frizzy like a bird's nest, partially curled falling down her shoulders. She looks up and half smiles, forcing herself, but her energy is not into it. She thinks I'm not worth the effort. I respond in kind.

The others, Emma and Jess, jump up and push their chairs back with loud shrieks as they make their way over for hugs.

"You made it!" they exclaim in unison.

As excitable as they are, I can tell something is different. Not only is Val sulking in her corner by the window, but the other two are acting stranger than normal—awkward.

No one speaks for a minute as we all sip our drinks, lost in our own thoughts. I notice Val is drinking a ginger ale. Curiosity peaks my interest, but I let it go. It doesn't look good to ask too many questions. It makes you seem vulnerable, unintelligent, and desperate. In time, the answers will come. I will find out what she's hiding.

I turn around and grab a nearby chair vacated by one of the frat boys who is going for his fifth piss of the night. I try not to over think the reason behind the stickiness of the seat on the wooden chair as I sink down onto it.

My legs are grateful for the break; my boots are already killing my feet.

I peel off my coat and unwind my scarf to drape it across my shoulders as though it's a warm shawl. The nearby window and exterior doors are making it chilly. I don't handle the cold very well, never have. I definitely prefer the warm summer over the dead winter that is slowly creeping its way toward to us.

Thoughts of home come flooding in as a popular song plays on the loud speakers. Memories of my older sister Fran and I enjoying the last few days of summer before school, so many years ago. Grade eleven for me, last year of college for her. The two of us lying on our backs tanning on colourful bright blue and pink beach towels on the scorching hot sand in the summer sun one afternoon.

Suddenly, I'm nostalgic missing all of it. The shiny deep blue water that gleamed like millions of tiny diamonds dancing under the sun's rays and the blissful heat. The sand, a mixture of rocks and sea shells, washing ashore. Sand stuck to us in unmentionable places, Fran propped up on her elbows, hair flowing behind her and under the small of her back as she leaned back her head, chest up. I even miss the sound of the annoying seagulls who would squawk loudly high above us, making us fear they would drop unwanted gifts on our perfectly tanned bellies.

Us, together, laughing.

She was only three years older than me, but I thought she was so cool, so mature. She wore make-up and short skirts. Her hair was naturally blonder than mine, no expensive dyes required. She was a true beach bum, her skin, a healthy caramel colour. Every spare moment she spent on the beach or in the water. Neither of us really did any sports, no surfing either. We just walked and ran a lot.

She taught me how to run. How to pace my steps, and how to run on my toes.

53

More like prancing than running—the same as a deer. I'll never forget her face that day at the beach.

"You'll get a sexier butt that way", she'd pointed out. "Promise me you'll leave this place", she'd added after a moment of us staring out into the white caps.

"I promise", I'd replied.

That was the last time I saw her. The next day, she packed up her things and left while I was in the shower.

That was it. She never came back.

Where did you go, Fran?

9

CLAIRE

It takes three sips of my wine in silence for the first one to burst.

"OK, seriously? Are we going to stay silent all night? Because this is bullshit," Emma sighs irritably, looking between Val and me.

I laugh to myself at Emma's attempt at being annoyed. Emma, the peace keeper. Anger doesn't suit her well. It's comical really. I feel like she will burst into a large grin at any moment. She doesn't know the definition of serious. She's cute, actually—a free spirit. She doesn't like conflict. It makes her uncomfortable.

"You know what she wants to hear, Claire. Just save us the drama and say it," Jess coaxes me.

They want me to apologize.

I realize this is almost certainly what this entire night is about. Mending a friendship. What a bore. I should have stayed home. But the thought of going back to my dark apartment tonight makes my skin crawl. I guess if I have to choose between being in this dingy bar or going back to my unsecure apartment, the bar wins.

Goose bumps suddenly appear on my bare arms. I move my blanket scarf closer to my body, holding it close to my chest with my hand while my other one never leaves my wine glass. The very act of having something to hold onto tightly creates an odd and nostalgic feeling in me.

They seem to be taking this gesture as an act of remorse or a way for me to gather my thoughts before I speak. I want to tell them about the apartment, about my gut feeling that something very bad is about to happen, but I don't. They were talking behind my back when I walked into the bar, teaming up to take me down and forcing me to apologize. None of them can be trusted with my most sacred secret.

Not even Jess.

Losing patience just as I expected, Emma slams the table with her open palm, her shiny black nails reflecting the candle light. I know she just wants to rebalance the tables. She's always trying to keep the peace.

An artist, she calls herself—a make-up artist. Even though she completed her arts degree with the rest of us, she decided to get a certificate in college afterward to build more of a hands-on career. While I'd rather work with a computer in a private office and see as few people as possible, Emma has always been great working directly with people. She wants to work with her hands and build relationships with clients. I guess she found something that suits her.

She's actually very talented. I've seen her social media page— over one thousand likes. Not bad for make-up. I wouldn't get one thousand likes if I combined all my accounts. Luckily, getting likes is not a concern for me as I don't have any media accounts. I'm not that vain or that stupid. I've always argued that social media profiles were for narcissists and people with low self-esteem trying to prove something to strangers.

Never let a stranger determine your worth, Emma. People share too much about their personal lives on social media.

Too much private information is flying around ready to be grabbed at any moment.

Emma seems to be very successful in her business. She pays a lot of attention to detail and she's very gentle with her clients. But as I face her now, I see a new side of her. Her patience wearing thin, I realize she's not playing a game anymore.

This is real, she is very angry. Interesting. Funny enough, this makes me respect her more.

Why so on edge, Emma?

"Come on, Claire! This has gone on long enough." She steadies her breath trying to regain her composure.

"Please apologize to Val," Emma begs in her annoying whiny voice, open hand, palm up in Val's direction.

"Just drop it," Val voices after a beat speaking more to the window than to us. "She's too proud to admit she's wrong." She faces me now, daring me to contradict her.

I don't. She's right—I am too proud.

We sit there at a standoff. There is fire in her eyes, but she won't dare take it further.

Val has always been a dreamer. Dreaming of the perfect man, the perfect life, and the perfect friends. Lately, I think I'm muddying the waters for her. I no longer fit in her perfect life, her dream life. But all she ever does is dream. She always moans about wanting this and that, travelling far away, and starting her own soap-making business. But it's all talk and no action.

I believe in action. I act on my goals and I achieve them.

I think that's why she's envious of me, of my get-it-done attitude and my success.

She doesn't understand that her own expectations of what she wants out of life are what bring her down every time.

When you set attainable goals, you can reach for them and achieve them. Don't wait and listen to everyone else tell you why it can't be done. Someone like me loves to tear down people like Val and their unrealistic dreams. Tell them why it won't work out. Like a dream ninja, I slash into their hopes and plans, and leave a tiny doubt there—small, unnoticeable. Sometimes I even camouflage it as a compliment. Then, I hide it, bury it like a seed in the ground. Water it every so often, and let it grow. Just big enough to multiply into hundreds of doubts that will overwhelm the mind and block the dream from ever being achieved.

Why? So I can make them trip up. So I always end up on top and win.

Unfortunately, over the years, my hurt and lack of trust in others have made me bitter and harsh, a sort of defense mechanism I've developed to keep people at a safe distance. Yet, even as I think this, I have a sour taste in my mouth. This isn't me.

No one speaks for a minute. Jess breaks the ice by talking about the latest drama with her newly single father and his new girlfriend. She can't stand anyone being silent for too long or for there to be any tension for that matter. I guess she and Emma are the same that way. Val on the other hand, is always seeking for drama, always causing trouble.

Thankfully, Jess draws us all in as per usual with gossip about her father's new relationship and the tension in the group slowly dissipates.

I watch her closely, how she pretends to be embarrassed by her father's dating game.

Her cheeks flush pink, her high cheek bones rounder than usual as she senses my stare boring into her. I'm giving her a longer stare than is normally acceptable, as though I'm trying to start a fire on her skin with a magnifying glass. I know what she really wants to talk about, and it's not her father. She's bursting to tell us about her new guy—the man she was kissing.

But she doesn't mention him, not yet. She wants to keep it private and I respect that, so I drop it and let her.

A small dance party erupts in the pub. Some of the frat boys have become louder and are dancing to "Save a Horse, Ride a Cowboy". They have foaming pints in their hands held high above their heads dancing around a group of young girls. A few of them spill the white froth onto the floor, sloshing their beers while imitating holding mics in their hands, serenading the girls. *Charming*, I sarcastically think to myself as I try to keep the sneer off my face.

What do women find attractive in men anyway? They are chimps—all hair with brains the size of a pea when drunk, stumbling around, suddenly losing the ability to walk. I used to enjoy gawking at their hard muscles, be fascinated by their strength, but now it's what keeps me awake at night.

The bar owner—Richard, I presume—comes out into the bar from a door at the back. His glasses are on the top of his jet black hair, his sleeves rolled up. He's sporting a dirty apron with streaks of food on it.

There is a shuffling backwards as one of the frat boys falls back and lands on his butt laughing.

The other boys bend over to help him up, spilling half the contents of their beers in the process.

Some of the honey liquid falls on top of their friend's head and some onto the floor.

They are acting like complete idiots.

Richard gives a stern look to the barmaid with the big boobs, the one who was flirting with the boys earlier. His gaze seems to insinuate that she should have cut them off three beers ago. Last chance Debbie. That's what she resembles anyways—a Debbie. Pointy nose, piercing eyes. She almost appears bird-like.

Richard returns his attention to the boys. Unimpressed and tired of this disturbance, Richard rubs his forehead. His features are grey and saggy. He looks like he's been working overtime for three consecutive months and the last thing he needs is to deal with immature shit-heads. He proceeds carefully as he gently but firmly ushers them all out.

You never know how drunken men will react. You can never be too careful. I admire his tactic. He is direct but cautious and insistent that they need to call it a night. He seems tired and burnt out.

Poor Richard. Just trying to run his own business, make a living, and some stupid drunks have come to spoil the party as they always do. What were you thinking, Richard? I can imagine he's reconsidering his new wooden chalkboard sign advertising "Monday Student Nights."

The action in the bar seems to have given Jess the build-up she needed and time to gather her thoughts.

Not sure why this particular moment with the drunken men has brought this up for her, but she decides this is the perfect moment to bring up the fact that she's officially been dating someone for two weeks.

She earns herself a clap and whistle from Emma and Val. Val leans in, obviously dying to hear details, hopelessly romantic as she is. Jess doesn't date often—very rarely in fact. She usually doesn't let her guard down. This must be quite the man for her to decide to tell us about him already. Jess smiles a wide smile as she talks about him. She's completely smitten, unguarded.

The honeymoon phase, I call it.

It's the annoying one, but not the most dangerous one. It's the phase in the relationship when you accept all the other person's flaws. When you see their faults as minor issues and tell little white lies so that you don't rock the boat, but this almost always leads to disappointment on both sides.

The most dangerous phase comes later. After trust has been built-up and is expected. Never expect anything from anyone else. No one owes you anything. In fact, people often think we owe them. So they keep taking.

I'm not interested in this new guy, but I'm interested in Jess's behaviour. She's typically not the boy-crazy, girly-girl type like Emma. She doesn't usually gush over men. But this guy hits all the points on her check list, she claims.

A tight smile runs across my face before I can hide it. Of course she has a list. Good old, predictable Jess. So organized, so thorough. Tony Andrews is his name.

"He is smart, gorgeous, and into the same shows as me! He likes to read and is not scared off by my job." In fact, Jess adds, "He too is detail-oriented. He is tall and has dreamy deep blue eyes and thick spiky dark brown hair," she smiles. "He started working as a mail clerk at my office recently and asked me out. We've been inseparable ever since."

She finishes her gushing by announcing that she's invited him over tonight to grab a drink and meet her best girls.

"So can we please pretend to be getting along, all of us?" she begs, her eyes turning directly to me.

I haven't offered one word since I ordered my wine which is long gone but I don't bother ordering another. I don't want to meet this guy. I already disapprove. Plus, I've already kind of seen him so that's enough for me.

"Speaking of good news...," starts Val, ignoring me and turning her attention to the other two.

Annoyance runs through me. What now?

I'm now thankful for my position facing the window instead of the rest of the bar. Jess looks disappointed to change the subject so soon but hides her dismay well. Her eyes are downcast for only a brief moment before she regains her composure and puts on a smile. The others don't seem to notice, but I do.

Of course, Val never allows others to have the spotlight for too long before she steals it back and claims it as hers—demands it, actually.

"I bet you've all been wondering why I didn't order a real drink tonight...," she trails off as she gazes down to her stomach. Emma and Jess shriek in accord while I roll my eyes and wince at the high pitched sound.

"OMG, Val! Are you pregnant?" Emma almost yells, her drink long gone as well.

A pause then. The bar is silent in my ears. The word seems to echo off the walls and bounce indefinitely around the dark space. Every other noise goes mute as the scene in front of me seems to pause in a tormenting hell.

Time stands still for a moment. The only sound I feel rather than hear is the pounding of my own heart, deep and so loud, I'm almost convinced Richard can hear it from behind the bar.

Blurred images flash before my eyes forcing me to close them at an attempt to steady myself. I'm on the verge of falling off my seat, not trusting the stickiness of the chair to hold me in place. My mind is spinning. They don't know, of course. No one does—I've made sure of that. But it doesn't mean it doesn't hurt in the deepest parts of my soul. They think I don't even want kids, assume I don't have kids.

I don't, of course—well, not anymore.

"I'm not. Well, not yet. We're trying." I hear Val answer in the distance of my mind.

Far away, the sound of her voice brings me back to the room. Oblivious to my sudden distress, she keeps talking. I hold my breath and open my eyes.

None of them are looking at me. It's as though everything froze and then unfroze to right where we left it, but just for me.

As though I'm not even here, like I'm a ghost.

Maybe I am.

We're trying. Val is beaming.

But who's the other part of the 'we' is she referring to? I think back to the last fling she had months ago. Jeff, was it? Or was it Josh?

I can't remember. I don't even care because it won't last.

This "trying to get pregnant" thing is a trick many couples use to try to fix their relationship—to salvage what's left. Val takes a quick glance at me and smirks.

I win, she winks.

She played her card of this most unexpected news to win the attention of the others. Her smile makes me sad. She's doing this to prove herself to me. To prove she's interesting and because of what I said last time when I called her an attention whore. Always lost in another dream, a fake.

Oh Val, you dumb bitch. I still win.

Seconds into her announcement, my phone rings in my purse. It's Phil, my boss. Thankful for the interruption in the middle of all the pregnancy-related questions, I grab my purse and fling my coat over my arm as I move through the bar distancing myself from the girls.

"Hello?" I speak loudly into my phone knowing the bar is too loud for him to hear me properly.

I make my way to the outside doors, phone to my ear pressing a finger to my other ear to hear better. He's speaking in a low tone, but I can barely make out what he's saying. Something about Sandra and news. He's asking me if I've heard the news from Sandra, I hear him mention before I step outside and the call cuts out abruptly.

Crap. My phone lays dead in my palm. Just a black screen giving me no information but reflecting the semi-crescent moon above my head.

What does he mean, news about Sandra? What's happened?

Not bothering to say goodbye to the girls, I make my way to my car and head back to my apartment to find my phone charger.

Jess will understand.

The others can suck it.

10

CLAIRE

Speeding through the dark streets ignoring the puddles this time, my mind is racing faster than the speedometer on the dashboard. I need to know what Phil was telling me before the call was disconnected. There was an edge to his voice—a quivering below the calm. As though he was trying his best to remain professional when one word might have sent him overboard.

With one hand gripping the wheel my long nails digging into the leather, my other hand reaches for my necklace, but comes up empty. I almost blow a red light at the realization.

My necklace. The curse.

I knew something was going to happen, but what exactly has happened? So many questions run through my mind. Was Phil referring to Sandra and Matt or the fact that I gave her the afternoon off? Was he mad about that? Or was it something more serious?

I think back to the conversation we had and try to conjure up Sandra's state of mind. She was distraught, upset about her fight with Matt, but was there another emotion there?

Phil wouldn't call me to reprimand me, especially this late at night. He'd be in bed, most likely in flannel pyjamas, reading a book under a thick duvet with his bedside lamp on, next to his wife.

Phil wouldn't be able to deal with the anxiety of confronting me about anything. Not directly anyway.

He would have emailed me with three key points and that would be it. No follow-up conversation to make sure I'd read it. Nothing but a "read-receipt" to secure my acknowledgment of his passive discipline. Then he would just leave it be, never to be discussed. Just a meek hope that I wouldn't do it again.

No, this is different.

I step into the elevator, my feet loud on the metal floor, my anxiety coming off as anger. Catching my reflection in the mirrored walls, I see fright on my face.

Why do I care? I ask my reflection, but I know I do. I feel it in my gut—something is wrong. I know, or rather, I suspect the worst, always.

Something bad has happened to Sandra.

Once the heavy doors open up to the brightly lit hallway, another perk of a modern building, I make it to my apartment door in seconds. I push the keys in the knob, not remembering taking them out in the first place. I'm on autopilot in a moment of stress. Good. So my training is paying off. I can do mundane things and not blink or think twice about it.

The same Ralph Lauren cologne smell from earlier hits me, still floating around the apartment, but I push it aside. I quickly scan around, only to confirm that I'm alone. I find my phone charger next to my bedside table and plug in my phone.

It's at 3 percent battery. Crap! I'll need to leave it for a few minutes while it charges. I pace around the room. Go to the kitchen for a glass of water, drain it immediately, and slam it slightly too hard on the marbled countertop. My body is reacting to the stress of the unknown.

I've never liked being left in the dark.

I make plans in order to avoid surprises. I prefer knowing when something is happening, having all the facts. My nerves are sparking like tiny fireworks all through my body. My mind is racing. I try to conjure up less dramatic reasons why Phil would call me at this late hour on a Monday night to talk about my assistant.

I grab my phone once more, click the button to boot it up, but it will be a few moments before everything is working properly. Impatiently, I walk to my living room window, open up the curtains, and stare at the busy street down below. The white lights of the nearby apartment keeps the town awake even at this late hour on a week night.

I've seen a lot of these lights lately as it's been hard for me to get enough sleep. I stifle a yawn with my cupped hand, getting lost in the display of lights in front of me when my focus changes to something being reflected in the window.

My chess board.

I brought it with me from my childhood home all those years ago. I used to be a really good player, before graduation. My father, a stickler for education, used to make Fran and I play every evening, one game every night after dinner.

It was his idea of keeping us in line. He used to claim that he learned how to speak English while playing chess. According to my father, chess was what allowed him to immigrate to Canada from Germany. That, and my mother marrying him, of course.

I haven't played it more than a handful of times since moving into this apartment. Rebecca and I played after we had finished unpacking my few personal belongings. A welcome wind-down after hours of moving and unloading heavy boxes.

I've always liked the feel of the tiny wooden pieces in my hands. I just love the carefully crafted details, the time and care put into each piece. My father brought the set with him from Germany, a gift from his old boss when he got the job transfer to Saint John, New Brunswick.

I stare at the reflection of the board now in the large, blackened bay window. The black and white checkered board, the small pieces standing alert, waiting for instructions. I turn slowly, careful not to step too heavily as I approach the chess board sitting on a glass coffee table by the couch. I stand above the square board, my head slightly tilted back, looking down my nose as I focus on what I'm seeing. Something's different.

Someone has moved a piece, but only one—the queen pawn.

My hands are shaking, unable to maintain the facade any longer. Someone is sending me a message and I'm pretty sure I know who.

In the distance my phone rings, the mobile finally charged enough to receive incoming calls. In a trance, I turn my back to the chess board and run across the small space to the bedroom to retrieve my phone before the call goes to voicemail.

"Claire here," I respond, out of breath, not from the run, but from the fear taking residence inside my mind.

"Claire, it's Phil," he hesitates. "I'm glad I reached you. I'm not sure how much you heard before we got disconnected...?" He waits, but I don't answer so he continues, his voice catching. "I'm afraid I've got some bad news." A beat then. "Sandra died today." He releases the last words as though he's been holding on to them in a breath.

"Oh my God!" I gasp, my throat swelling with emotion.

69

Phil continues but I only catch a few words here and there. Something about a car..., not close to home..., something strange about the accident..., doesn't make sense. Through the fog of sadness I catch something I need him to elaborate on.

I interrupt Phil's train of thought, "What do you mean, something strange?"

"Well, for one, why was she not working this afternoon? And second, what was she doing by the water when she lives downtown?" he ponders as I'm collecting my thoughts. "Did Sandra seem...depressed to you?" he asks nervously, surely afraid for the reputation of the office.

"No," I respond immediately, my voice cracking. Then I remember our last conversation and add "Well, she was having a fight with her boyfriend, Matt. She was rather upset so I let her go home early to gather herself."

"Ah, I see." As though that was the solution to this problem.

"Well, regardless, there's something just not quite right going on here. The police have been calling me, asking questions about Sandra's work habits, who she interacted with. They asked to speak to you, as Sandra reported directly to you. Inspector..." he hesitates, and I hear him riffling through paper, "...Riley. Inspector Riley. That's it. He implied he needed to clarify some details about this accident as it wasn't a standard hit-and-run. They wouldn't tell me anything else, but said there were reasons for his team to believe there could be another reason for her death."

I feel sick to my stomach as I thank Phil for the call and tell him I'll speak to the inspector when he calls me. I end the call and slump down on my king size bed, my mind buzzing.

Sandra is dead?

I feel a pang of sadness heavy over my heart. How did this happen? What does all this mean? Phil said that the inspector thinks there's another reason for Sandra's death. That this guy wants to talk to me, but why? What could I possibly know about all this? How can I help them figure out what happened? What do I have to do with why or how Sandra died?

As I twist my body to grab for my phone to see if I've received any text messages, my eyes meet my reflection in the mirror inside my open closet door. Even in the dimly lit room, I can see it. I'm hit with a wave of memories I'd tried hard to push far away. I trace a shaking finger over it. Suddenly, I know who's doing all of this.

11

ELISABETH

The needle punctures my bronze skin 3,000 times a minute, the gold rotary machine pushing the needle into the fatty part of my back near my underwear line.

"Fuck! That hurts!" I swear as I grit my teeth, while squeezing Ethan's hand.

Ethan laughs softly as he leans closer to brush his lips to mine. He smells so good that I lose myself in his kiss. I'm floating somewhere far away for a moment until the tattoo artist adds more black ink to the needle and resumes scarring my body forever.

"Don't laugh at me!" I moan lying on my stomach, head cocked to the side gazing into his beautiful and kind blue eyes. "You're next, you know!" I add, reminding him with my eyes that if he wants support, he better give it to me first.

"I know, babe. You're just so cute. I still can't believe we're doing this!" He beams as his hand gently touches my hair.

"This has been the best year ever! Well mostly...," remembering how I still haven't heard from my sister Fran since the last day of summer almost a year ago.

I met Ethan in Mr. Sutton's chemistry class last semester and we flirted with each other before becoming official after the Halloween dance. Now it's July—my birthday month. I'm turning seventeen, and we are starting grade twelve at Kateri Tekakwitha High School in September.

Ethan's older brother Steve booked this appointment for us as we're minors and would've needed a parent's permission. *Thank you, Steve!* I make a mental note to punch him in the shoulder next time I see him—his payment for my pain. But seriously, I'm so happy to finally be getting a tattoo, I should consider being courteous to him next time I see him. Ethan and I had wanted to celebrate our eight months together with something big. I've always wanted to get a tattoo and it didn't take much convincing to get Ethan on board. He's always up for whatever makes me happy.

The machine's buzzing is ringing in my ears.

The seaside shop is pretty quiet for a Wednesday afternoon. I am slightly wary of the quality of the tattoos because if a company accepts forgery as proof of I.D., what else do they overlook? I shut my eyes for the last little bit, biting down hard on my lip, tuning into the music playing off the computer in the lobby. I zone out until the tattoo artist lets his foot off the pedal and wipes at my bloody back.

"All done." He declares, emotionless—just another day for him.

He's got a long pointy beard falling down to his chest, but a bald head. Why is it that as men get older, they get more facial hair and less hair on their heads?

"You're next, kid," he announces, peering at Ethan as I shift myself off the table carefully.

We exchange a quick panicked look at his use of the word "kid". It's as though he's letting us know that he's on to us but doesn't really care.

My back is screaming in pain.

I'll be sore for a few days, but it's worth it.

Ethan's face contorts as though he's about to lose consciousness, shuttering as he stares at the fresh needle on the table. Eyes wide, mouth partly open, face drained of colour, he looks like he's about to be sick.

I gently put my hand on his shoulder and turn him towards me so I can look up into those blue eyes. I reassure him that it'll be over soon and doesn't he want a tattoo to match mine? Yes, he confirms as I plant a kiss on his warm mouth. I playfully run my hand through his thick black hair so it messes it up, breaking his concentration long enough for the fear to dissipate.

I press my body to his reminding him of what's to come. We've promised to lose our virginity together on graduation day. I'm nervous but also excited about it. I wish I could talk to Fran. She would have a way of giving me advice on how to get the best orgasm, all while lecturing me to wait until after I'm married.

I already know I want to marry Ethan. He's the One, and he says I'm the One for him too.

We professed our love on Valentine's Day by saying 'I love you' for the first time and it was magical. We even developed a secret way of telling each other without actually saying it out loud. We just need to catch sight of each other and blink twice, and we just know.

We're the most popular couple in school mainly because we've been together the longest.

Ethan lays down on the table, arms under his head. He presses down his forehead not wanting to see what's about to happen. The now familiar buzzing resumes and I extend my hand to him.

74

Unable to move a muscle, Ethan just squeezes his own arms, crisscrossed under his head. He won't allow himself to scream like I did. He has to show me he's more macho than me. He's competitive that way. Or rather, he just wants to seem manly.

After about ten minutes, Ethan's tattoo is done. As the tattoo artist is wiping Ethan's back clean, I lightly run my fingers over my own back. The swollen skin rises slightly under my touch. I find a long vertical mirror at the back of the shop. I want to get a glimpse of the tattoo before it gets covered in gauze.

I slowly raise my grey t-shirt, biting down on my lip while holding my breath. Freshly inked in black is a drawing of a crown.

A crown for a queen.

Queen Elisabeth.

12

CLAIRE

Queen Elisabeth. That was the pet name Ethan had given me. Growing up on Princess Street in Saint Andrews and with my name being Elisabeth, Ethan had thought it was cute to call me his queen.

"My queen", he used to call me all the time when we were alone. I used to call him "My king".

That was why we had decided on matching king and queen crown tattoos, to commemorate how loyal we were to each other and as a promise of how we would stay together forever. Until death do us part, we used to swear.

It was cute back then but now the nickname makes my stomach turn. My name back then, before graduation, my real name, had been Elisabeth Claire Smith.

I'd changed it before attending college in Saint John to Claire Martel. I didn't want anyone new to know about my past and who I used to be.

New year, new me—literally. I hadn't wanted to be found. I'd wanted to hide from Ethan and ended up running away from everything and everyone I knew.

I legally changed my name to Claire Martel and chose a new personality to go with it. I even made new friends and left the other ones in the dust.

I wonder sometimes if Fran left me because of something similar to what had happened to me.

I'm still convinced that my parents have an idea of where she is now, but for some reason they refuse to admit it and claim ignorance.

Martel is my mother's maiden name. She changed it to Smith when she married my father after he emigrated from Germany one year before Fran was born. My mother is a typical French-speaking woman from New Brunswick, Acadian accent and all. She has lived in New Brunswick her whole life along with her two brothers. She apparently hadn't wanted to change her last name, or believed in the tradition to do so when she got married. My dad always speaks of this with pride, that he finally convinced her to change it. About how he got her to see that it would be best if she changed her last name to his for the children's sake. He had argued that school pick-ups and general appointment-making on our behalf would be that much easier. In the end, my mother had caved, wanting to have the same last name as her girls.

Growing up so close to the province of Quebec where most women don't change their last names after marriage, my mother found it difficult to adjust to her new identity. After all, my parents were slightly older than most new parents when they had Fran and me. My mother had been closing in on thirty-six with Fran and thirty-nine with me. Both of her pregnancies were considered 'at risk', simply because of her age.

The year I moved away to college, I changed everything about myself. I stopped talking to everyone from my past with the exception of Rebecca and my parents. They were the only ones who knew my new name.

Although, I'm starting to doubt if that is still true.

***

I get up off the bed slowly and walk over to the mirror like I'd done so many years ago when the ink was still glistening under my raw skin in that run-down tattoo shop in Saint Andrews. I'd almost been able to put that day behind me.

The tattoo on my back, also behind me; a metaphor of my past. A time I wish I could forget—escape. It seems very clear to me now that my past has caught up with me.

13

CLAIRE

My heart is racing. I don't know what to do with my hands. I clench them into fists and release, repeating this five times, taking deep breaths. So someone from my past knows my new name and where I live. So what? But then someone had taken a great risk breaking into my apartment, taking important steps to make it appear undisturbed.

Seeing the queen pawn makes everything clearer. The gears are aligning.

Someone wants me to know.

They only changed things that no one else would notice. That no one else would ever suspect. They only want me to know. Whoever it is, they are sending me the message that they are watching my every move, that they know my routine.

A shiver runs up my spine as I recall the day's events. The broken necklace that started it all. The strange light in Devon's office, the disturbed clothes in my room and the pulled shower curtain in my bathroom.

The clock now reads eleven p.m. How can I possibly go to sleep now knowing someone has access to my apartment? Should I call my parents? Get in my car, make the one-hour drive back home, and come back in the morning for work? Who am I kidding? Work isn't important right now. My safety is on the line. A creeping feeling washes over me.

Sandra is dead.

Am I somehow responsible for her death? Did the same person who broke into my apartment kill Sandra?

As I consider the implications and think of the days ahead, I realize there will be no important meetings tomorrow. My team will all be mourning the death of Sandra. This Inspector Riley will undoubtedly come around to the office and talk to everyone in order to get to the bottom of all of this, myself included.

Sitting on top of my bed still plugged into the wall, my cell phone rings breaking the silence of the night. It does little to break through the noise building up in my mind. The display announces a private number.

I hesitate a few seconds, worried it might be the same anonymous caller from before at my office. Quickly, I remind myself that the previous caller had called my office line, not my cell phone. I quickly rationalize that it's most likely the inspector calling as Phil had warned.

"Hello?" I respond, my voice barely above a whisper. The caller could have assumed he had woken me from sleep, but it doesn't seem to matter to him that he is calling me so late.

"Hello, is this Claire Martel?" Barely giving me the time to respond, he continues, "This is Inspector Gary Riley with the Saint John Police Force. I'm sorry to call at this late hour but I'm afraid I've got something pressing to discuss with you. Is this a good time to talk?" His tone demands attention.

I can tell he's not usually declined an opportunity for discussion. I'm about to protest the time of night, but think better of it. If I want to learn more about what happened to Sandra, now is the time. Before I can offer anything in response, he continues.

"It's my understanding that Sandra Reed was an employee of yours in the Communication Department at the University of New Brunswick." He wants my confirmation, and I comply.

"I'm sorry to tell you that Sandra has been found dead this evening." He pauses out of respect before continuing. "She was found by an elderly couple out for an evening stroll. They caught sight of Sandra's pink coat just a little way off the walking trail. The body was discovered by the water's edge near St. John River." Without skipping a beat, he asks in a seemingly casual manner, "Are you familiar with this area?"

"Sure, I run near there all the time," I answer, not understanding how that's pertinent.

"Were you running near there this evening, Miss Martel?" he asks.

A moment passes before I answer. "Yes, I was out running earlier this evening." I curse myself immediately for not having a vaguer response.

"Do you happen to know at what time you went running and which route you took?" he inquires.

Not liking where this is going, I query, "I'm sorry, Inspector Riley. If Sandra was hit by a car, why would you need to know if I was running by the bay this evening?" Before I let him answer, I remember Phil's comment. "Do you have any reason to believe that there's something else going on here?" I question, in one breath. Anxiety runs through my body and my right eye lid begins to twitch uncontrollably.

I try to picture what this Riley guy looks like and for lack of imagination, I find myself visualizing him as the typical stereotype of an overweight, hairy-chested, bald man in his fifties with a striped, short-sleeved dress shirt with the buttons about to pop off.

"Miss Martel, I understand your concern. I'm sure this is very difficult news to hear. We are working hard to get a clear picture of what exactly happened today. In order to do so, we need to talk with everyone Miss Reed was in contact with throughout the day to see if anything can help answer some questions. We are contacting people she is regularly in touch with to find out their whereabouts today to see who was the last to see her alive. We have reasons to believe Sandra's death was not an accident but that she was murdered."

His last words echo in my mind.

Murdered.

Quiet, compliant Sandra.

Phil had insinuated that she had been depressed, suicidal even, that maybe she had thrown herself off the path and into oncoming traffic. But why go near the bay in the evening when there wouldn't be much traffic? What was she even doing near the bay so far from her house?

Murder did seem like the more plausible option.

But who would want to hurt Sandra? I immediately think of Matt, her boyfriend, who she was fighting with earlier this morning. A sense of urgency to get the words out overwhelms me and I blurt out Matt's name into the phone, but Inspector Riley assures me that Matt has a solid alibi. Apparently he'd been at his parents' house all day after spending the weekend with them in their home in Nova Scotia.

Lost in thought, I almost don't hear the inspector continue.

"We believe you are the last person to have talked to the victim before she was found dead. I have a witness report who recalled a rather emotional conversation between yourself and the victim this morning in your office. In fact, Miss Reed was seen exiting the office in tears wearing her pink coat." He pauses, "She wasn't seen again until later when her body was found. Our witnesses can attest that you were in your office until about 4:30 this afternoon when they left to go home." He falls silent now.

Am I in trouble? Should I hang up and call someone?

"Miss Martel, I do require an answer as to your whereabouts for this evening. At what time exactly did you go for a run and where?" he presses.

"I ran by the bay but..." and then I pause. A cold sweat goes through my body. "Wait...am I a suspect?"

My breathing is heavy. I feel hot all over. I hadn't taken any phone calls or written emails for an hour or so before leaving work. How would I prove I'd been at work?

"As I mentioned, we are simply trying to identify everyone who was close to the victim, and to determine their location and activities for this evening. As the last person to have spoken with Miss Reed, we are extremely interested to learn what the conversation between you and the victim was about. You are not currently a suspect in this investigation."

Victim.

That's all Sandra is reduced to now. He doesn't even use her name.

I hesitate before I reply. It definitely sounds as though I'm being interrogated.

Don't they usually bring people into the police station for these kinds of questions?

"She was upset about a fight with her boyfriend, Matt," I explain curtly.

"And can you confirm your whereabouts after you left the office tonight?" he probes.

"I can't remember precisely," I begin, my tongue sticking to the roof of my mouth. "But I left work around 5:30 p.m. and I went out running shortly after at around six this evening," I finally respond, feeling slightly light-headed from the sudden build-up of stress.

I can hear Inspector Riley writing this down presumably in a black notebook like on TV shows. Another stereotype I'm picturing over the phone.

"Thank you, Miss Martel. What did you do later this evening, after your run?" he questions.

"I went back to my apartment and showered, and then met some friends at a bar for a drink around 7:40 p.m." I answer nervously remembering when I checked the clock upon spotting Jess outside of the bar.

"I see." he reflects while reviewing the information I've given him. "Did anyone see you between when you left work this evening at 5:30 p.m. and 7:40 p.m. when you met your friends?"

Silence as I understand the weight of his question.

I don't know if I should hang up now and find a lawyer or answer in order to seem less suspicious.

If no one saw me, it means there's no way for me to provide an alibi for those hours. Two hours is enough time to follow and murder someone.

I could be wrongly accused of something I didn't do, only because no one saw me. I know I can't keep silent much longer and that they're going to find out eventually.

"No, I was alone," I finally answer as I exhale silently at what I may have just done.

This simple answer may have given Inspector Riley the "person of interest" he's been fishing for. What if I *was* the last person to see her before she died? I'm panicking now, hating myself for working late tonight.

I know I'm innocent and the best thing to do now is to stick to the truth. If I start to lie now I might not be able to get my story straight later and trip over some facts.

"So you cannot provide an alibi for your whereabouts for this evening between the hours of approximately 5:30 p.m. and 7:40 p.m. Is that correct?" he inquires seemingly casually but I know where he's heading. I picture him sitting up with his back straight, on the edge of his seat, phone pressed tightly to his ear.

Gritting my teeth so hard I fear I might loosen them, I reply tightly "No." Feeling defensive, I start asking him questions of my own. "But why does it matter where I went running this evening? Sandra lives on the opposite end of town. Surely you've been given her address?"

"Miss Martel, the victim's body was discovered by the St. John River, near your apartment building." Without missing a beat, Riley continues, "I've done a preliminary background check on you on our system and it's my understanding that Claire Martel is not the name you were given at birth. Is that right?" he asks in a friendly manner that's not friendly at all.

At this, I almost drop the phone. All my senses freeze in time, my breath catches, and the room begins to spin.

How does he know that?

Those records were supposed to be sealed. Only my parents have a copy of the original birth certificate, as a keepsake, locked away in a safety deposit box at the bank. But I guess the police can easily find out this kind of information.

"Yes, that's correct. But how is this relevant?" I ask bewildered, my voice quavering.

I try to keep my tone in check and not give in to the angry ball of fire building inside of me. How can he know so much about me already? My mind is in a frenzy trying to put together all the new information I've learned. I should start writing some of this down.

"Can you confirm that you used to be called Elisabeth Claire Smith?" he asks.

"Yes, but this is absurd! How could you possibly know all this?" I demand losing patience.

Who is this asshole? I need a lawyer and I should really hang up now.

"Some markings were found on the victim that are concerning to us," he continues, unfazed by my angry outburst.

"I assure you, I had nothing to do with Sandra's death!" I scream into the phone now, detaching it from its charging plug and moving out of the bedroom. I pace into the living room and pull at the curtains, covering the large bay windows, paranoid that I'm being watched at this very moment.

"We are trying to understand and eliminate all possible connections," he relays calmly as I let out a frustrated grunt.

"Yeah, well, I'm done talking to you! Next time we talk, I'll have my lawyer present."

"No problem. I completely understand. Thank you for speaking with me this evening. I'm very sorry for your loss. I look forward to meeting you in person soon." He pauses before adding, "And one more thing, Miss Martel." A beat as I feel my blood boil. "Don't leave town, OK?"

I don't even bother to answer him. *Asshole*, I curse to myself as I press the End button, my hand shaking. It's not half as satisfying as slamming the phone down onto its receiver. I send my phone skipping on the hard surface of the island countertop. My hands support my shaky body as I lean on the cold granite counter inside the U-shaped kitchen.

I quickly go over the facts. Someone has killed Sandra. Someone knows who I am—who I really am—Queen Elisabeth. Someone has been inside my apartment. Someone has moved my clothes, moved the queen pawn.

The message is clear. They are coming for me next. They saw Sandra as the queen pawn, a way to get to me, and took her out. But it's really me they're after.

I say *they*, but I know it's *he*. I guess I knew most days that he was still after me. The markings related to my old name have just sealed it.

I force myself to believe that Ethan is the one orchestrating all of this even though my heart pulls at me, challenging me to believe that he couldn't possibly be the one doing this. But it has to be him. I remind myself that I was wrong about him back then and I can't make the same mistake now.

He's getting back at me for what I did to him all those years ago. Graduation Day. The day when everything changed. The day I changed. Head down, my hair falls like a waterfall around my face, a sheet of curtains I try to hide myself behind it.

I would disappear if I could.

14

CLAIRE

Panic grips my shoulders bunching them up high, tight around my face. I want to break things, scream and hit the wall. All these years of successfully and skillfully misleading everyone. All the work I did to hide out in my new life has suddenly been for nothing.

All evaporated into nothing. I feel helpless and angry.

A thought occurs to me. I wonder if this inspector works with Jess. Maybe she's in on this somehow. She was late for our girl's night after all, but then again, she was with Tony.

The fact that I've had my name changed most likely doesn't help the fact that I know the murder victim and was in the same area of town where she was found. It makes me look suspicious. The park being near my apartment building and with markings that connect me to her... What does that even mean, "markings"? All point to me becoming a prime suspect.

This is no coincidence.

All these events happened today. They're all connected somehow to me. Why?

Ethan.

I guess I always knew he might find me someday. But why now?

He has to be the one orchestrating all of this. He wants revenge. I was stupid enough to believe I'd gotten away from him. That I was free. That I had a chance at freedom.

This was a train wreck of a way to remind me just how fragile freedom really is. One minute it's yours, and the next you're fighting to get it back.

Inspector Riley has instructed me not to leave town, but my gut is screaming at me to do just that.

Screw it, I can't stay here tonight.

More and more, I'm convinced a psycho is out there, tormenting me by messing around in my apartment. And now Sandra is dead and I'm being framed for it for some godforsaken reason. Speaking of God, where is He now? He's been extremely silent today, it seems. I'm sinking and he's a quiet bystander just like all those years ago when I needed Him and He wasn't there.

Any time you want to jump in and help, God, give me some direction, maybe a miracle? That would be great!

Feeling I'm alone in this, tears fall down my cheeks. Why am I always running away from my life?

A voice in my mind quietly reminds me that I knew this would happen eventually, that he would find me. I can't talk to anyone about this or they will turn on me just like the inspector. If I talk to someone, how can I avoid talking about my past? And how can I get clarity on why I'm a suspect for Sandra's murder without giving myself away?

No. I can't talk to anyone. I can't trust anyone. Ever again.

In fact, I can't exist anymore. I need to make myself disappear.

For good this time.

Hot tears run down my cheeks as my mind spins with what comes next. I know how this goes. I've done this before.

I run into my bedroom and dig under mounds of clothes in my closet to find my black gym bag with a shoulder strap. I begin frantically stuffing clothes into it, not paying attention to what goes in, hoping it will sort itself out. My eyes are blurry from the tears. I had a beautiful life here. I had friends here. Even if they were fake, the company was appreciated.

I wasn't all alone, but when I leave now, I will be.

I run my hands between the mattress and box spring and grab all the cash stored there for emergency purposes. This is clearly one of those times. My rent is already paid for next month, so that part is taken care of, but where I'm heading, wherever that might be, I'll need some cash to get by. I haven't counted the stack in several months, but I know there's over five thousand dollars there.

My safety net.

I'm glad I never let my guard down too much and kept stashing bills away over the years. It'll come in handy now.

Hastily, I grab my purse and take out my wallet to see if there's any extra cash hidden in it, or anything else that might help me right now. Desperate and running out of time, I shake it upside down.

I must be quite a sight with my hair damp on my forehead from stress, eyes manic and wide, tears staining my cheeks, makeup running down my face. As I shake my wallet, receipts and change fall out and so does my broken necklace. It had been an omen, just as I had predicted. For some reason, I can't leave it behind. I still believe having it with me will bring me good luck. I don't care that it's broken, it's irreplaceable to me.

I wrap it around my wrist in two quick swoops and make a small knot, using my other hand and my teeth to tighten it.

It appears secure enough that I'm sure it won't accidently fall off. I glance around my bedroom one last time before I move on, furious about leaving my comfortable life once more.

I wipe the wet black smudges of mascara from under my eyes and rush to the bathroom to pack the few toiletries I have. I make sure to only bring enough to fit into the one gym bag. I switch out my leather high heeled boots for my pink runners. I don't care that they are flashy. If I have a killer following me, I will need to be able to make a run for it. Whether or not my shoes put a bright pink spotlight on me, they're my best bet.

My mind spins as I exit the washroom and turn to grab my phone still lying on the kitchen counter, but I think better of it and toss it on the sofa. Best not to give anyone an obvious way to track me down. If I'm going to disappear, I can't be reachable.

I cannot be traceable.

I swallow the hard ball in my throat at the thought of leaving everything behind me, shut the heavy wooden door on my life, and exit my apartment building.

I've thrown on a loose-fitting black hoodie and matching pants to hide any identifying features. I twist my hair back and pull the hood over my head to hide my long blond hair. The hair and the shoes will make me stand out in this season of heavy black coats. I can cover up my hair for now, but I'll need to find a more permanent solution for that soon.

I start making a check list in my mind of what I need to do. First on my list is transportation. I need to get away from here and fast, but I can't take my car, for obvious reasons. I need to blend in with the crowd.

I don't know the bus schedule as I've never had to use it before, but I remember seeing a single mom from my building waiting at the shelter near my apartment every morning around 8 o'clock. I can't possibly wait that long, but I imagine the night bus is on a sparse schedule. It was about eleven when I got the call from Inspector Riley and that was almost two hours ago.

I'm sure morning will come soon.

Without a way to tell time, I stare up to the night sky. I was always one for being minimalist. I didn't need accessories like watches because I found their use too limiting, and besides, my smart phone did it all for me in one simple device. I have to admit, a watch would be very useful right about now given I've opted to leave my phone behind. There's something invaluable about old, timeless technology, about devices that can function without a transmitter and a wave length. There is freedom in using something that doesn't need a wall charger to run properly.

I make a mental note to buy some supplies. A hair dye kit will be necessary, as well as a watch, and maybe a burner phone. The rain still falling hard on the top of my hoodie sends a shiver through me. The temperature outside must be a few degrees above freezing tonight, or maybe I'm just reacting to the shock of tonight's events.

Either way, I need to find some sort of shelter away from the rain before it freezes me to the core and this whole mission goes to waste. I can't let a little rain ruin my plans to escape this hell. But I can't risk going to my parent's house or getting Rebecca involved. I need a fresh start. I need to go somewhere where no one knows me. Where they don't know my past or my real name.

There will be time to figure that out later.

I try to put as much distance between me and my apartment as I can. I begin a slow jog and feel my leg muscles tighten at the memory of my earlier run. I know I can go a little while, but I can't possibly run as far as I need to tonight, not after my extra-long run earlier this evening. My muscles would go into overdrive and start to spasm into a painful throb.

I won't make the same mistake as last time.

I will get away from this place. But I will need to pace myself. Sometimes patience is better than acting too quickly and losing it all.

Gazing up at the stars and the darkness of the apartment behind me, I estimate the time to be around 1 or 2 o'clock and I remind myself that I really only need to figure out a plan for the next six or seven hours. I need to be careful not to lurk near public places that would have working security cameras. I need to blend into the shadows.

I walk along the water's edge, a million thoughts bouncing around in my mind.

Why would Sandra even be in this area of town? She didn't live near here. What were she and Matt arguing about before she died? Before she was murdered, I remind myself.

As I wander through the dark, I hug my shoulders and rub them trying to keep myself warm. I need to find shelter. Somewhere I can stay dry. Somewhere I can think.

The wind picks up over the water and I smell the same faint wet grass smell from my apartment. There's no doubt that whoever killed Sandra was also in my apartment.

I spot a kids' park nearby and start making my way to it.

At this time of night, I could encounter drug addicts, sex-crazed runaway teenage couples or worse. But on a rainy, chilly night like tonight, I'll take my chances at the park being empty. Thankfully, there is a small wooden wall where children often hide, pretending to play in a house. Along with the platform above to access the big yellow slide, the structure creates a makeshift shelter. I figure this is as good a spot as any.

My legs hurt from my earlier push at jogging and they are getting colder with the rain drenching my pants. I sit down in the cold sand and start gathering it around me as an improvised blanket. The sand gets colder as I dig deeper with my hands, my fingers growing numb as I work the hard ground, but I don't care. I need shelter from the water or my skin will chafe and it will hurt to walk.

Leaning on one of the wooden structure's walls, I cross my arms over my chest and make sure the hood of my sweater is hiding the exposed side of my face as I rest my other cheek against the wood. My thoughts run as wild as embers in a dry field, and I'm not expecting to actually get any sleep when suddenly my brain shuts down into blackness.

15

Well, that was a lot easier than I thought.

You're not so careful with your keys when you're working at the office. I would have believed someone like you would have known better than to leave your purse and house keys unattended during your important meetings. Lucky for me, I guess, you're just not that smart.

See, I'll always be one step ahead of you. I'll always be the smarter one.

But now you know I'm here. You know I'm watching. I revel in that image—you glancing over your shoulder.

You know you have no choice but to play my game. Now you know I've made the first move and that I'm watching. Removing your queen pawn was easy enough. That fat ass was so annoying; I didn't think I could handle her pathetic little pleas anymore. Luckily, I didn't have to.

You made it so easy for me to find you. Now, I've made my move, and it's your turn to play. I know you will try to outsmart me, but you can't—you never have. This is my game after all and I always win.

When you figure all this out, I know you will run. You always run and I'll be right behind you.

16

TUESDAY, SEPTEMBER 16TH

CLAIRE

A ray of sunlight makes its way through a crack in the wooden platform above my head and shines directly into my eyes.

I'm jerked awake by the sound of a barking dog not too far away. It takes me a moment to realize where I am and why. I must have fallen asleep despite the cold due to stress and exhaustion. In the light of the day, I will need to take extra precautions to blend in and remain unseen. But the rain is gone and the sun is shining—I take this as a good sign—the light returning after the cold dark night. A new beginning of sorts.

Maybe God has heard my cry after all and is watching over me.

If my neck was bothering me yesterday, today I feel an entirely new level of pain. My neck is pulsing to its own beat in slow agonizing thumps. What was I thinking, falling asleep while sitting up against a wooden play structure?

I carefully turn my head slowly to the right, then to the left, gritting my teeth through the painful motion, unable to keep my eyes open during the exercise.

I try to think of anything else, remembering the bar last night, feeling guilty about taking for granted the simple pleasures of grabbing a drink with some friends. It's a luxury I won't be privy to for some time now that I'm hiding out.

Trusting myself to have regained some basic neck functions, I start to wipe away the sand from my legs. The heavy logs attached to my body feel tingly like millions of ants are crawling under my skin, nearly numb from remaining still all night. I stand cautiously, not wanting to bang my head on the roof of my makeshift shelter as I carefully scoot out, Quasimodo-style from my hiding spot.

I warily scan the park, fully alert, but only spot a lone, early walker being led by his dog, far in the distance. Even from this far I can tell he's a few decades older than Ethan.

It's not him. Good.

But there's still a chance it might be an undercover cop. It's doing me no good to hang around here. I need to change location and quickly. I'm sure Inspector Riley and his team will be making their way to interview everyone at my office this morning, and they will be expecting me to show up as well. For a second, fear overwhelms me and my breath catches in my throat as I think of how it will look when I don't show up for work and that I'm nowhere to be found.

Guilty, that's how it will look.

I shake my head slowly and push the thought away. No negative energy today. This is my fresh start. A chance to start over, to be a new me.

I'm making the right choice for my life. If I had stayed and gone into work as usual, who knows what would've happened?

I may have been questioned, embarrassed, accused, possibly arrested, or worse. No, this is the only way to keep myself safe. I'm the only one I can trust.

As I walk through the park, I wince as my feet make loud crunching sounds on the fallen leaves in my path. The morning dew is not wet enough to have soaked the leaves through. The sound intensifies with every step, reminding me of the life I'm leaving behind, the further away I get. All the friendships I've worked so hard to make in order to appear normal, the credibility I built for myself, the work I did for the university—none of it matters now.

It's all gone.

The wind coming from the St. John River whips at my face, making me shiver again. But for the first time in twenty-four hours, I'm confident. I'm taking my destiny into my own hands, not waiting around, weak and afraid. I'm creating a new reality for myself. Some might see it as running away, but I choose to see it as surviving. Who knows? Maybe this time I'll become someone nicer, friendlier, and popular even? I'll have a lot of time to make up a new personality during my journey.

I finally let out a long breath as I reach the edge of the park and gaze into the dark waters of the river. The waves match my breathing as they roll in and out. The water seems to be the only constant in my life—always there to be counted on wherever I end up. I am leaving all this behind for a chance to be free. I have to keep reminding myself that there is no other way. I look up at the sky once more, the sun taking up temporary residence as the day begins to get warmer.

People will be making their way to work now. I need to hurry. I don't want anyone to be able to identify me.

Before I drifted off to sleep last night, in my mind I sorted through all the travel options available. I decided I'd hop on a city bus. It's the most populated option, but that might work to my advantage. More people around usually means it's less likely I will be noticed. If I'm seen, no two people will provide the same description of me.

It's my best bet.

Morning commuters are still half asleep, some actually dozing off. Usually people are focused on themselves and their days ahead, or they have their noses glued to their cellphones reading the latest post from one of their hundreds friends. Although I'll be amongst a crowd of people, if I keep to myself and don't act too out of place, I'll blend right in and not bring attention to myself, hiding in plain sight so to speak.

The city bus is also the most cost effective way to travel, other than walking, of course, but walking wouldn't get me very far. And most likely I'd be seen or spotted on a traffic camera later on. Riding the bus will also make it harder for anyone who might be tracking me to know which connection I'll be making and where I'm heading. Although, I'm not sure how someone could know or anticipate my next move because I'm literally making it up as I go. I know this seems unprepared and foolish, but it's actually a solid strategy. They won't know where to find me next.

At this point, I have to anticipate that someone is watching me. Inspector Riley works for the Saint John Police Force and he's not working alone on this case. I take a quick glance back; the only time I allow myself this momentarily lapse in judgement.

I must never look back again, even if the hair on the back of my neck stands up and my gut screams that I'm being watched and followed. I would be easier to spot that way. If I keep glancing back, I risk my face being seen by someone who's searching for me. It also appears suspicious.

Better to let them think I don't know they're coming.

I exit the safety of the park and walk alone on the sidewalk for a few minutes until I spot a few teenage students walking in a group ahead of me. For teenagers, they seem very awake at this time of the morning. They also seem excited to be going to school. They toss their backpacks up in the air, while yelling insults at each other.

Oh, to be young again! As annoyed as I am being slowed down by these idiots, I decide this will work perfectly for me until I find a bus shelter to sneak into. I blend right in with these high school students despite my height and the fact that I'm in my thirties. My attire goes a long way. The bright shoes and black hoodie seems to be in right now. Perfect for me. I stay a few steps back to not raise any alarm but near enough to appear as though I'm just another student going to school.

I re-adjust the strap on my left shoulder and carefully tuck a strand of blond hair back inside the hoodie. I didn't put much in this bag, but the strain on my neck and shoulder is already bothering me and I know it'll be intolerable later on. I might need to ditch it and buy a real backpack similar to the ones the kids in front of me are throwing above their heads.

I spot the shelter for the bus line in the distance and casually scan the loud street to my left trying to make it look natural.

The air is thick with fog from early morning commuters stuck in traffic, the gas emissions lifting slowly into the atmosphere. One reason why I always made sure to leave for work early—the ten minute commute could easily take me an hour if I left only a few minutes behind my usual schedule. A trivial issue now, compared to my current situation.

I'm barely five blocks away from the park, but I can still see my building, its tall brick tower casting a shadow on the road. It's as though my past is reaching toward me trying to pull me back in. *It's not too late to turn back*, my mind reminds me. But I know it's just the fear talking. *That's not the way to freedom*, I think to myself.

No. I need to keep moving forward. I can't go back now.

They want to dig into my past, arrest me, and lock me up. I have no interest in waking up my demons. I can't let them do that—I won't. I shut the door on that part of my life a long time ago. Suddenly a terrifying, yet very important realization occurs to me.

Maybe all this time, my demons had been growing and not dying.

17

ELISABETH

I spot Ethan in the cafeteria and have to stop myself from skipping over to him. I love him so much, with his big grin, his wavy hair, and those baby blue eyes. Thankfully for me, Ethan is just as crazy about me as I am about him.

That's what makes us so great together.

When I finally reach him, I put my plastic tray down on the table with a thud as it's barely holding my steaming mac & cheese and a can of Coke. I throw myself into his arms for a bear hug. Immediately, Ethan puts his hands on my back and pulls me into him for a kiss. I sink right into him, feeling his hard abs beneath his blue Ralph Lauren polo shirt with his collar pulled up instead of down. Ethan is the prep guy and I'm the beach babe. It's so cliché that it just makes sense.

We're perfect together.

"All hail the king and queen," Rob mocks with a roll of his eyes without looking up, before stuffing mashed potatoes in his mouth.

"Shut it, Rob," I hissed, parting from Ethan's embrace only for a moment to give Rob a death glare which, of course, he misses entirely.

"You guys should get a room," Rob adds, risking a glance up at me from his seat, a grin forming on his face.

"See, babe, I told you it would stick," Ethan states at the mention of our new nicknames. He smiles as he brushes a strand of hair away from my face and grabs hold of my hand before adding "My queen".

We settle into the seats across from Rob to eat our lunches. Our trays are so big; they stick out on either side of the metal cafeteria table. I'm sitting across from Rob and his potatoes and carrots, with Ethan on my left. He's got a burger today.

Normally, I would have chosen the same, but when I saw the cheesy gooey goodness of the mac & cheese, I had to have it. I never get amazing comfort food like this at home. My mom doesn't believe mac & cheese is real food, telling me that it's so unhealthy. She would scoff at me and force me to eat eggplant with goat cheese and honey with a fresh house salad before she would let me eat this garbage. But sometimes, I just want to eat normal food like any normal teenager, calories and all.

It's called comfort food for a reason. Plus, I can barely keep the weight on as it is—I need all the calories I can get.

I've been running so much since school started. Mostly to keep in shape, but also to clear my mind. I'm nervous about school, choosing a college or university, and nervous about what will happen to Ethan and me after we go all the way. Will he leave me once he gets what he wants?

What we want, I remind myself.

I could just as easily leave him. I try out the thought in my mind coyly, but I immediately shrug it off. Who am I kidding? I know I'll never dump Ethan. He's my soulmate, my partner in crime, the love of my life.

No. I can't.

The thought of leaving him makes my stomach turn on itself and I'm hit with a wave of nausea. He means too much to me and we're good together. We're so good.

Thankfully, the boys didn't seem to notice my body shaking when the idea of leaving Ethan crossed my mind. Thank God! If Ethan even suspected what I was thinking, he'd have a fit! He would go ballistic! Still, it's difficult for me to imagine Ethan ever being mad. He's always so bubbly, so silly. But he's also able to be serious when it's just the two of us. I love being the only one who sees that side of him.

I watch Ethan and Rob exchange the latest sports stats about last weekend's football game and I swallow a yawn. I can't appear bored. Ethan is the most interesting person in the world and we have so much in common except for sports. I leave those discussions to Rob.

Watching them now, you'd think they were brothers. Same tall, lean, and muscular build—football players, both of them. Both have clear blue eyes and squarely defined jaws—typical jocks. The only visible difference is that Ethan has thick floppy black hair, while Rob's thin brown hair is styled into medium length bed-head-like spikes. That, and Rob almost never smiles. While Ethan is funny ninety percent of the time, serious ten percent of the time, Rob is the opposite. After being friends for years, the two seem to just get each other. They're always together.

When I started dating Ethan, I knew I would have to be friends with Rob too. He's likable enough, but I don't have anything to say to him.

Some days I wish I could just go sit with my girlfriends and talk about things I actually care about rather than sports—especially not football. I barely see Ethan as it is, because we have no classes together this semester.

The girls will understand. They know this is the real deal. Most of them wish they were as lucky as me. I'm sure they talk about us behind my back though. Girls can be such bitches sometimes.

18

ELISABETH

After lunch, and a steamy make-out session against Ethan's locker, we separate to go to our respective classes. Chemistry and history for me; physics and calculus for Ethan.

Despite what everyone thinks of Ethan, he's also a genius academically. Not only is he great at sports and one of the most popular guys in school, he can also do complex equations in his head, without a calculator. He also constantly debates with his science teacher, Mr. Farrell, on the laws of physics. That's what I love so much about him—he's such a surprise—with so many different talents. I can't wait to unravel each layer until I know him completely.

Once school is done for the day, Ethan, Rob, and I are heading down to Irving Nature Park's saltwater marsh for a boardwalk stroll. This park is part of the Fundy coastline and features many various ecosystems.

My parents used to take Fran and I here when we were kids. It's where Ethan and I had our third date so many months ago. It's pretty, quiet, and free, so it's been a favourite hangout spot since.

The peaceful marshes go on for a long time, and I always feel like I can breathe more easily after our walks. Maybe it's the sea air. We might all be popular, but none of us enjoy the chaos and noise of a busy school day.

We're mostly introverts. We all like to connect with nature whenever we can. The boys prefer playing outdoor sports and I like to run. This walk won't be as active as that. However, it's outdoors, so it's a good compromise for all of us to hang out together.

I'm definitely not going to burn off my carbs today, but whatever. I'm sure Ethan will still think I'm beautiful.

I spot him with his backpack slung over his shoulder. He's leaning on my locker, and texting on his phone. I frown slightly as a sting of jealousy courses through me, wondering who he's texting. But then, he glances up and smiles, and all my fears disappear.

He's still mine. Always will be. I'll make sure of it. I won't become one of those lazy girlfriends who doesn't want to have any fun and who just wants to stay in and cuddle. I shiver at the word. Ugh. Cuddling is for losers. For kids. We're not kids anymore. We're practically adults. We're in love. When we hold each other close, we embrace. Our love is pure and we're saving ourselves for each other. And when we go all the way, we won't say, "We had sex", we'll say "we made love".

I feel Ethan's breath on my neck as he pulls me in for one of his famous bear hugs. I inhale a deep breath and catch a waft of his cologne that makes me feel things down below, pleasures that I can only guess at.

"You ready?" Ethan whispers in my ear, his mouth so close it makes me giggle.

I pull away from him only to grab his hand in mine and pull him down the hallway to the exit. As I'm making my way to the buses, Ethan pulls my hand tighter and tugs it the opposite way. Confused, I give him a searching look, only to find a smirk across his face.

Ethan, full of surprises.

I spot his mom's Honda CRV in the school parking lot and shriek with joy. Ethan got his license a few months ago and he's now finally able to drive alone without his parents.

He casually gets the car keys out of his dark blue jean's pocket and swings them into his palm, acting like an old pro. So cool. I'm still staring at him when I spot Rob coming around the passenger side window.

I wish Rob wasn't coming today, but I quickly shrug it off. Time with Ethan is still time with Ethan, even if I have to share him with Rob. And besides, if Rob's there, Ethan will pay even more attention to me, trying to make him jealous.

So, win for me.

We all hop into the CRV and buckle in. Once the car is in motion, we roll the windows down despite the low temperature and bring up the music loud on the speakers.

We're free. For the evening anyway.

"So, I texted my mom and she asked me to bring the car back by nine tonight, so I guess we'll need to leave the park by eight so I have time to drop you guys off," Ethan explains with one hand on the steering wheel, the other resting on my lap.

I feel a slight disappointment that we have to leave earlier, but I try my best to appreciate the time we have together. As we drive on, I day dream of kissing him in my bed, rolling around the sheets, discovering each other's bodies. A tingle of excitement courses through me as I imagine the months to come with Ethan. I look over to see his easy going smile and sigh.

He's so sweet.

And it must have been his mom that he was texting earlier. *See Elisabeth? You had nothing to worry about,* I scold myself. Ethan was simply doing the responsible, mature thing, as any decent adult would do. That's why his mother trusts him so much and lets him borrow her car.

I wish my parents would let me borrow theirs, but they don't trust me. I haven't even done anything that bad. But for some reason, my parents have always been extra hard on me. It's not fair. They never treated Fran that way. She got to do so many things and stay out later than me at the same age.

As I stare out the window at the flat plains of grass approaching as we leave the city and edge closer to the nature boardwalk, my mind escapes to thoughts of Fran. Before she disappeared, we had packed her oversized suitcase with her life for the last two decades, including clubbing dresses and high heels. While I was more comfortable in runners, Fran had always been about showing off her curves and her long legs. And did she ever have long legs! She always looked great, even without make-up—a natural beauty. Fran was so smart, too—a real catch. Her laugh would make everyone in the room smile. She just had such a presence about her.

My heart aches as I remember her on that day at the beach, not knowing it would be one of the last times I'd ever set eyes on her.

I miss her so much. I wish she could see me now.

Me and Ethan. She'd be so proud. Although, she was never that interested in a serious relationship, I know she would be happy for me.

***

Ethan parks the car in a nearly empty lot and the three of us exit the vehicle. I wrap my green knit cardigan tighter around my waist as the breeze coming from the water's edge of the Bay of Fundy whips at my face and blows right through me.

Thoughtfully, Ethan takes notice. He immediately removes his thick leather football jacket and drapes it over my shoulders to warm me up. He's such a gentleman. The walk isn't a long one, but it's peaceful.

We've spent many days here during the summer. It's a place we can let our guard down. We come here to forget about our lives, our failures and expectations, or just to forget, even for just a moment, who we are.

19

CLAIRE

I only have to wait ten minutes before the first bus shows up. I walk behind the shelter to a tiny shed-like building to buy a ticket for the bus line called Maritime Bus. Avoiding eye-contact as I set some bills down on the counter, where a clerk hands me my change and a one-way ticket. Grateful I wasn't asked many questions, I make my way back to the shelter to wait for the bus.

I have a general idea of where it's heading as I had a few minutes alone to study the bus route map. This bus line can get me either to the United States, the rest of Canada or more nearby, to Halifax. I decide to stay in Canada as I didn't think of packing my passport. I don't want to be in a public place for too long. My focus is on getting away from this place and fast. I can't risk anyone recognizing me. I decide that I will travel to Halifax first. Not too far, but travelling to a different province should be far enough to lose Ethan, assuming he's the one chasing me.

I step onto the bus with its blue and green stained carpeting and find a spot near the back, two rows up from the restroom. Thankfully there is no one else in this two seater row. I plop myself down heavily, exhausted by the adrenaline crash. I bring my legs up and lean my feet on the edge of the seat ignoring the stares from the passengers on the opposite row.

My wet shoes make the seat soggy and I instantly regret pulling my feet up.

I flop my gym bag onto the seat beside mine, my only friend in the world and my only tie to my past.

Finally, feeling reassured by the little privacy the row of seats provides, I allow myself a few moments to release some of the tension building up in my neck. I adjust my hoodie and lean my head on the cold glass to peer outside. The glass feels so good against my skin. I can feel the cold slowly beginning to numb my forehead. I'm the only one getting on the bus at this stop. The next stops are Quispamsis and then Hampton. I have no idea how long I will remain on this route or where my destination will be after Halifax.

As I settle into my seat, the padding under me feeling no thicker than a thin strip of paper, I finally allow myself to freak the hell out for the first time since the call from Inspector Riley. That call rattled me to the core, and it almost made me forget about the other strange things that had happened yesterday.

Was it only yesterday? It already feels likes weeks ago.

So much has happened since my meeting at work. How is all of this connected? I'm so shaky that I'm having a hard time concentrating. I need food and sleep. I really need to be at the top of my game right now—not weak.

I lose myself in thoughts, remembering the events from yesterday. It doesn't take me long to figure out Ethan's message. The queen pawn had been Sandra. She was my assistant and she was in the way. She was the only one I kept close, the only one who knew my schedule. Ethan knew this.

He knew that Sandra would stay loyal to me and not give out information unless extreme measures were taken. He needed to get rid of her in order to get to me. But to take a life?

I never thought Ethan could be capable of something so crazy, something so terrifying. Then again, I never truly knew what Ethan was capable of. I tremble at the thought. To think I'd once trusted him! He's a psychopath; he has to be. No normal person would kill for fun, only to send a message to an ex-girlfriend from over a decade ago. I search my memory for any signs in my past with Ethan that would give me clues as to whether he would be capable of killing someone, but I come up empty. I must have been stupid and too much in love to notice what was right in front of me.

My mind traces back to that night. How could he have broken my trust in such a way?

The pre graduation party...When blackness and evil lurked, when all hope for our future disintegrated. Like a fire consuming a house, the flame burned brighter than any amount of water could wipe out. The trust was severed, never to be put together again.

Ethan betrayed me—he broke us.

I made him pay for it, but now, he's trying to make my life a living hell.

The slow rhythm and gentle sway of the bus along with the steady soft buzzing of the motor, rings in my ears as I drift to sleep, slowly falling into the black abyss and into the unknown.

20

CLAIRE

"Amherst!" I hear the bus driver yell in the distance.

I blink away the sleep in my eyes and feel dampness around my chin. Gross! I wipe away the drool that seems to have accumulated there. Did I fall asleep? Oh no! How did I let myself fall asleep?

I'm suddenly very awake and glance around quickly. I'm relieved to find that I'm still alone in my seat, my bag, untouched, still beside me, a loyal companion.

I rub my dry eyes as I open my mouth wide to yawn. I guess I needed sleep. It's funny how your body can shut down when you need it to and somehow manages to block out all thoughts and fears.

Never mind the gnawing fear that's overtaking me every moment, eating me alive from the inside out, seeping out of my pores.

The fight or flight reaction takes over—a reflex. Some people believe that when faced with any situation of stress, we always default to one or the other, that our personality will automatically always choose the same response.

Every time.

But what happens when everything we've ever known in life has changed? When everything we once knew is no longer true? When we've built a new personality, a new identity?

I guess you could count my actions in the last twenty-four hours as a flight response to stress. I should probably admit to myself that this has always been my go-to reaction.

I run. It's what I do.

I'm sure Ethan has already figured that I would. I should have done something completely out of character, even for this new me. But to be honest, I don't think I could have. That would have been too much, to change something so genetically a part of me, such as my response to stress. I don't know if I would have been capable of changing my reaction even if my survival had depended on it.

My mind drifts back to the bus driver. Amherst, Nova Scotia. How long have I been asleep? That's at least a two-hour drive from Saint John. It might be good to stop here and have some breakfast. My stomach is rumbling, making loud whale-like sounds in approval, the gurgling so disruptive it's distracting me from making a solid escape plan. As the bus slows to a stop, I stand up carefully so as not to hit my head on the overhead compartments and sling my bag over my shoulder while walking the aisle accidently hitting an elderly woman in the head with my bag as I pass.

"Hey! Watch it!" she exclaims with a dignified cry.

"Sorry," I mumble, trying to stay hidden under my hood.

A gust of fresh air swirling towards me from the bus's open doors. Relief hits me and I take a deep breath. I wasn't made for confined dark spaces with moldy air. The outdoors is my home. I allow a hint of a smile on my face as I step down to the sidewalk. Several other passengers trickle out behind me and I move to the side to get my bearings. It might not be the States, but it's the furthest from my childhood home I've ever been.

I adjust my bag on my shoulder, the strap already starting to pull at the sore spot on my neck once more. I spend a few minutes taking note of my surroundings. An old-fashioned, cast iron clock is ticking loudly nearby and lets out a deafening chime announcing that is it presently noon. *Well, there you go stomach, you were right.* Before I can even think about food, my head throbs with a familiar aching. My brain needs food too, only in the form of liquid brown gold— coffee.

I scan the area quickly and I'm surprised to find a large map of the town. I locate the "You are here" red star and scout out nearby restaurants. I keep my fingers crossed for a Starbucks, but I spot none. No recognizable coffee chain in the near vicinity.

Crap.

I start to bite the skin on my lip, shut my eyes and let the wave of anxiety course through me as I inhale and exhale carefully. *It's fine. It's fine.* I repeat it like a mantra. Any food will do. I scan the list of available restaurants, skipping the sushi place and the pizza joint.

I happily spot a seemingly suitable alternative—Backman's Coffee House. Well, what do you know? It has 'coffee' right in the title. I hesitate briefly and realize I don't have many choices.

How bad can it be? I decide it's my best option and begin making my way over to it.

My stomach is gurgling so loudly, I half expect people to run out onto the street for fear of an earthquake. I cross Main Street and carefully walk up some creaky, wooden steps onto the porch of the coffee house with anticipation and gratitude.

Someone has worked hard to make this place appear welcoming and quaint.

Two plastic navy-blue Adirondack chairs sit on the porch as though in conversation, each with an elegantly padded chevron cushion leaning against the back. Yellow mums spill out of a large plastic flower pot sitting in the partial shade on the step. It appears someone has taken pride in the details here as the porch seems to be regularly swept clear of dead flowers and dirt. A welcome mat on the ground invites me to wipe my paws and I oblige. I may be breaking the law today by running away during an ongoing murder investigation where I may or may not be their prime suspect, but that doesn't mean I need to be disrespectful.

I falter at the door knowing it's risky to stop by a small mom and pop store such as this, but I'm counting on the fact that they must get several customers a day from the bus line and that I haven't made the news yet. I push through an old wooden door, brightly painted red, and trigger a chiming bell overhead, announcing my presence to the whole place.

Just great. *Way to go unnoticed*, I mutter quietly.

I get a few stares before I realize that in this kind of quaint setting someone could easily recognize my face should Inspector Riley question them later. But taking my hood off is likely better protocol for blending in rather than drawing attention to myself by keeping my hood on.

Thankfully, the café is mostly empty. Apparently the other few passengers from the bus who got off with me have wondered into different shops for lunch. I don't recognize anyone as I make my way to the wooden counter.

Smells of warm, fresh, homemade bread and strong espresso swirl up my nose, and I close my eyes briefly inhaling their goodness.

I haven't had anything to eat since my tuna salad at four o'clock last night in my office.

No wonder I'm starving.

As I peer over inspecting what other customers are eating, I'm pleased to notice that the food here seems promising. Deciding to continue on my streak of breaking some rules today, I skip over the salad portion of the blackboard menu above the register and settle on the turkey chili on basmati rice with garlic toast on the side. The rain has left me chilled to the bone and a warm bowl of spicy chili is sure to fill me up until I stop to eat again. Who knows when that is going to be?

A small wooden stove glows in the corner of the room and surprisingly, there is no one sitting by it. I slowly make my way towards it, tray in hand. I place the heavy tray on the small circular tree stump table and bring my chair up as close to it as I can manage despite the comically large size and low seating of my chair. Clearly this cozy spot wasn't designed with eating in mind, but I can't complain. I have a magnificent, warm fire and a steaming bowl of chili all to myself for the next twenty minutes or so.

Careful not to burn my tongue on the chili but eager to dive into my meal, I start with the garlic toast. I take a large bite of the crunchy buttery bread, and crumbs fall on my hoodie—a visible contrast to the black colour. I brush them to the ground immediately feeling guilty for the mess. The dark-stained pine floor here is as immaculate as the porch outside. I risk a glance up at the counter, but the owner doesn't seem to notice my bad manners, that I'm eating like a pig in a barn.

As I finally dig my large spoon into the chili, mixing it around to make sure I get rice in every bite, I think over my next steps. I'll need to find a pharmacy or a grocery store to buy some supplies. Nothing more than what I can carry, of course. I'm not looking forward to adding weight to my bag, but I need to make preparations.

As I eat, I watch the flames rise inside the wood stove as they engulf a dry log. For a moment, it feels like the flames are melting my sweater onto my forearm, sending a hot sensation through me. I move my arm quickly, as though the flames have burned my arm from inside the glass container.

Fear courses through me. Even when I'm at peace, I cannot rest. Maybe I really am entering a living hell.

21

Text from Sophie Mariner on Tuesday, September 16th at 8:15 a.m.

O.M.G. Claire! Can U believe Sandra is dead? Did U know? Of course U know. U were probably the 1st they called. Do U know what happened? So sad.

Text from Phil MacEwan on Tuesday, September 16th at 10:05 a.m.

Hi Claire, Phil here. Just wondering why you didn't show up to work today. Everyone is pretty shaken up by Sandra's death. Could really use your female intuition here. Are you taking the day off?

Text from Jess Levac on Tuesday, September 16th at 11:00 a.m.

Yo, what the hell was up with U last night? I can't believe U just ditched us like that. And that silent treatment with Val? It has to stop!

Text from Jess Levac on Tuesday, September 16th at 11:03 a.m.

And U totally missed meeting my BOYFRIEND Tony. I'm kind of pissed at U for leaving like that. Not cool.

22

CLAIRE

I leave the café with a chill covering my entire back. Even though the café was warm and inviting, I wasn't able to relax one little bit in there, thinking about what's ahead.

That he's coming after me.

I know everything about Ethan and he knows everything about me. That's the scary thing. He knows all my flaws and my habits. He knows I will run and that I need to plan everything. I'm not the spontaneous type, making it up as I go. That's just not who I am.

Part of me wonders what Ethan looks like now.

Are his blue eyes still that same dreamy deep ocean colour? Or have they clouded over with anger. Does his hair still flop down the way he used to wear it? Or does he wear it short now? Quickly, I shake the thoughts out of my mind. He's not a good person, I remind myself. For God's sake, he's a murderer, and he wants me dead.

Focused now with a plan in mind, I walk over to the pharmacy just a few stores down. Another small business where they have exactly what you need, and nothing more. Where everything is overpriced, but like everyone else, you fall for the trap because, well, let's face it, you're desperate.

I take a green plastic basket and make my way through the aisles. I pick up a few granola bars, a couple bottles of water, and gum for my nerves and my breath. Gross. I'm still embarrassed that I drooled on a public bus. I stop, glancing around the little store. Only about five rows of merchandise here, and I seem to be their only customer. The sign up front proudly announced, "Sullivan and Son. Open since 1956." How does a place like this even survive? I have no clue, but more than likely I'm not the only desperate passenger in need of gum to pass through. Can a store survive on one gum sale a week?

I grab a watch off the end aisle and make my way quickly to the hair colour department. I scan the boxes, landing on the most boring colour—dark brown. I need to transform into someone who won't stand out since I'm trying to blend in. Brown is one of the most common hair colours and is sure to cover up my expensive blond hair. A shame, really. My hair dresser would be appalled.

On impulse, I grab scissors and some maxi-pads on the way to the cash register. My hood still up, I take out two twenty-dollar bills and pay for my items. The old woman at the checkout doesn't pay any interest to my rush or my strange appearance. She's too busy watching a re-run of *"The Young and the Restless."* She doesn't bother glancing up when she hands me my change.

Dear God! That must mean it's the afternoon now. I need to get back on that bus, and soon.

I run back to the bus stop. The plastic bag neatly tucked inside my gym bag goes unnoticed by the other passengers waiting in the bus shelter. My gym bag makes crinkling sounds as though it's trying to share my escape plans with the world. Thankfully, the bus doesn't take long to reappear.

123

For the first time since I left work yesterday, I've done something right. Ignoring the stale air smell and the faint odour of urine, I gladly step back onto the bus that will shuttle me out of this dead town and take me far away from my hellish past.

23

HIM

The plan seems to have worked. I was able to follow Elisabeth, or Claire, whatever it is she goes by these days. I was right on her trail as soon as she made the choice to run. She never saw me as I knew she wouldn't. I had scouted out my position long before killing her assistant.

Yes, that was me.

Are you surprised? You probably hate me already, don't you? You don't even know me, yet you've already judged me. Most people do. They don't bother actually talking to a person before making their assessment of them.

It's easier that way.

I grip the wheel of the truck as I make my turns and press harder on the accelerator. It feels so good to be out in the open and have no one running after me, no one suspecting me. All signs point right to her. That was the plan all along.

She needs to pay.

It makes me sad to think about her dead, but this is how it has to be.

I saw her running out the front doors of her apartment building. She didn't even try to hide or leave by a back door. She used the fucking front door, but I was ready. I saw her run into that park where I stayed and watched until morning.

I watched her get on that bus too. I was peering through the window while she enjoyed her little lunch in that stupid forgotten town.

She couldn't have gotten far. I watched her from my spot in the bushes at the back of the store. At first, I thought she'd spotted me when she randomly started looking around her like a scared little kitten who'd heard a loud bang. I hid deeper in the bushes and took the opportunity to take a leak. When I glance up again, she was gone.

That was a stupid move, dick head. Mad at myself that I've started making mistakes, I kick at the ground. The absence of something to punch makes me even angrier.

I walk on the open sidewalk and peer into the stores. Not spotting her, I start making my way back to the restaurant thinking that maybe she was using the bathroom or something. Like a creep, I start examining every face, trying to find hers amongst the crowd, but I don't see her.

I was surprised to see she hadn't changed much since I'd last seen her. Still beautiful, still lean—obviously she's taken care of her body. She looked all confident and wore expensive clothes. That's not how she used to be when I knew her.

I didn't like it.

I recognize her better now that the fear is taking over her body, and she is hunching down and lurking, just like me. We were always meant to be together, she and I. Too bad it can't be that way now.

I step in a puddle as I miss the sidewalk curb and drop into the street.

Damn it!

As I'm shaking out my pants, I happen to glance up and spot her just as she's getting back on the bus.

Gotcha, I whisper under my breath.

I quickly make my way to my truck, parked in the shade on a side street. I pull up the bus schedule on my cell phone as I follow three cars behind, carefully keeping my distance, remaining successfully hidden for now.

I will show myself soon enough.

She will know her fate soon if she doesn't already.

24

CLAIRE

The bus bounces me around in my seat as I cross my arms tighter around my body trying to hold myself together. My stomach feels like a thousand butterflies are trying to get out. The chili isn't enjoying its stay, it appears. I shut my eyes, afraid one more pothole will completely unglue me.

There seems to be a lot more people on the bus with me now. A lot of students. I notice one of them is wearing a thick gold ring with a deep black X on it, a symbol belonging to St. Francis Xavier University. I didn't realize this bus could take me to Antigonish, home of that university.

I ponder my options for a few minutes and decide that might be the best place to stop. I need to figure out where to sleep tonight and where to stay for a few weeks until the investigation dries up a bit and people stop searching for me.

The irrational part of me thinks that maybe when this is all over, I could apply for a job there, but who am I kidding? Phil would never give me a solid reference, not when I'm now a prime suspect in a murder investigation. I'm screwed, utterly screwed. I will need to learn some new skills and get a job that pays under the table. Like a criminal, I will need to lay low for a while, leave the luxury behind in lieu of survival.

That's something I can live with.

I rest my head on the cold glass as I peer out at the scenery before me, absent-mindedly biting the dry skin off my lip. It's not the best of views. It's more about getting people somewhere than about enjoying the ride. I wish I had my iPod with me right now—music always seems to calm me.

A few hours later, the bus pulls up in Antigonish and almost half of the passengers exit onto the dark fall streets. As I step off the bus, a weight is lifted off me and I decide I will make the most of this new life. I will leave my past behind once and for all and not live in fear.

This is a new start. A chance at true happiness, I lie to myself—overdoing the optimism a smidge. Rounding the corner, I spot a black truck with its lights off parked in the shadows of the street. The hair on my neck rises, my instincts kicking in.

Is it me or is there someone in that truck? And are they looking at me?

25

CLAIRE

The old fear reflex to escape makes my head throb and my ears ring so loudly that I need to fight hard to push back the instinct to cover my ears.

And I run.

I run so fast, I push through the crowd of students who just left the bus nearly knocking a young girl to the ground in my wake. My hood falls and my long blond hair floats behind me like a cape. I'm pretending to be brave, when I am actually terrified.

I need to get my bearings. I've never visited the campus before. I spot a sign for a bathroom in the arts building that I'm hoping will be isolated. But is isolated the best option when I think I'm being followed? Putting that thought aside, I realize my options are limited. I need a place to hide and fast.

I run towards the arts building and crash through the doors, receiving a few stares from annoyed students. They can tell I'm older than most of them. What is this adult doing here, I imagine them thinking. It wasn't so long ago that I would have been one of them. From my appearance it's clear that I'm not a professor late for a lecture. People quickly move aside, unwilling to get involved, noting my impending panicked state.

Spotting the bathroom sign up ahead, I scurry down a flight of stairs and find the bathroom that I was seeking. I do a quick check under the stalls but soon discover that I'm alone.

I let out a breath and swiftly lock the main door behind me. Without wasting any time, I spill the contents of the gym bag onto the floor. It's the first time I've actually been able to see what I packed in my frenzy to leave my apartment.

The result is quite pathetic. A couple of shirts, one pair of underwear, and two pairs of shorts. In this cold fall climate? What was I thinking? I'm forced to keep my pants and hoodie on for now until I get a chance to stop at a store and buy new clothes, maybe new underwear and socks. With the amount of running I'm doing lately, I'll wear a hole through this pair fast enough.

The items I picked up at the pharmacy have also scattered all over the floor. After waiting a moment to make sure that no one is coming in, I grab the box of hair dye and open the package. I snap on the latex gloves provided and shake the colour into the clear little formula tube until it becomes almost black. I take a deep breath and stare at my blond self in the mirror, one last time. I extend my gloved hand over my head, close my eyes, and begin to squeeze out the black liquid dye onto my hair.

I'm too mad to cry, but my hair means so much to me. I've never had it darker than a chestnut colour before. Now that Ethan has found me, I've got no choice but to do something drastic and change my appearance.

Asshole, I mutter.

I glare at my reflection, as though it's him. I wish I could confront him. He screwed everything up! We were perfect together. We were so in love. I wanted to marry him! I guess it's a good thing I didn't. Who knows what he would have done to me if I'd stayed with him. In a way, he did me a favour, showing me his true colours.

I feel some black liquid ooze down near my ears and wipe it up with toilet paper. Once I've massaged the dye all over my hair and I can't see a single blond strand left, I lean my back against the cold blue brick wall and slide down all the way to the concrete floor careful not to get any of the dark dye on the wall. I slip on the watch and count down the ten minutes.

I take note of my other wrist to inspect my broken necklace. The tiny gold chain is wrapped tightly around my small wrist, but it's not difficult to notice the clasp is completely broken.

Damn it!

This necklace has always been a good luck charm for me. The delicate circle represents karma. My sister Fran gave it to me for my birthday the summer before I started high school.

God, I miss Fran. Where is she now?

I don't understand what happened, or why Mom and Dad never bring her up in conversations. I think they know more about what happened to her than they let on, but they won't tell me. They keep me in the dark about everything.

Oh God, Mom and Dad.

I haven't even told them what's going on. Inspector Riley will surely have gotten hold of my parents by now. They will lose their minds when he tells them I'm gone.

Crap! I didn't think about this. Like my parents need to worry about another missing daughter. It wasn't enough that I'd left them and changed my name. Now I've disappeared, just like Fran, without a word.

Great. I'm officially the worst person in the entire world.

My painful ten minutes of waiting is finally over and I stand up slowly.

Still stiff from my night in the park, I remind myself that I will need to find a proper bed or even a basic sofa to lie on tonight, not that I will sleep well. Insomnia will surely have followed me, even here.

My once pretty, light blond hair now resembles a dirty nest of black gunk on my head. I fight the tears. I lean over the sink and dip my head under the tap to let the freezing water wash all the dye out. After many minutes of rinsing and scrubbing, the water finally runs clear and I lift my head to take a look at the damage. I bear a resemblance to the girl in The Ring, white faced, long stringy dark hair and big purple crescents under my eyes.

I stuff a hand inside the hair dye box and grab the conditioner. I lather it on and rinse my hair again after a few minutes. I walk over to the hand dryer and squat under the vent, letting the scorching hot fan blow dry my hair. Without a brush to untangle this mess, I run my fingers through the dark tresses as a make-shift hair brush. Relieved to see the black colour has now transformed into a more natural rich brown, I breathe out slowly as I dry the ends some more.

Box dyes are always a gamble. I think dye companies take pleasure in making women panic at the sight of the dark colours during the application, only to magically lighten it up at the blow drying stage.

Once my hair is completely dry, I stand up straight, stretch my back and let out a deep groan. My legs are killing me from squatting all that time under the hand dryer. *So much for being in shape*, I think as I run my hands along my thighs trying to get the blood back into them.

Shaking out my long legs, I walk over to the sink that transformed me from a blonde to a brunette. I don't like this sink. I hate it actually. It appears to be mocking me with its gaping mouth, laughing at my distress.

With disdain, I rinse out the traces of the dye, scrubbing my fingers into the sink near the overflow and the plug. Once satisfied that all the dye is gone and all the evidence is washed away, I take a good long look in the mirror. I'm startled at the huge change a small cheap box of dye can make. But it's not enough—I'm still recognizable.

If Ethan is following me and if that was him in the black truck, I need to be extremely careful. No cutting corners now. I need to be on high alert. *He is dangerous*, I remind myself. He's not the guy I fell in love with all those years ago. He's a psychopath who wants to kill me.

I pull out the scissors from my bag, this time, letting the tears fall. I start snipping away chunks of my hair, hoping pieces of my past get chopped away at the same time.

26

CLAIRE

I seem lighter with my new haircut, I feel a little less like a rat that needs to hide and scurry in the corners of the room. I slowly exit the basement bathroom.

I glance to my left and my right. The long yellow hallway appears to be deserted. I make my way up the checkered black and white steps, holding tight to the wrought iron railing, pulling myself up at every step. My hair is shorter and weighs less than I'm used to, but my body feels heavy with exhaustion. My shoulders are tight and aching from my bus travels. The pressure from running away has caused my muscles to bunch up in knots in the top part of my back.

The noise of sneakers running down the ceramic glass tiles to my right sends a bolt of energy through me. Fully alert now, I twist my entire body to survey the direction of the noise, only to notice a young student running out of a classroom, the steel door shutting loudly behind him. I wonder what he's running away from in such a hurry.

Maybe his demons are chasing him too.

I don't stand around long to find out. I make my way down the empty halls—most classes are over by this time of night. The sun has completely set, and I'm met with my own reflection in the darkened glass of the outside door.

Still shocked by my new haircut, I run a hand through my freshly washed and dried hair.

I decided to cut off several inches of hair and give myself bangs. Instead of my classic thick straight blond hair going past my breasts, I now sport a disheveled medium length, dark brown shaggy bob with bangs.

It doesn't look as bad as it sounds.

The brown actually matches better with my eyes and eyebrows. It's quite natural, in fact. I'm surprised a twelve-dollar hair dye box managed to hide all of my expensive salon treated blond hair in a matter of minutes. I hope that the darker brown and shorter cut will be enough to trick Ethan.

Leaning against the exterior door, I feel the cold evening air seeping through the base of the door. Time is ticking by and I'm no closer to finding a place to sleep tonight. Will I find a safe place? Or spend another night in the harsh elements? Maybe I could sneak back down to the basement and sleep in the bathroom without being noticed.

Contemplating my options for tonight, I spot an old cork message board in a corner on the opposite side. I slowly make my way to it, feeling pulled towards it. I begin to franticly scan the adverts browsing it to find out what had caught my eye in the first place. The noise from earlier keeps me on high alert, my rapid heartrate reminding me that I am not alone in this building—this is both frightening and reassuring.

Most of the papers advertise class manuals for sale at half the price of new ones. Others offer tutoring. There are posters on student rights and one against bullying. A pair of students seem to be looking for someone to rent their two-bedroom apartment, and there is also an ad for the local police help line.

Underneath this, I spot an older advertisement. Yellowed by the sun, the ad is sticking out, some of the cut-out slips missing.

Room for rent, $350/month, located in Salt Springs.

That is less than an hour from here. I check my new watch for the time—7:40 p.m. It's worth a shot. I rip off a slip of the paper with the phone number and pray the information is still accurate. The ad appears really worn and it's been covered up many times by newer ads. Maybe they have already rented the room and just forgotten to take down the ad.

Thankful for the old building's amenities, I grab the pay phone, slide two quarters in, and hold my breath as I dial the number. The ringing seems to go on forever. Finally, on the third ring, someone picks up the receiver on the other side.

A loud cough rings in my ear and I pull the phone away from my ear quickly, wincing at the noise.

"Hello,...hello?" a man answers.

"Hello?" echoes a woman's voice, sounding farther away.

"Anna, I already picked it up!" yells the man with a weak attempt to cover the phone.

"Oh, ok, sorry!" and she hangs up her receiver.

"Hello?" I question hesitantly, already regretting making this phone call.

"There we go. Hi there, how can I help you?" the man offers in a friendly tone.

Encouraged, I ask him about the ad and if the room is still available.

"Oh, that ad! I had forgotten all about it!" he laughs as my heart sinks at the thought of having to find another place before it gets too late. I'm about to thank him and hang up when he adds, "We put that ad up years ago, but as a matter of fact, the room is still available."

I sigh loudly, immediately relieved.

He follows by asking me if I'm a student. Lying, I answer that I am—an arts major—the truth.

I ask him if it would be possible to move in this evening. I hear him cover the phone with his hand again as he asks Anna her thoughts. I hear her yell something back, presumably from down the hall in the kitchen as I can make-out the faint sound of pots and pans in the background.

"You are more than welcome to come over this evening, my dear." He proposes in an endearing tone.

I feel hot tears run down my cheeks as I thank him for his kindness. His voice reminds me of my Poppa, my grandfather, who died ten years ago. His kindness is a drastic contrast to my father's gruffness and business-like discipline.

He tells me his name is Stewart Davidson and his wife is Anna. He offers to come pick me up at the campus as he assumes I don't have access to a vehicle. I happily accept and we end the call.

A fresh hope grows inside of me that I might have made it and found a way to hide out until this mess sorts itself out. I rub my neck as I imagine the promise of a hot shower and the soft comfort of a warm bed to rest my aching muscles on tonight.

I sit on the cold floor underneath the old pay phone and wait. The sense of relief I was just feeling is immediately replaced with extreme fatigue and hunger.

I reach in my bag to pull out one of the granola bars I stashed there earlier and devour it as though I haven't eaten in days. My brain feels foggy and I can't think straight. This always happens to me when I don't get enough sleep. I was already running on only a few hours of sleep a night. After getting the call from Inspector Riley, I haven't managed to get any decent sleep. The rest I had in the park and on the bus didn't help me much.

Oh God, what if he's followed me here? What if it was one of his guys in that pick-up truck?

I hope I don't get sweet Stewart and Anna in trouble.

I quickly entertain the idea of calling Stewart back to cancel the agreement, but then realize that he's most likely already on his way to pick me up. I can only hope that I don't transfer my bad luck over to them. That's the thing about being a criminal. You become like a disease and begin infecting everyone around you.

PART
TWO

27

ELISABETH

Breaking rules, twisting the truth, and being disobedient. That's what most teenagers do when they reach a certain age.

I certainly saw this crazy streak with my sister Fran. She was a wild one, always going out with one guy or another, nothing steady or serious like what Ethan and I have. My parents never knew this, of course. Whenever they'd question her, she'd always assure them that she wasn't interested in boys. She always voiced her deep desire to remain free, to belong only to herself and to the sea. Maybe that's where she ended up in the end—free as a fish, swimming into the deep ocean, singing songs of love and celebrating the joys of being alive.

All I remember is a loud and mumbled argument between my sister and my dad in the dining room while I was getting out of the shower before bedtime. And then, I never saw her again.

Every time I confront my parents about it, my dad immediately gets defensive and angry. I can't talk to him about anything. Since Fran left, he's closed off, drinks more and laughs less. My mom isn't much better. She worries about everything, always asking me where I'm going and with whom.

I have a cell phone for the sole purpose of texting my mother reassuring messages about my whereabouts. So that's why this little white lie about where I'm actually going tonight is so thrilling.

My parents think I'm going for a quiet movie and sleep-over at Rebecca's tonight when in reality, I'm heading over to Ethan's for a pre-grad party. Everyone is going to be there.

I've taken care of planning my appearance for tonight and I must admit I'll be looking pretty sexy. I'll need to keep everything hidden in my overnight bag so that my parents don't become suspicious. I've spent quite a bit of time on my hair which is naturally straight, but now it's really straight, not one single hair is out of place. I've used an entire container of hair spray on it. In a way, it makes me seem older and I like it.

It makes me resemble how Fran used to present herself. Confident. Bold. Sexy.

I'm waiting until I'm in Rebecca's car to add the finishing touches to my make-up and change clothes because my parents would never let me leave the house looking the way I will end up looking tonight. In my large tote bag is a pair of sparkly, black, open toe heels that I'm praying I can pull off. I found them in Fran's room. I'm not sure why she decided to leave them behind when she disappeared. They are gorgeous! I'm not used to wearing anything so high, but I figure there won't be much walking around, so I should be able to pull it off at least for tonight. While I was scavenging in Fran's forgotten closet, I also found this amazing tight leather mini skirt and black sequin short sleeve top. I can't wait to see the entire look put together.

Rebecca arrives to pick me up at 8 p.m. I wave goodbye to my parents as we head down the long narrow drive onto Queen Street and then onto the county road.

The ride is a bumpy one, the gravel road filled with potholes, but we have the music cranked up loud and the lights on inside her car so I can get ready and put the finishing touches on my outfit.

I clumsily take off my dark skinny jeans to a whistle from Rebecca and pull on the leather mini skirt. My smooth tanned legs look like they are shiny in the street lights bouncing off of us through the windows. I slip off my plain grey t-shirt and throw on the sequined top, tucking it in the skirt, as best as I can manage. I finally refasten my seat belt and lean over to pull on the heels.

Turning on the overhead light, I pull down the tiny mirror to apply black shadow across my eyelids. Waiting between bumps on the road, I hesitate a moment before drawing a perfect black line at the edge of my lashes and add several swipes of dark mascara. I've chosen to go with a simple pink gloss rather than the bright red lipstick I brought with me. I find when you play up both the eyes and the lips it can be too much brightness for one face. Plus, I know that as soon as I get there, Ethan's lips will be irresistible, and any lipstick will end up smeared across his face which is so unsexy. This way, I don't need to be careful where I place my lips. I can just be free to kiss him as much as I want, anywhere I want.

Tonight is a big night. Ethan and I are waiting until our graduation day. Since it's a pre-graduation party, the rules might get blurred if the mood strikes.

When we turn onto Ethan's road, we can already hear the shrieks of teenage girls in the distance and the growing roar of a party. We spot his house in the distance, lit up like a Christmas tree.

Every light in the house is turned on and people have started to spread out onto the yard and the front porch.

The front door is ajar, casting a bright light onto the small gatherings of smokers on the lawn, an open invitation for people to come and go as they please.

A familiar thrill runs through me as the beat of the music penetrates my soul. The bass on the speakers is so loud it seems to both control and mess up the beating of my heart. I know I will have a pounding headache later on. Still, I get out of the car with the same anticipation and excitement I always feel when I go to parties.

The energy is contagious. It's going to be a night to remember. I just know it. I can feel it deep in my gut and with every fiber of my body.

28

CLAIRE

I must have fallen asleep again, too weak to wait for that kind old man, Stewart, to make the forty-minute drive. A bright light beams through the glass of the exterior door, shining through brightly across the white tiles and exposing me, a black lump on the floor. I squint and bring my hand to my eyes, a granola bar wrapper scrunched up in a ball still in my fist. I must have fallen asleep with it in my hand.

I quickly grab my gym bag and make my way through the doors. A wall of cold air hits my lungs and for a moment, I cannot breathe. My hair is flying all around me as the harsh wind whips at me, making me stumble slightly backwards. Punishment for getting this innocent man involved in my mess, surely.

When I look up, the car's only working headlight is still shining directly at me, but now there is the shadow of man in front of it. In the dark, it's impossible for me to make out any facial features, but his shadow does tell me a few things. He is a tall, moderately built man, leaning slightly to the right, and he's wearing a cowboy hat.

At nighttime.

Oh, gees. Who are these people? What did I get myself into?

As I make my way over to him, his features begin to appear. I see a weathered, kind face, crooked teeth, and bushy grey eyebrows.

He's wearing very large oval glasses and has a thick grey handlebar mustache. He's not wearing a coat, just a thick plaid button-down shirt. He holds out his large hand to shake mine and takes me in with one long look. He doesn't let go of my hand for a long while. Uncomfortable, I look down at my feet, hoping he can't tell that I'm hiding something. Unfortunately, his intuition seems to win out.

"You're not really a student here, are you?" he concludes, a knowing look appearing on his face.

Not threatening, but curious.

I decide I might still have a chance at this rental agreement if I just tell him the truth. I confirm his suspicions and tell him that no, I am not a student, but I do need a place to stay, a warm meal and a hot shower.

He looks me over once more, dropping my hand, trying to decide what to do. His hesitation doesn't last long as he turns on his brown leather cowboy boot heels and opens the door to his run down green and white Ford pick-up and waves me in.

Stewart seems to be in bad shape, both financially and physically. His truck has rust spots on every surface, one of the headlights appears to have burned out, and he is limping as he makes his way to the driver's side.

I throw my bag in the passenger side on the rusty floor, a small hole showing through to the ground below. I squeeze the bag in between my shins and sit on my hands to avoid twisting them nervously. The zipper of my gym bag is not fully closed and some of the pads fall out onto the floor of the truck, but I'm not paying attention, too nervous to move.

He pretends not to notice me looking at him as he backs up onto the road and starts making his way down Highway 104 to Salt Springs. The ride is mostly silent other than the occasional cough from Stewart.

He doesn't ask who I really am, probably assuming I wouldn't tell him the truth anyway.

He's right.

He whistles to no particular tune and rests his left arm on the window ledge even though the window is up. The heat is cranked up to the max, but there is still a draft coming in from the bottom of the truck through the rusty hole. I rub my hands up and down my legs in a weak attempt to warm myself up.

Soon, I'll need to buy myself a good winter coat. Snow in the Maritimes comes in massive storms and can hit at any moment. It can, without warning, cut off entire towns of amenities for days or weeks. I will need to find something to do for money while I'm out here as well. Maybe I should become a waitress or something. Not that it matters. I doubt I will be staying in this place for too long. The best thing is always to keep moving around while staying under the radar. Never give your true name or any identifying details about your family, yourself, or where you come from.

***

Less than an hour later, we pass the sign to Salt Springs. Stewart, who had been whistling the entire ride, suddenly goes quiet. Instinctively, I know something in him has shifted. I don't know if it's just my experience of being a daughter, but I know that Stewart is about to have some sort of important talk with me. I brace myself for what might happen.

The air in the cab of the truck suddenly feels heavy. The silence, which had previously been comfortable, now feels tense. The energy is different. Stewart is holding himself much taller, his back straighter. There is nothing casual or relaxed about his posture now. No more charming, welcoming nature.

I feel the pace of my breath increasing, my pulse rising. Have I put myself in danger? What do I really know about these people?

"Our house is just up this road up here," he explains slowly, pointing at the black space ahead. He scratches his moustache pensively, obviously leading up to the real reason he's suddenly speaking to me after an hour of silence.

He vaguely waves his hand towards the direction of the house and suggests, "When Anna asks you for your name, let's just pretend that your name is Beth. Just Beth. No last name. She won't ask more. Just tell her what you told me, that you're studying arts. She'll know better than to question it." Still looking out the front window, never meeting my eye, he continues, "Anna has a big heart, but she doesn't pry. She understands privacy."

Then, as though he had been listening to my inner monologue from earlier, he adds finally, "And if you need money, I might be able to get you a part-time job somewhere nearby. Doesn't pay a lot, but it's something. It's a hard job, though. You need to be a strong person, but you look like you could handle something like that."

He ends with a sideways glance in my general direction, a small smirk on his tight lips. Too shocked to argue, I nod slightly. I learned a long time ago that if you don't say anything or openly disagree, then you are agreeing.

Grateful and confused by this new dynamic and connection, I feel tears prickling, threatening to fall. For so many years, people thought of me as weak for running away like I did. Like I still do now. But here is this man, this stranger, who just met me and who's only known me for one hour, understanding me better than most people ever did. He's only ever known this version of me, scared and withholding information, but yet here he is calling me strong. He's willing to keep my secret and lie to his wife. His willingness to do that for me has me feeling extremely grateful. No one has ever wanted to lie for me before. No one has ever put their faith in me before.

This makes me want to trust him, maybe just a little bit.

I twirl my gold karma necklace, wrapped tightly around my wrist, as I think. The habit is still present, even with the change of placement. As I think over my options, I feel a creeping smile on my lips.

Yes, maybe my luck is changing.

29

ELISABETH

I play with the dainty chain hanging off my neck, running the small gold circle sideways on the chain a few times, biting my lower lip while standing in front of Ethan's door, hesitating.

Anticipation of the night ahead is building up inside me. I take a deep breath and then stroll through the open door, careful to walk slowly so I don't trip in these crazy high heels. Strangely, the music seems to stop right as Rebecca and I enter the warm room. We didn't bother to bring our coats in from the car and I'm glad for that now. The coat pile is so large that, many of them have fallen down to the floor. A couple has taken residence on top of the pile and is engaged in a heavy make-out session.

I feel both repulsed and excited. Things are already so far along and it's still early in the night. I'm suddenly very aware that I'm stone-cold sober. I'm behind on the drunkenness level. I'll need to hurry and catch up to the rest of the partiers.

As I finish scanning the first room, the music starts up again and gets louder with each verse. I spot my friend Terra by the stereo, playing on her phone, a USB cable linking it to the speakers. She always gets stuck with the role of DJ at parties, but I think it suits her just fine. She's kind of a quieter girl, but she sure knows her music.

I can't help but move my hips instinctively as she starts the next song.

She looks up, sensing my stare, and winks at me as she drops the phone back on the table and dances over to me.

"Hey, beyotch!" she screams over the music. Apparently even Terra has gotten into the hard liquor quite early tonight. Speaking of which, where are the drinks?

"Hey, yourself!" I shout in her ear. I'm not drunk enough for it to be cool to scream. My ears are ringing. I need a drink. "I love this song!" I beam at her.

"I know. I saw you guys coming up so I switched it for you. A queen needs a grand entrance." She bends over, does a curtsy, and I laugh, slightly uneasy at the undertone of rudeness.

Terra is sure coming out of her shell tonight. Wary that I may have spotted a touch of resentment there, I choose not to focus on it tonight. Normally I would spend hours analyzing what someone had said, the tone they used, and the meaning behind it, even days after the interaction.

But not tonight.

Tonight is an important night—my big night with Ethan. Possibly. We haven't decided that yet. Not officially anyway. But I think I'm ready.

"Hey, Terra, have you seen Ethan around?" I ask in her ear, her head swaying, eyes closed, lost in the music blaring through the room.

"The king?" she smirks, one eye peaking up at me, inquisitive. "Yeah, he's over there." She waves over to the kitchen as she twirls away, leaving me laughing at her back.

Oh boy, I'll be holding her hair in the bathroom when she throws up later, I'm sure.

I shake my head and make my way slowly to the kitchen. During my short interaction with Terra, Rebecca had wandered across the room and I spot her in a corner speaking with some of her other friends. I wave my hand to get her attention and gesture drinking, followed by pointing to the kitchen to let her know I'm leaving the room to get a drink.

There is a strong smell of pot in the air that I'm sure Ethan is freaking out about. His mom would never allow drugs of any kind to cross the threshold of their home.

The lights in the kitchen are bright in comparison to the low-lit room I just left. The kitchen has dozens of recessed lights making the room feel exposed and clinical. There is a serving station set-up on the marble island. A variety of hard liquor, pop cans, and red Dixie cups are littering the wet surface. There aren't many people hanging out in here, which is surprising. Yet again, it's only a refill station, not a prime party spot.

I think the vivid lights Ethan's mom loves so much for her meal preparation are simply too intense for a party scene. It completely changes the vibe. Without a dimmer option, the space is too exposed and, by no fault of its own, not intimate enough. When people go to parties, they want to find the darkest corners to escape to, to hide in. Those corners are where you mess around. No one wants to do dirty stuff under this bright lighting.

Whereas most people have filtered out to the other rooms of the house, I'm not surprised to find Rob lingering here in the glaring light. Not one for the party scene, he prefers the quiet.

He is staring at nothing, a pained look on his face. Part of me feels bad for him as I make my way further into the kitchen over to the red Dixie cups.

He must have spotted movement in the corner of his eye, because just then he looks up and our eyes meet.

For a moment, I think I see a small sparkle in his eyes as he looks at me, his smile lopsided. It makes me see him like the handsome guy Rebecca and the other girls are always going on about. Rebecca has always had a secret crush on Rob. I've been trying to hint to Ethan that we should go on a double-date with them so they could get to know each other romantically, but it hasn't happened yet. They're both so shy. They'd be perfect together.

While I only have eyes for Ethan, who is in my opinion, the hottest guy in the school, many of my girlfriends think that Rob and Ethan are equal on the hotness scale. Though the boys do look very much alike, their personalities couldn't be more different. Ethan is outgoing and friendly. He also has that amazing smile that makes me melt. Rob, on the other hand, is mysterious and quiet.

I guess I can see the appeal of that now.

Tonight, I feel his eyes on me and I see him differently. I stand there, paralyzed, frozen under his gaze. He looks different tonight in this light. He's not hiding in Ethan's shadow for once, and I can see him more clearly. I'm stunned to admit to myself that he's a very good-looking guy.

He starts making his way over to me, his lips pressed together, head down slightly, eyes intent on me. His intensity is making my heart skip a beat involuntarily.

I match his slow stride and back up slowly, carefully, until I feel the cold marble countertop behind me. He's almost reached me, when cheerful, drunk Ethan sweeps in and cuts Rob off right as he is closing in. Ethan almost steps on Rob's shoes, he's so close to him.

Was Rob leaning in for a kiss? What was that look he was giving me? My vision blurs for just a moment as I readjust to Ethan's face, closer in proximity.

With a huge smile on his face, Ethan sheepishly looks at me, his puppy eyes adorable. I'm so happy to see him, but I can't help but wonder what Rob was going to do once he'd reached me.

Sensing a presence close behind him, Ethan turns around and comes nose to nose with Rob. The two seem to have a tense silent conversation using only their eyes. I swear they could be twins. Rob has been growing out his hair lately and both his and Ethan's are styled the same way tonight. Rob might even be wearing one of Ethan's shirts. It wouldn't be the first time. Rob usually stays over at Ethan's after school before a party so they can get ready together.

What a bunch of girls! I smile at the thought. They have quite the bromance going on.

Rob's family doesn't have extra money for things like cars and clothes, so Ethan is always lending him clothes and driving him around whenever he needs to go somewhere. There is an underlying respect and affection between them that I will simply never understand. They are as close as brothers, but now, that closeness seems to be jeopardized by Rob's closeness to me.

Ethan's strong stance and broad shoulders, tell Rob to step back. The tension doesn't last long. Though no words were spoken, the point was made clear with a simple eye contact interaction. Ethan slaps his hand on Rob's shoulder and spills a bit of his beer onto his shoes.

"Damn it!" Ethan mutters as he walks to the counter for a sheet of paper towel and throws it on the ground to wipe up the mess with his shoe. "Sorry about that, man."

Whether it had been deliberate or purely accidental, I'll never truly know. Those two agree on mostly everything and never let anything get between them.

Except me, for some reason.

As Rob wipes up the beer from his shoes, Ethan takes the opportunity to grab a refill. What is it about parties that no one takes off their shoes? I guess house rules like removing your shoes when you enter seem silly and irrelevant what with all the other rule-breaking going on—music too loud, underage drinking, sex, and drugs. Either that or most people are like me and their shoes simply complete their outfit and they are too proud to remove them.

When Ethan comes back, Rob is leaning against the counter next to me, looking behind Ethan to the living room at a couple making out on the couch. I find myself glancing in the same direction and spot Terra, drunk, dancing by herself, Dixie cup held high. Well, at least she's having a good time tonight. Maybe she decided to let loose, this being the last party of the year and all.

"Damn, babe, you look hot!" Ethan mumbles, slurring a little bit near the end.

Oh geez! Any hope I had of having sex with him for the first time tonight evaporates right then. Tipsy Ethan is sexy, but drunk and sloppy Ethan is so far from it. He comes closer and plants a wet kiss on my lips, his mouth stale with the smell of beer and cigarette smoke. I gently push a hand on his hard chest—damn he's in good shape.

"Ethan, you're drunk." I laugh. "And I need a drink!" I push past him, knowing he will be staring at my ass as I lean over the kitchen island to pour myself a rum and coke.

I take a slow sip of the cold, sweet drink before I turn around again. Just as I was expecting, Ethan is staring with gawking eyes like a cartoon character whose mouth is wide open and whose jaw is hitting the floor.

I laugh.

Good. He likes the outfit. At least one thing went according to plan tonight. Before I can stop myself, I chug the drink like I'm the bravest girl here and turn right around to pour myself another.

30
WEDNESDAY, SEPTEMBER 17TH

Text from Phil MacEwan on Wednesday, September 17th at 11:00 a.m.

Hi Claire, Phil here. Look, I don't know what you're doing, but the investigation into Sandra's death is leaning to murder. Now they are asking me questions about you.

Text from Phil MacEwan on Wednesday, September 17th at 11:03 a.m.

Claire? It doesn't look good that you conveniently disappeared on the same day Sandra was killed. I think they're trying to peg you as a suspect…

Text from Phil MacEwan on Wednesday, September 17th at 11:05 a.m.

Look, just call me when you get this.

Text from Jess Levac on Wednesday, September 17th at 1:00 p.m.

Claire, what the hell? Where are U? No one's heard from U since U bailed on Monday. What's up with that?

Text from Jess Levac on Wednesday, September 17th at 3:15 p.m.

I just called UR work and they said no one's seen U since Monday. And that your assistant was murdered? WTF? CALL ME.

Text from Emma Beaufort on Wednesday, September 17th at 4:01 p.m.

Claire! I just got a call from Jess. UR assistant was murdered? OMG! Are U ok?

2 Missed calls from Emma Beaufort on Wednesday, September 17th at 4:03 p.m.

Text from Emma Beaufort on Wednesday, September 17th at 4:04 p.m.

Why aren't U answering my calls? Where R U? Jess said U haven't been @ work?

Text from Emma Beaufort on Wednesday, September 17th at 4:05 p.m.

Look, I'm RLY starting to freak out! I need 2 know UR alive!

31

CLAIRE

Stewart pulls into the gravel driveway, his one working headlight pointing towards a small white farmhouse. In the night, I can barely make-out any details about the property. This doesn't help me decide whether or not I can trust him.

He drives slowly up to the house and cuts the engine. If I hadn't heard his wife's voice on the phone when I called earlier, this scene would totally freak me out.

I pick-up my gym bag and throw it over my shoulder as I step down to the ground and contemplate my new temporary home for the first time. Most of it is only faintly lit by the high moon in the sky, the night already far past midnight.

Fitting that I should see this house for the first time in the dark. To someone who is always trying to hide and run away, darkness becomes a friend—a safe place. Where I don't need to pretend to be someone else. Where I can relax, even just a little. Even now, when darkness has betrayed me so many times.

Then again, how many people keep going back to things or people who hurt them? Like addicts—no matter how bad the drug is, they keep wanting more. That's darkness for me. I still trust it, even after it's let me down.

After a moment of standing outside, in the cold, I decide this place is perfect and I smile. Stewart, standing next to me, looks over and smiles too, as though he's heard my thoughts once again.

On cue, Anna opens the front door and turns the porch lights on, telling us crazy people to come on inside and warm up some. I'm surprised to see her. I had imagined she'd be in bed at this time of night. But looking at her now, her relaxed posture, her greying hair loose and shoulder length, flowery button down shirt, she's got hospitable written all over her.

I like her already.

She holds the door open wide and I walk through followed by Stewart. As I remove my shoes, a feeling of bliss overwhelms me. It feels so good to be out of these damp running shoes. As I take in the old peeling wallpaper and the small size of the farmhouse, I sense Anna's eyes on me. I feel her assessing me, silently making up her mind about me.

She's no fool.

She raises one eyebrow in question to Stewart, but he's avoiding her eye contact. Fantastic! Thanks for leaving me hanging, man. He's leaving me to fend for myself, I guess. That's to be expected. Under heat, people rarely rise up to help others when they feel they could also get in trouble. So I'm back to being on my own. That's just fine. I'm used to it.

"So, what brings you here to Salt Springs on this cold fall evening?" she asks, seemingly amused.

Damn! She knows. Following Stewart's advice, I lie.

She plays along and nods a few times. After a while, she laughs and shakes her head. I haven't fooled her, but for now I've won. I can tell she won't be pushing me further tonight.

She remarks the evening is all but gone and she's put dinner away already, but that I'm more than welcomed to help myself to a bowl of beef stew in the refrigerator and heat it up in the microwave.

I thank her, and then she shows me to the basement stairs.

"This is where you'll be staying," she gestures to the stairs. "I've made up the bed for you and there's a small desk down there, for your books," she offers, peering over my shoulder to my single gym bag, skeptical once again of my real reason for being here.

She waves the thought away and continues as though this is a well-rehearsed speech.

"There's only one bathroom. It's upstairs down the hall, second door to the left. I'm afraid we all have to share it. You know these old farmhouses and their amenities. Hell, we're lucky we even have a basement!" she laughs. "That was one of my conditions for moving way out here. Needed a spot for my Christmas tree decorations!" she adds as an explanation.

I laugh along politely while trying to see down the steep staircase. Impatient to settle in and get a good night's sleep, I stand in front of her quietly for a moment and she seems to get the message.

"Alright, well, you must be exhausted. I'll leave you to it. We'll see you in the morning. Breakfast is at seven a.m.—sharp. Good night, dear." She pats me gently on the shoulder, a familiar and sweet gesture.

Touched by their generosity and hit with a wave of extreme tiredness, I thank them both and make my way downstairs, eager to find my new room.

The basement is divided in two parts; one side is reserved for the utilities and storage, while the other is semi-finished and dry walled. A door leads to a simple double bed with a green and yellow quilted bedspread.

The walls are a soft dandelion colour and there are tiny knickknacks and porcelain figurines littering the shelves and the top of the single dresser. I imagine they were trying to make the cold, damp basement a more joyful and homey place, but it honestly just creeps me out. I drop my bag onto the grey shag carpet and look around the room. I spot a small closet in the corner of the room and find an empty shoe box on a high shelf. I immediately begin to clear the room of any dolls and figurines, placing them carefully in the box and returning it to the top shelf of the closet. I turn around and assess the room once more.

There, much better. This might work after all.

I empty my bag right onto the quilt. What's left of my past lies in a sad pile before me. It's slim pickings, pathetic really.

For someone who made so much money, I have nothing to show for it now, proof that money isn't everything. I open one of the drawers of the dresser and begin transferring my clothes in it. It takes me less than a minute to barely fill one drawer full. This is all I own now. What a change from my expensive apartment and car back home.

Home. What a complicated word.

I swallow the hard ball forming inside my throat.

Relieved to find there is a lock on the inside of the bedroom door, I turn the lock before I turn off the main light to the room. Guided now only by a small bedside lamp glowing orange, I undress until I'm only wearing a t-shirt and underwear before sliding under the covers to warm up.

My stomach is growling and my body aches for a hot shower, but my eyelids are heavy. I need sleep more than I need anything else right now. But as tired as I am, I cannot get comfortable.

Sleep doesn't come until two in the morning. When I finally fall asleep, I cannot rest. Even the knowledge that I'm safe and not alone doesn't give me peace. I have nightmares and run through endless hallways, constantly heading towards emptiness.

32

HIM

I followed the city bus until I saw her get off at St. Francis Xavier University. Why in the world would she decide to stop there? Maybe she wants to hit up a frat party and end up sleeping in someone's bed for the night.

Unlikely. Claire doesn't trust anyone.

Not like she used to when she called herself Elisabeth.

I saw her get off the bus, but just as fast, I lost sight of her. The rain and the descending darkness mixed with my lack of sleep these past few days made it impossible to see clearly. This isn't good. I've been tasked to locate and take down Claire.

Eliminate her. Strike her out of the story.

A pang of sadness grips me at the thought of ending Claire's life. I loved her so much when she was Elisabeth. Sweet, innocent, kind Elisabeth. I thought she loved me too, but something changed. She became bitter, accusing. She spread rumors and became angry. I didn't like that version of her as much.

She became dark. Complicated. Not the housewife type I had pictured for myself.

And then, there was the baby. To her the baby was a complication, a mistake. To me, it was a blessing, a miracle.

A reason to be together forever.

When she rejected me and did the worst possible thing—killing the baby, she broke all ties with me and what we could have been. All those feelings of rejection and inadequacy lurk around me in the shadows and I instinctively retreat into myself as I used to do in those days.

Before I grew up and became the man I am now. Before I could fight back—protect myself and fight for what I wanted.

Thoughts of my past envelop me in the dark space of my truck when I see a flash of light that's heading towards the Arts building. For a moment, I'm transfixed by the blinding single headlight as it shines directly into my cab, making my face immediately visible to the outsider heading right towards me.

I take cover, afraid to be seen. I duck my head toward the passenger's side and hover over the stick shift for a few moments until the light slowly turns to shine on the doors of the Arts building.

I'm parked far away, but I can still make out that the vehicle is an old truck. I feel like I recognize it, but as I'm trying to make out any defining features through the rain, I see a woman exit the building. For a moment I think its Claire, but this girl has shorter dark brown hair with bangs. I squint to see better. Something about her walk seems familiar. Confused, my eyebrows grow tighter together. The woman has the exact same built as Claire and she's also wearing the same ugly bulky sweater Claire was wearing earlier. Excitement grips me and I let out a surprised chuckle.

Damn, that's Claire!

Nice try, Queen. Thought you could fool me, but I see you.

As I'm looking at the two illuminated silhouettes in front of the old truck, my phone rings in my leather jacket pocket.

I grab the steering wheel with my left hand and reach in with my other hand to answer the call.

"Hello," I respond without emotion in the slim phone.

"Hi. It's me. I...I need you," she murmurs into the phone, her voice strained like she's been crying.

Crap! I've gotten this call before.

It must have been a bad night. I tell her to hang tight and that I'll be right over. Me, the hero. Always there to save the day.

If only Claire could have seen me like that when she had the chance.

33

ELISABETH

The room is spinning around me as my body goes numb. Too much. I've had too much to drink. I stumble around the living room and bump into several people on my way to the bathroom.

Oh God, I'm going to be sick.

How humiliating.

I barely have time to think as I clumsily grab the doorknob to the bathroom, but it doesn't open. Confused, my eyes blurry, I pound a fist on the door, stating it's an emergency only to receive a rude and blunt "Fuck off" from the person inside.

Knowing my chances of making it to the upstairs bathroom on time are slim, I try anyway. Taking the steps two at a time, I realize my high heels have gone missing somewhere between midnight and two o'clock but I can't be bothered with that now.

Screw the heels. I'll find them later. I feel too nauseous to care. I begin dry heaving as soon as my knees crack against the bathroom tiles.

Just as I lift the lid to the toilet, I vomit into the cold bowl, a few drops splash back into my face making me dry heave again.

God, that's nasty!

I feel awful but better at the same time, even though I know I'm nowhere near done being sick for the night. At least I'm alone here. No one will hear me being sick. Just then, I hear a faint knock at the door.

"You OK, babe?" Ethan asks through the thick wooden door.

Shit! Ethan!

I moan in desperation at my own patheticness. He heard everything! I guess there's no coming back from that one.

Still clinging to the toilet bowl, too weak to stand, I flush and reach into the cabinet under the sink for a towel. From my position on the floor, I reach up to turn the faucet on and wet a corner of the towel with cold water then run the towel on my forehead, the back of my neck, and on my inner arms and wrists.

"Babe?" Ethan asks hesitantly. "Rebecca said she saw you running up here. She said it looked urgent. Is everything ok? Are you sick?"

How does he do it? How can he act so sober when he's so drunk? He's had way more to drink than me and yet, he's taking care of me.

When we became official, I had promised myself I would never become that girl. The clingy girl. The one who needs her boyfriend to save her.

Ethan likes to feel needed sometimes, but he likes me for my resourcefulness, my independence. Immediately thoughts of losing him take over me. He won't want anything to do with me now! Ethan likes me strong, not this puddle I've been reduced to. Every time he looks at me from this point on, he'll see vomit all over me. He'll see weakness.

Oh my God, does this mean we're going to break up? We can't break up! We just can't. I love him too much.

With panic and fear of losing Ethan, I gather all my strength to stand up from the floor. I splash some water on my face and swipe under my eyes where my mascara is running.

I swish some water in my mouth and spit into the sink. So classy. I do a quick check around to make sure there's no real evidence of my mishap and let out a slow breath, gathering all my strength before I unlock the door to face him.

I find him leaning on the opposite wall by the staircase as I walk out. He takes one look at me and rushes over.

"Ah, babe, you don't look too good! You should probably sit down. Can I get you anything? Maybe some water?" He watches over me, brushing my hair slightly to tuck it gently behind my ear.

Ethan's touch always reassures me.

He has a way of making even the worst situation feel light and like no big deal at all. I nod slightly, too shy to speak for fear of having any residue vomit breath.

He puts his hand on the small of my back and leads me to his bedroom. I know it's his because we've fooled around in here on many occasions when his parents were out. He helps me remove my shirt and skirt, lays me down on his bed, and fluffs my pillow like a real gentleman.

"I'll be right back, my queen," he winks, trying to make light of the situation and make me feel better. "I'll go get some water. You just have a little rest. You'll feel better soon." He adds as he kisses my forehead and closes the door behind him.

I smile sheepishly. What a sweetheart he is. Who knew he could be so cool about me being sick?

Maybe I had it all wrong.

The floor vibrates with the music down below. Thank goodness Ethan's neighbors are travelling in Europe or they would be having a fit right now.

Even with the beat pumping through my ears, the darkness envelops my every cell and I drift into a deep sleep.

***

I wake up as the door opens slowly. The hallway is dark apart from a small glow from a window reflecting the moon. My eyes take a moment to adjust to the shift in light. I spot the bottle of water on the nightstand. Next to it is a bottle of aspirin.

How thoughtful of Ethan.

The alarm clock states it's now 3:30 in the morning. I've been asleep for just over an hour. I still feel like a bag of shit and I'm not doing a great job of keeping my nausea at bay. With my eyes closed, it feels like the room is spinning out of control and bile rises in my throat.

I'm nestled under the thick duvet in Ethan's room. Right now, if the world ended, that would be quite alright with me. I don't want to move from this spot right here—my own fluffy cocoon of warmth.

I've just about fallen asleep again when Ethan carefully walks into the room. The faint sound of music and feet shuffling below fill the room and quickly disappear again when he shuts the door behind him. For a moment he just stands at the end of the bed and I wonder what he's doing. Is he going to come to bed? Confused, I'm about to ask him, when I see him removing his shirt and then his jeans.

I shut my eyes again, wanting to savour this moment. This will be our first night sleeping in the same bed together. I feel so giddy, but I don't dare move. I don't want to screw this moment up.

Besides, I'm afraid the butterflies I'm feeling in my stomach have nothing to do with anticipation, and everything to do with nausea that might cause me to be sick at any moment.

I feel him slide under the covers and make his way over to me. I'm only wearing my bra and underwear and I feel his warm chest against my back. He's cuddling me like we normally do, on the couch, him the big spoon, me the small one. But then I feel a hardness between my legs.

My mind starts racing. Could this be the moment? I guess I haven't turned him completely off after all.

Not wanting to pass up this opportunity, I try to muster the courage I will need to do this and do this right. I've heard that the first time is painful. I'm not sure how much I can endure right now as I've been in and out of consciousness for a few hours now.

I want to remember this moment forever.

I feel his hand trail up my naked thigh and his hot breath on my neck as I push myself against his body. His movements get faster as he moves his hand all over my body. There isn't one inch of me he doesn't touch. Still facing away from him, I feel him slide down my underwear. I let him slip them off my legs and drop them to the floor by me. An action so ordinary usually, but tonight, it's the sexiest thing ever.

I feel his fingers rubbing my inner thighs and then he slips a finger inside of me and I gasp. The anticipation is killing me, and I feel myself arch towards his hardness in pleasure. I then feel him release the clasp from my bra and toss it next to my underwear on the floor.

Suddenly and without warning, the energy shifts. The room spins as he uses a strong grip to flip me onto my front and lays over me. My mind racing in excitement, I quickly release the expectation that my first time will be romantic and more missionary style. I guess it doesn't really matter which position we do it in the first time. We will have the rest of our lives to try out different ones, I tell myself.

My face is pressed against the pillow, and we still haven't said two words to each other, when I feel a sharp pain between my legs as he penetrates me in one quick motion. I grit my teeth in pain. I had anticipated some level of pain, having been forewarned by more experienced girlfriends, but I hadn't expected him to go inside me so fast.

I wasn't ready yet. I wasn't wet enough.

Wasn't there supposed to be some sort of foreplay first? That's what all those teen magazines always go on about.

I lift my head slightly to tell him to slow down a bit, when I feel his hand on the back of my hair, jerking my head backwards aggressively, arching my back awkwardly. I'm left fighting for breath. He roughly pushes inside me again and I feel like something is tearing. The pain shoots through my body and I let out a muffled cry.

What is he doing? What is the big hurry? I'd heard guys were quick to get it over with while girls needed more time to reach a climax, but this wasn't fun at all for me.

I don't want this. Not like this.

It should be slower. More romantic.

We should be staring lovingly in each other's eyes, but there is none of that tonight. Just quick, hard thrusts entering and exiting me, no pleasure in any way for me.

I'm sore and terrified when I finally gather enough breath to ask him to stop, but he doesn't. Thinking he's too lost in pleasure to hear me, I begin screaming and beg for him to stop. His response is to shove my head down into the pillow with force, nearly suffocating me. I push my head to the side and gasp for breath. Tears are running down my face, snot making it impossible to breathe through my nose. My screams are completely muffled.

His body is so heavy over me, the alcohol making my movements weak and slow. I can't lift my head. I feel like I'm on the verge of passing out. Surely this isn't normally how people have sex? What the hell is going on? Why is Ethan doing this to me? Grabbing at every bit of strength I've got left, I beg him between sobs,

"Ethan, stop! You're hurting me. Please, stop!" I cry out to him as loud as I can above his grunting.

"Shut up!" he responds before pushing my face onto the pillow again. He sounds angry and distant, so unlike himself that I barely recognize him.

There are quicker movements, more panting from him and then the movement stops completely, and I feel him quiver on top of me, but I'm completely numb.

He pushes himself off of me and climbs out of the bed clumsily, turning his back to me to scoop up his pile of clothes from the floor.

I gulp in air between sobs as I spot his crown tattoo, a perfect match to my own. He exits the bedroom as quickly as he entered it, leaving me once again in the dark, sinking into the abyss of the giant bed full of my tears and my blood.

34

ELISABETH

When I come to in the morning, my brain is buzzing. My mind and body aren't attached, and my head is pounding. My eyes hurt and feel swollen. My pillow is soaked and my mouth is hanging open. I peel myself from my pillow in disgust at the thought that I must have drooled like a dog last night. When I look up, I'm slightly disoriented.

Where am I? Frantically, I look around for clues. I see navy blue painted walls, a plaid blue and grey duvet, and a basketball hoop fastened to the wall.

Ethan's room.

My eyes shift to the nightstand and begin to focus on a tiny white thing—the aspirin bottle Ethan brought over to me last night along with a bottle of water. I should feel grateful to have such a caring boyfriend and even feel excited to have spent last night in his room, in his bed, but I don't. Instead, I feel confused. As though there are tiny holes burnt in my brain, my memory is so foggy.

Damn, my head hurts.

How can I not remember getting in Ethan's bed?

I feel like that is something I should remember. It's kind of a big deal. I feel hot tears forming in my eyes, upset at myself for forgetting about last night. Lying awake, I slowly try to place bits and pieces from last night.

Alright, think! Piece the hours together, I tell myself.

Right, I drank way too much—I do remember that. I also remember not feeling well, but was I sick? I can't remember. I do remember, however, having a splitting migraine last night. Immediately, I feel an agonizing pain, as if remembering has made it intensify and make its presence known. Otherwise, I don't remember much about last night. I know I had a few rum and cokes in the kitchen and that I danced, a lot. But I can't remember much more than that.

Come on, think!

I blink a few times, as though the memories will somehow materialize in front of me like a movie. The feeling of not remembering several hours of last night is giving me major anxiety. My breath starts to catch in my throat. I never wanted to be one of those girls—the ones who can't remember anything the next day. What's the point of going to a party when you can't remember it afterwards?

What if I hurt someone? Or said things I didn't mean? I've been told I get mean when I drink, but if I have too much, I'm usually sloppy and just get sick. I feel like last night was way too much. Who knows what I did when I crossed the line of sloppy and sick?

I turn over onto my back and feel a sharp pain in my lower abdomen. Cramps? Am I getting my period now? Seriously? But I'm not due for another week. That's strange.

Feeling someone stirring beside me, I turn my head slightly to the right and startle at seeing Ethan's naked back. The sight of his bare back brings a flash of some distant memory from last night. I shut my eyes to try to remember better, the memory just out of reach.

Unfortunately, all I can remember is the sensation of heat and the colour red. That and this strange feeling of anger bubbling up inside me. I feel mad at Ethan, but I can't imagine why. He brought me aspirin for my head and was nothing but sweet to me in the kitchen last night, from the little I can remember. Still, I can't help but feel resentful towards him some reason.

Jumbled thoughts crowd my mind. Did I have a dream that we were fighting or something? I seem to remember being afraid we were going to break up. Did we break up but then get back together? Why can't I remember past dancing last night?

Every time I close my eyes, my mind spirals, and I can only see snippets. Everything is all mixed up. Nothing makes any sense right now.

Ethan rolls over and faces me. His eyes are partly opened, and I can tell he's got a bad hangover as well. Neither one of us makes a move to go shut the blinds in his room where the bright sun rays are shining down announcing the start of a new day.

I look at the clock and notice its 9:08 in the morning.

Did Rebecca stay over too? She was supposed to be my alibi for staying over at Ethan's last night. I do a quick glance around the room, but I can't find my tote bag. I have no clothes here. Not even shoes.

Where are my shoes? I seem to remember something about looking for shoes. And why am I naked? Where are my bra and underwear?

Oh my God! Did Ethan and I do it last night? With a start, I sit up on my elbows and practically slip right back down to the mattress, flat on my back. Pain hits me like a truck.

"Mother fucker!" I yell through gritted teeth as a wave of pain mixed with nausea hits me. Once again, the room begins to spin around me and I fear I might be sick. What the hell happened last night? My eyes are still shut tightly as I try to keep the room in focus and bring all of my attention to remembering what exactly happened last night.

I feel Ethan's hot breath on my right cheek, and I open my eyes. He's propped up and looking down at me with a worried expression, fully awake now, crusts of sleep still in the corner of his eyes. Somehow he still looks handsome. His dark full lashes blinking rapidly as he looks from one eye to the other checking for clues about my outburst.

"You OK, babe? What's wrong?" he asks, and his hand gently caresses my arm which I've now placed under my head as support.

Support of what, I'm not sure.

I feel the tears coming and I'm embarrassed that he will see me cry. This is so not how I wanted our first morning waking up together to be. I decide I can tell him I'm in pain, and gross him out by talking about my period, or I can just lie as still as possible until he decides to get up to shower.

I prefer my second option.

"Oh, nothing, I'm fine." I smile weakly. *Am I?* I wonder to myself. "Sorry I scared you. I just remembered I never said good night to Rebecca last night. She must have left with all my clothes when she went home," I add, hesitantly, still wondering what to do about the fact that I have no clothes to go back home in, my alibi blown. Ethan lets out a small sigh of relief.

"Oh good. I was wondering if you were still feeling like shit. You looked really bad last night. I checked on you a couple of times, but you were sound asleep," he explains with a smile.

He kisses my raised elbow in an attempt to calm my racing heart.

"Now before you start getting all anxious about what to wear today, I can help you," he winks.

Unfortunately, Ethan's idea of help probably means that he's thinking of lending me some boxers and a large white t-shirt, but before I can protest, he adds, "Rebecca helped me clean up last night, or rather, this morning. She left your tote bag downstairs next to your shoes and coat before she left for her house."

His face mocks seriousness before he asks me in a very concerned manner, "Why weren't you wearing your shoes last night?" before breaking out into laugher.

Now it's my turn to laugh. Thank God for Rebecca. At least I have clothes. I'm trying to remember if I packed some tampons, but I'm not sure. I usually pack some, always being so over prepared.

"I think they were getting in the way of me getting my groove on," I giggle.

It feels so good to be getting kissed by Ethan and laughing together. We are so carefree, so happy in this moment. All the tension I was feeling seems to float away from me and right out the window.

Ethan leans over and kisses my cheek, then my chin, my neck, my nose, and my forehead before his lips land over top of mine for a long moment. He pauses after our kissing ritual before holding my gaze intently and proclaiming completely genuinely,

"I love you, Elisabeth Claire Smith." Still so serious in his expression, he leans in closer. His mouth meets mine in another deep and beautiful kiss. He lets me taste his tongue a few times and teases mine with his teeth before his lips leave mine wanting more. He winks at me, all seriousness gone. He sits up and I see that he is also naked, no boxers lining his bottom.

Why are we both naked? I'm about to ask him if we had sex last night, but just then, he turns to me, his bed head hair, so sexy with his sideways grin and announces, "Alright, babe, I'm going to shower. Are you going to be alright here for a few minutes?" It takes everything for me not to reach out and pull him over to me, but I remember the pain and the possible period and I don't move.

I don't think Ethan would be very turned on if we started getting all hot and heavy and it turned out I had my period.

Oh God, what if I bled in his bed?

I need him to leave so I can inspect what's happening and clean up whatever mess is going on down there before he comes back. Suddenly eager to be apart but trying to play it cool and nonchalant so he won't know anything's wrong, I respond as confidently as I can muster, "Yeah, for sure. Don't worry. I'll just go grab my stuff and meet you in the kitchen when you're done." I add a convincing smile.

A smile goes a long way in deception. It's my strongest weapon. Ethan takes the bait and walks out of the room, bare bum exposed, all confident and tight. I feel myself biting my lip as I stare after him.

35

ELISABETH

With Ethan gone, I can finally inspect the source of this pain and try to get some answers. Hoping it's nothing, I slowly attempt to sit up. Expecting the pain seems to help me push through it somehow. It's the unexpected that hurts the most.

I won't be caught unprepared this time.

Now that I know what I'm in for, all I need to do is try things out to see which movements hurt and where I have more flexibility. Once in a seated position, I bring my knees up to my chest slowly, afraid of what I'll find. Carefully and hesitantly, I lift the bed sheet up to uncover the spot where I was just laying down.

I see a dark red circle where my ass was, and I cringe. Shit.

Exactly what I was afraid of, and just like that, I'm on the move. Pain be damned. Adrenaline is rushing through me. Oh no! Oh no! How could this have happened! How can I already be having my period? It's usually so regular, like clockwork. Anxiety spikes through me and quickly turns to anger. Crap! Of course this happens on the first night I sleep at Ethan's house!

Not wanting Ethan to see my blood on his sheets—not ready for that kind of relationship intimacy level yet, or ever for that matter—I begin frantically scooping up the sheets in my arms. I hold my breath until I see the mattress is miraculously unstained.

As I stand there gathering the sheets and pillow cases in my arms, I feel a trickle running down my leg.

I look down and see bright red blood making its way to the hardwood floor.

Damn it! I glance rapidly around for a box of tissues and grab a handful so aggressively the box falls from the dresser onto the floor with a thump. I begin wiping at my legs and cleaning myself up. I need some water to get the stain of the blood off my skin. When I reach to pick up the box of tissues, I spot my underwear on the floor, next to my bra.

Weird. I don't remember taking them off. I must have been really out of it last night.

Not wanting to waste any time, I huddle the blankets and tissues in my arms and practically sprint to the stairs. I pray the sun's glare won't let any prying drivers see inside as I walk around Ethan's house naked. I use the bundle of sheets as a makeshift buffer. On my way to the stairs, I have to pass the bathroom where Ethan is still showering and naked. I push the thought away quickly.

He won't be long now.

I need to hurry.

Every step down is so painful, I need to grab onto the railing for support. I finally reach the bottom step and I feel like it's the biggest achievement of my life, but I hold the cheering for later.

Very aware of my naked body and that more blood is dripping down my leg, I walk quickly to the laundry room and drop the sheets in the washing machine. I find my bag of clothes in the living room. Thankful for this little piece of my own stuff here, I hastily grab the bag and rush to the powder room locking the door behind me.

I sit on the toilet bowl as I scavenge my bag for a tampon all the while praying that I've packed one.

I've never had a period so heavy before and the cramps are terrible.

Finally, I find one and begin putting it in hoping it will stop the bleeding, but I stop almost immediately, unable to go any further. A pain so intense envelops every cell in my body so terribly that I feel I might black out. My knees buckle and if I weren't already sitting, I would surely have collapsed right onto the bathroom tiled floor. With my arms outstretched on either side of the small power room, I try to keep calm and not lose my cool. I need to think clearly. I shut my eyes to consider my options. This is no ordinary time of the month.

What the hell happened? What is going on?

Maybe I should call my doctor?

I decide very quickly that a tampon is definitely not going to work now. I grab a long row of toilet paper and fold many layers over each other to make a temporary pad. Hopeful, I decide to wait until Ethan is done in the shower. Then I'll go into the upstairs bathroom and see if his mom has any sanitary pads up there. Until then, I'm stuck with what's available in this bathroom. I decide to clean my legs and tame down some of the stray hair on my head while I'm in there.

My long blond hair is still pretty straight considering the hellish night I seem to have spent. My make-up, on the other hand, is quite atrocious. I wet some more toilet paper and clean my face as best I can. The cheap thin paper practically turns to pulp in my hand, but I don't have anything else to work with.

Thankfully, my make-up is in my bag since I got ready in Rebecca's car last night on the way to the party. I reapply a little bit, but my eyes are still fairly red.

I'll drink a lot of water this morning and I should be back to normal. By the time noon comes, I'll be able to go home. I hear the water stopping above me and I know Ethan's done his shower.

All dressed now and finished in the bathroom, feeling proud of getting myself together with almost nothing, I exit the tiny room and slowly creep upstairs. I have to time this well. I need to check his bathroom cupboard for a pad while he's getting dressed in his room across the hall without him seeing me.

I hear him whistling in his room, drawers opening and closing. He's left his door slightly open. I rush over the creaky wood floor and reach the bathroom unnoticed. Now, I need to open up the cupboard without a sound. As I pull on the handle, a loud creak resounds and echoes in the small room, and I suck in my breath. The whistling stops. I wait. Both of us at a standstill, but only for a moment. Before long, I hear the familiar creak of someone sitting on a bed, pulling on socks, surely. I let my breath go and peer into the crack of the slightly opened cupboard, not wanting to risk making the creaking noise again.

Relieved, I see what I'm looking for, and I extend my long arm to grab one.

I hurry back down the stairs and shut myself back in the powder room to install the pad. Just as I'm leaving the bathroom, I hear Ethan's whistle following him down the stairs. I scoot over to the laundry room, put some soap in the washer, and set a cycle, and then make my way to the kitchen to sit down on a stool at the island just as Ethan rounds the corner of the kitchen.

"Are you washing the sheets?" He asks with a smile playing on his lips.

"Yes, I thought it would be nice for you to have clean sheets."
I lie with my best smile.

"Thank you, my queen," he beams as he leans over to kiss my
forehead. A shadow of a smile crosses his face. Whether it's from
him hiding a secret or a muffled pleasure at the idea of me washing
his laundry, I'm not entirely sure.

"Now, let me fix you some breakfast!" he grins and shuffles
over to the fridge wearing the sweatpants that make his butt look
sexy.

Only this time, it makes my stomach turn.

36

ELISABETH

After breakfast, I agree to Ethan's offer to drive me home, but only if he drops me off a block from my home. I'm supposed to be with Rebecca, and I don't want my parents to suspect anything. Even if they question me, I wouldn't know what to tell them actually happened last night.

I'm not sure if I'm more afraid of my parents finding out I slept at Ethan's or of not remembering what happened.

As Ethan drives me home, I'm distracted by the many thoughts that enter my mind. The car is silent, and there is no music playing through the speakers. Both of us seem to appreciate the quiet ride—our heads are still pounding painfully. Our egg and toast breakfast hasn't yet settled down our raging hangovers to a murmur we can tolerate.

I feel an unsettling distance between us. Even though Ethan's hand is laying on my thigh, I can't shake off the unease I sense. Such a simple, normal gesture for a boyfriend to do with his girlfriend—there's nothing obviously wrong with it. Typically, I revel in this small touch. Any of Ethan's touches usually bring butterflies to my stomach—but not today.

Something doesn't make sense. It feels off.

I feel an anger so deep, all I want to do is scream. My throat is dry and raw, as though I have been screaming all night long. Instead of enjoying his touch, I'm repulsed by it.

His hand on me makes me cringe. Instead of being tender, it feels like he's holding me down, like he owns me, as though I've become just another one of his possessions. His silence, rather than being comforting, is making me nervous.

There's a wedge between us, but he's acting like nothing is wrong. I feel out of control, like everything is falling apart. Ethan's hand on me and his unusual silence makes me feel like he's trying to control everything.

Is he silent so that I won't find out the truth about last night? Or is he acting normally, but it's me who's changed?

I must be imagining things. This is Ethan I'm talking about. Sweet, loyal, dependable, predictable, and respectful Ethan. Then why does my skin feel like crawling away and hiding from him at his touch?

I look away from his hand on my thigh to take a look at his profile. Ethan's jaw is clenched tight. A little subtle stubble has started poking through his chin. He's looking older today, more like a man. Usually this thought would thrill me and leave me day dreaming about the next years of our lives. For so many hours throughout our relationship, I've dreamt of marriage, kids and finding a place to live together. But today, those dreams are making me feel like a child, as though they were simply a fantasy and will never truly happen.

It makes me feel lost, like suddenly we're not so perfect. Like suddenly, we're not the same. Now, he's the strong one and I'm the weak one. As though he's this older man who wants to harm me and I'm a lost child who doesn't understand what's going on. When did he suddenly grow up and leave me behind? What happened to make him appear more like a man suddenly?

Also, why am I bleeding so much? I wish I was home already, because I'm in so much pain, I feel like I just need to lay down and fall into a coma until I heal whatever this is.

As I stare out the window at the large fields of corn and wheat blurring past, I feel Ethan's hand burning into my skin, so hot to the touch, as though his hand is on fire. I push it off of me in a rushed movement, startling both of us. He looks painfully at me, as though I've somehow wounded him. As though my rejection has burned him. His eyes dart quickly from the road ahead and back in my direction, but I ignore him. What it was that made me push his hand away, I'm not sure. All I know is that I didn't want him touching me.

I shut my eyes and try to remember anything from last night. I remember there were tears, lots of them. Then I remember heavy breathing on the back of my neck, or was that from this morning when we woke up? In my memory, the room is still dark, so I must be remembering some parts of last night.

Suddenly, frustrated at the gaps in my memory, I can't hold it in any longer. I need to know, now. If I can't remember, then maybe Ethan can enlighten me and help me make sense of all this.

"Babe, I know this is random, but I'm spacing a little bit about what happened last night." I swallow hard before asking him, "Did we have sex last night?" sounding more confident than I feel as I watch his face for a reaction. Trying to read more into his answer than he might give.

He looks straight at me, his eyes wide in shock and then laughs it off, "What? Of course not, babe. You were passed out—cold. Besides, we're waiting until graduation day, right?" he looks slightly concerned at my not remembering something so important.

"Right." I reply slowly, my mouth dry as I turn my gaze back to the window more confused than before.

This doesn't make any sense. If we didn't sleep together last night, then why the hell am I in so much pain down there, and why am I bleeding?

37

THURSDAY, SEPTEMBER 18TH

CLAIRE

The smell of fresh coffee, eggs, and bacon makes my stomach ache for food and I force myself to rise from the bed. The walls of my basement bedroom are softer in the morning light, inviting even. I don't feel as joyful as the paint though.

Actually, I'm pretty damn miserable.

It's been months, no, years since I've slept through an entire night from start to finish. I stupidly expected that if I was in a house with other people, then maybe I would feel safer. I guess I had reasoned that I could hide from my demons here.

Obviously, I was wrong.

Shame, guilt, and pain find me wherever I run to. They are embedded into my cells. They speak lies into my ears all night long. Fear is a steady companion also—it never leaves me alone.

Anytime I start to feel safe, it rears its ugly head, always there to remind me that I can't trust anyone. Not even Stewart and Anna, the sweetest couple I've ever met.

These wonderful people who went out of their way to bring in a deceitful schoolgirl late last night without doing a background check or even bothering to obtain my real name.

I look at my reflection in the small oval mirror of the dresser and take in the haircut and dark colour from yesterday. In this light, it doesn't look too horrible for a pharmacy hair dye kit and a cheap pair of scissors. I'm quite proud of my handy work. Maybe I should consider becoming a hairdresser for my next career. After brushing my new bangs to the side with my fingers, I slide on the same pants and hoodie from yesterday, pulling on the sleeves to hide the goose bumps on my arms and legs before making my way upstairs.

As I reach the kitchen, a welcoming warmth and an array of appetizing smells hit me. Anna is standing at the stove, wearing a blue knitted sweater with the sleeves rolled-up and a yellow apron tied snuggly around her waist. She is expertly cooking bacon and scrambled eggs simultaneously, all while dodging grease spatters. A fresh pot of coffee is brewing next to her on the counter and fills the room with the smell of what I can only assume heaven smells like. It's the kind of coffee you can drink black, without having to mute the taste with sugar and milk. I almost drool at the prospect of drinking a cup or two as I take a seat at the table across from Stewart.

At my arrival, he curiously peers over his local county newspaper just quickly enough to make an assessment of my quality of sleep.

"Didn't sleep well last night?" he asks, with an expression that's hard to read, but again makes me wonder how he can tell.

Before I can react or respond, he adds, "I bet you haven't had a decent night's sleep in quite some time." He's apparently unaffected by socially appropriate protocols of privacy or letting things go.

He's folding his newspaper, but I'm pretty sure he's not done reading it. I give him a questioning look, not sure if I should be offended or impressed at his remark.

"Look, I know trouble when I see it. You've got it written all over you," he states.

Taken aback by his tone and accusation, I go completely still.

I don't dare move.

How does he know all this? Who is he? Where's the sweet, understanding man from yesterday? Does he know who I am? Has he figured it out somehow?

"Look, I don't know who you think you are..." I begin, but he simply lifts his hand and with that simple gesture, he shuts me up immediately. Apparently I'm still the same person, always trying to please authority figures.

"Alright, look, where you come from or what's troubling you doesn't matter to us. Like I told you yesterday, if you need some money, I might be able to help you." When I hesitate slightly, he adds, "I need some repairs done in the shop out back and I could use an assistant. Are you up to it?" His question is spoken more like a demand.

"I don't know anything about fixing things," I respond, suddenly unsure of myself and of his angle. I sense he already knew I would answer that.

"Are you willing to learn?" he asks me, and without waiting too long, I reply, "Yes".

At that moment, as though she's been waiting on standby for my answer to determine if I deserve to eat at their table, Anna comes up behind me, and places a heaping plate of fluffy eggs, crispy bacon, and buttered toast in front of me with a curt nod of her head. Acceptance or pride in her culinary skills, I'm not sure. Ignoring their questioning stares, I dig into the meal as though this might be my last, because for all I know, it could very well be.

After helping Anna with the dishes, I follow Stewart to the shop in the backyard. He explains that the previous owners used to board horses there almost three decades ago. Stewart has since turned it into a very large carpentry workshop sustaining a decent side-business.

He gets me to sweep up the dirty floor and check all the mousetraps for any dead critters. I'm not sure what it is about talking to men while working alongside them, but I always seem to get along much better with them this way. The conversations are always less intimidating, less defensive this way. Maybe it's about keeping a safe distance, or working together, but separately on our own tasks towards a common goal.

At work, I only hire women, because I don't trust men, but women really annoy me. They never stop talking which is why this is a nice change.

However, I'm not sure why I'm comfortable working alone in this isolated shop with a man I barely know. Part of me is curious, while the other part of me, the intellectual part, wants to learn any new skill he can teach me. I've always had a thirst for knowledge.

As I sweep, I ask him, "Have you always worked in carpentry?"

"For as long as I can remember," he responds in a slow, easy way.

I can tell he's warming up to me.

"I learned from my father as a teenager." he adds. "I was always getting into trouble at school, and instead of punishing me, my father would teach me new skills on the saws." A sad smile plasters across his face at the memory.

"And what does Anna do?" I ask him. If I'm going to keep living here, I need to get to know them.

"Well, she's always been a house wife, never worked outside of the home. She studied nursing before we got married and was on her way to work in emergency care, but she doesn't drive, you see. Hard to keep a job when you can't get there. Driving scares her and she doesn't want to put that burden on me." He stops for a moment, collecting his thoughts. I can tell there's more to the story than he's letting on, but I don't push it.

"She likes it here," he continues. "She always manages to keep busy." He explains this with a strange expression on his face and I think he's going to stop there, but he adds, "We're foster parents, Anna and I." He looks straight at me now, and his hands suddenly stop moving. I stop working also, sensing this is a more serious conversation that needs all of my attention.

"We were never able to conceive naturally, but we've always loved kids. We saw an ad asking for people to get qualified to become foster parents a few years after getting married and it just felt right to us. We never had any biological kids, but we've helped raise over 200 kids." He pauses to remember.

"I have a talent for spotting people in trouble." There's a heavy weight attached to his statement. "When I saw you, I just knew you needed help." Avoiding eye contact now, he adds, "We haven't fostered in a long time. That ad you found must have been at least five years old, but I don't believe in coincidences. I think you were meant to find it. Somehow, we're all connected. We're part of your story." He looks directly at me now, dead serious. "I think you were meant to be here. I don't know why but I feel it in my gut and my gut is never wrong."

What the hell is this? This isn't funny.

At first, I thought this guy was crazy, but now, I'm scared. His gut is never wrong? That's my saying—that's what I always say.

Who is this guy?

And I don't need any help, thank you very much. I've been taking care of myself for over fifteen years, I'll have you know! Who is this guy to think he can help me? I feel the familiar anger bubbling up and I'm about to tell him just how wrong he is. But he's turned away again back to his workbench without another word about it and somehow, the moment's passed. *That was weird*, I think.

The creepiness of his comment still lingers in the air and it's as thick as the dirt on the shop floor. I decide to keep sweeping and think about how he said that we're all connected and there's no coincidences. Hopefully, when I get this floor cleared of dirt, the rest will clear up and make sense also.

38

Missed call from Malcolm Riley on Thursday, September 18th at 8:00 a.m.

Text from Phil MacEwan on Thursday, September 18th at 10:10 a.m.

Claire, look, this is serious. Inspector Riley just called me. No one's heard from you since Monday. They're going to classify you as a missing person tomorrow if you don't get back to me today.

Text from Phil MacEwan on Thursday, September 18th at 10:15 a.m.

If you need help, just call me. Please. We're all worried.

Text from Jess Levac on Thursday, September 18th at 1:03 p.m.

Claire, the girls and I are getting RLY freaked out. Where R U? I just heard from some Inspector Riley and apparently they're going to put in a Missing Person report for U!?

Missed call from Jess Levac on Thursday, September 18th at 1:05 p.m.

Text from Jess Levac on Thursday, September 18th at 1:07 p.m.

Claire, I'm so scared. I RLY hope this is all a big joke and that UR safe somewhere. But I don't know Y UR hiding away if U are. PLZ call me!

Text from Rebecca McNeil on Thursday, September 18th at 4:01 p.m.

Claire? Where are you? I'm in the area and I thought I'd stop by your place for tea. Let me know!

Text from Rebecca McNeil on Thursday, September 18th at 4:30 p.m.

Are you ok? I just stopped by your place and there's a uniformed officer there.

Text from Rebecca McNeil on Thursday September 18th at 4:32 p.m.

He didn't say much, but basically told me that you're missing. What's going on? He asked me all sorts of questions. I'm scared.

Missed call from Val Parker on Thursday, September 18th at 5:01 p.m.

Text from Emma Beaufort on Thursday, September 18th at 7 p.m.

Claire, UR freaking me out! Inspector Riley just called me to let me know UR going to be classified as a missing person TMW morning if no 1 hears from U! Call me PLZ!

39

ELISABETH

At school, I'm quiet and distant. At home, I'm angry and I've started acting out. I'm not sure why I do it, I'm just angry with everyone. I don't give a shit about anything anymore.

My parents tell me they don't know what to do with me anymore. I can see the strain I'm putting on them. My dad and I used to be close, but he can barely stand to be in the same room with me anymore. He's stopped asking me to play chess with him after school, afraid it'll just start a fight between us. We live under the same roof, but we're strangers now.

I lock myself in my room for hours after coming home from school and barely eat anything anymore. I can tell my parents are worried. They keep begging me to talk to them.

I don't know who to talk to about how fucked up I feel. Ethan used to be my go to for this sort of stuff. He was always the first one I called when I needed someone to talk to. He always knew how to make me feel better, but for some reason, I'm not sure I can really trust him. In a strange way, he's the last person I want to talk to about this. Things between us have been tense and awkward these last few weeks. He's been tiptoeing around me—avoiding me.

Maybe its nerves leading up to graduation day, but I sense there's more. I sense guilt. I can smell it on him as strongly as his cologne. What he's guilty of though, I'm not sure.

Rebecca's been avoiding me also. I think she's mad that I got so drunk at Ethan's pre-graduation party last month and unintentionally ditched her. I didn't mean to get sick—she should know that. For some reason, she's been giving me the cold shoulder ever since that night. Wait, did something happen between Ethan and Rebecca that night? Are they trying to hide it from me?

This is great, just great!

Immediately, I shake my head. Gritting my teeth, I'm angry at myself for even allowing such a thought to cross my mind in the first place. How did everything get so screwed up?

I'm seriously going crazy.

As I slam the front door of my home and stomp up the stairs to my room, my mom calls out to me from the bottom of the stairs. Her eyes have dark circles under them, her hair is in an unkempt and unwashed messy bun on the top of her head. I can tell she's been staying up late trying to figure out what to do with me. I can also tell it's eating her alive. She sees the change in me, but neither of us dares to bring it out in the open. Instead, we try to forge ahead like this is some phase I'll grow out of. I'm sure she's thinking its only hormones, but it's so much more complicated than that.

"Elisabeth, how was your day?" she asks as she plasters a forced smile on her face that doesn't reach her ears.

I don't feel like pretending to be civil today, so I just roll my eyes, turn away, and keep walking.

Nice try, mom. Try harder.

Part of me doesn't want her to stop trying to talk to me. She seems to be the only one trying to maintain the appearance that everything is fine. I could use a little bit of that normalcy right now.

It's like the world I used to know so well has drifted away, burnt up in flames and I'm left with ashes that will take years to rebuild.

I slam my door, unable to contain the anger I feel on the inside anymore. I need an outlet—a release.

I turn on some music on my laptop and crank it loud enough to drown out every other noise in my head. I'm not sure if it's just a regular teenage phase or what, but I feel so low these days. Does everyone go through a period where they feel like this—alone, unloved, ugly, stupid, and angry? I stand in front of my tall mirror and look at myself.

I barely recognize myself anymore.

I'm wearing a white tank top with faded jean shorts, socks, and black shoes. My wrists are littered with various bracelets, some I've made, some I've bought. I used to think it was a cool style, but now, it just feels heavy.

Everything feels heavy.

My hair looks washed out and matte as though it lacks proper nutrition. My skin is dry and I'm breaking out everywhere. I'm always itchy like I've suddenly developed eczema. I'm also constantly nauseous, and my mind is always spinning. I haven't had a normal night's sleep since before the party, only running on three hours of sleep a night. The same nightmare always wakes me up screaming, gasping for air. Spots of deep red, surrounding me, like blood.

I slump heavily onto my bed, crossed legged, and hear something crack under my weight—a picture frame with a photo of Ethan and me last summer.

Crap! The glass is broken. Just great! Why did I leave that there?

I'm about to throw the frame across the room but instead I grab hold of one of the sharp triangles-shaped shards of glass and rub it between my fingers. I glance at my wrists for a second and ponder how it would feel, but I don't have the stomach for it. I throw the piece of glass to the floor, drop my head in my hands, and begin to cry heavy sobs.

40

ELISABETH

I wake up at five in the morning, sweat drenching my forehead and butterflies in my stomach.

Oh God, I think I'm going to be sick!

I rush out of my room and run down the hall to the bathroom my parents and I share. I barely make it before I'm hurling myself over the porcelain bowl. I throw up a couple of times and wipe my mouth with the back of my hand. Most of what I've thrown up is bile because I haven't been eating that much lately. It's one of the only things Ethan seems to have noticed that's been different about me.

I feel so weak—so gross.

I don't feel like myself at all anymore. It's like someone has taken over my body and is killing me from the inside out. I flush the toilet, get up slowly from the cold tiles, and open the door to find my mother standing only inches from my face.

"Holy crap!" I swear under my breath at my mother's shocked expression.

Whether it's because of my swearing or my appearance, I'm not sure, she asks,

"Are you OK, Elisabeth?" Concern is ever so present in the shape of creases around her eyes and on her forehead.

From this distance, I can see new details about her that I would normally have missed.

With her head tilted this way, I notice that she seems to have a few extra grey hairs since last year. I assume this is because of me.

"Yeah, I was just sick for some reason. It must have been something I ate," I mumble as an explanation and wipe some residual spit off my chin, using the inside of my palm.

I need sleep so badly—I'm exhausted. I know I must look like hell.

I was already skinny, but now with all this throwing up, I'm beginning to look like a toothpick. It's not even sexy—it's too thin. I don't look healthy. In a moment, I see her considering our last meals in her mind. When she looks over at me again a moment later, I catch her analyzing me, looking from my hair to my feet.

Her gaze stops on my belly and I see her expression change as though she's making calculations in her mind. Her breath suddenly catches and tears begin to form in her eyes. She slowly lifts a small, shaking hand and covers her gaping mouth as she stares at me, waiting for me to catch up. Staring at her, confused, wondering for a moment why she's crying, I think back as fast as I can trying to make sense of this.

As a sex-ed class comes suddenly to mind, I feel my mouth gaping wide, mirroring my mother's, as shock begins to overwhelm me. The reason behind my strange behaviour, the change in my skin, the nausea, the lack of sleep, and the dry hair. It doesn't take me long to put together the pieces of exactly what is going on.

Now, I finally know the truth of what happened to me that night at Ethan's party.

A flashback so intense hits me, making me stumble backwards.

My back collides with the bathroom sink. A memory, darkened by low light and alcohol distortion is forming before me as my mother rushes over, her shaking arms extended as she helps steady me and lowers me down on the closed toilet lid.

Vivid images of that night flash before me. Ethan pushing my face down into the pillow in his bedroom and forcing himself inside me while I yelled at him to stop. That's why it had hurt so much the next day, and that's why I've unconsciously been mad at him since his party. That's why I feel disgusted whenever he touches me.

Ethan. *Oh God, Ethan, what have you done?*

How could Ethan have done this to me? My perfect boyfriend, my best friend, the one I've trusted with all my secrets has betrayed me in the worst possible way. He'd even lied right to my face the morning after when I asked him if we'd had sex.

My blood starts to cool instantly as another wave of nausea hits me. I stand abruptly and turn to lift the lid almost head butting my hovering mother in the chin as I stand. I fall to my knees and I'm sick again.

"Oh crap!" I cry, more to myself than to my mother. But as I say this, I know now that a horrible thing has happened.

Now I know the truth—that Ethan raped me, and then lied about it, and now I'm pregnant.

In that same moment, I also know that Ethan is a fucking asshole and that I'm going to kill him.

41

FRIDAY, SEPTEMBER 19TH

New Brunswick Gazette

Local Woman Missing

By Jordan Keller

Claire Martel, also known as Elisabeth Claire Smith, thirty-two, has been missing since Monday, September 15.

Miss Martel was reported missing after she failed to show up at work on Tuesday September 16. She hasn't been seen or heard from since Monday around 11 p.m. Miss Martel has worked for the University of New Brunswick in the Communications Office for close to ten years. She is very well respected amongst her peers and has been missed during her sudden absence.

The Saint John Police Force have reason to believe her safety is at risk and, therefore, needs to locate her as soon as possible.

Miss Martel is wanted for questioning in a recent investigation. She was last seen wearing a black sequined top, dark jeans, boots, and a large scarf. Miss Martel has brown eyes and blond hair, is 5 feet 8 inches, and weighs about 130 pounds.

The Saint John Police Force is urging anyone with any information to call Inspector Riley at the number below. Thank you for your assistance in locating Miss Martel and bringing her home safely as soon as possible.

42

ELISABETH

We spend the morning cleaning up the shop. It appears Stewart hasn't worked back here in quite a while. He mentions he likes to come here to learn new things about himself. That there is honest work in working for yourself and with your hands. I hold back the thought that drug dealers must tell themselves the exact same thing.

At noon, we walk back to the house for Italian minestrone soup and sandwiches. The cold air sends a chill through my body. Stewart seems to notice and without a word, grabs a coat from a nearby hook before we head back out to the shop and hands it to me.

I thank him and throw it on.

I still need to buy a coat before winter, but I'm not sure how to get back to town without having to ask Stewart for a ride. More and more, I'm beginning to feel like I'm too isolated out here. The beautiful flat golden fields don't offer much in the way of shelter. The only buildings for miles are the old, white farmhouse with its wrap around porch and green metal roofing, and the barn turned into shop. A real Anne of Green Gables dream house, minus the horses.

Later, as we re-enter the shop, we get right back to work. Stewart wants to show me how to change the burnt-out headlight on the old truck. He asks me to hand him a couple of screwdrivers from the glove box and we get the new light in.

Without a second thought, he throws the tools in the truck and wipes his hands on his green overalls before putting on his thick working gloves. After a few other odd tidying up jobs, he decides to call it a day.

My feet are aching. I'm used to running on them, not to standing still on them all day. Disappointed by the realization that my body has gotten used to an office job, I'm slightly too embarrassed to mention it. I bite my lip and walk slowly back to the house behind a limping Stewart. Perhaps his days standing on the hard concrete floor of the workshop are what's made him limp in the first place.

When we walk into the house, Anna is in her usual spot, hovering over the hot stove, cooking up another one of her delicious meals. I surprise myself by thinking that I could really get used to this. On the menu tonight is a pot roast with boiled potatoes slathered in butter and steamed carrots. The aroma is mouthwatering with fresh thyme, rosemary, and garlic. A farmer's dinner, I think to myself. Grateful for the thoughtfulness and the care that it took to prepare this meal, I wash my hands and offer to set the table.

Anna is beginning to warm up to me. She's let her guard down around me. She's smiling more and not afraid to make eye contact. She's so quiet, but helping people has always been a passion of hers. She was in a very severe car accident in her teens that made her afraid of driving, and that's why she still doesn't drive now. Stewart mentions that she doesn't feel the need to. He is good to her. He gets her everything she needs, and she has no desire to leave the house.

Tonight, with the warm lights inside the small kitchen and the dark fall sky outside, the little house has a cozy feel. It almost feels like home.

I'm brought back to memories of my own childhood. My mother in the pure white, clinical looking kitchen, with white counters and white shaker cabinets, busying herself with scrubbing every surface of the counter. She was constantly dusting the light fixtures and baseboards, throwing away abandoned wrappers or papers—anything left on the counter for longer than an hour. I'm feeling anxious just thinking about it. It was difficult to relax in that house.

I never gave much thought to why she always needed the house to be clean. Was it a control thing? Or maybe it was more of a metaphor. Maybe she felt messy, unclean, or guilty about something, so much so that she would scrub clean any surfaces she came in contact with. Trying to clean up her messes wherever she went. Unable to stand any sort of disorder in the house.

Cleaning—the only thing to push out the demons in her head—her way of dealing with a lifelong battle with depression.

Keeping a clean house was a way to cope with her ever present anxiety. A crumb on the floor had the power to make her come completely unglued. A stack of unattended bills on the counter would send her into a spiraling cyclone, and it never stopped there. She could spend hours cleaning, often forgetting to eat once she'd started. She wouldn't stop until every surface was spotless, clutter-free, and shiny. In some way, making her home clean was her way of solving her problems—an escape.

Most of my memories of my childhood home involve my mother cleaning something. Unable to stop, she'd often clean while trying her best to be present and spend time with family.

Whenever she made a meal, she would rarely sit down and enjoy it with my father and me. The meal wouldn't be out of the pan for two minutes before she would plunge the scorching dish into the hot soapy water to clean it immediately. Dishes were almost always cleaned and put away, long before she finally allowed herself to sit down to eat her cooling meal, only to stand up again seconds later with some excuse of needing to grab the peppershaker or a napkin.

My mother always needed to keep busy. It was her way of restoring peace in our house, cleaning whatever disorder landed there. But she was so busy scrubbing the floor when she should have been spending time with me.

I think about the warm, soft bed downstairs and begin to make my way across the kitchen floor to prepare for bed when Stewart, still sitting at the kitchen table, asks me if I'd like to play a game of chess. Glad that all they can see is the back of my head, I'm unable to hide the shock on my face.

A game of chess? My heart skips a beat.

The queen pawn. Sandra.

Could that be a coincidence?

Rationally, I try to reassure myself. It's an old game, a traditional game. Many people know how to play it. It could mean nothing. Besides, recent threats aside, I do love the game. I like the strategy of it, the long pace of it. It might be fun to play a round.

Oh, what the hell.

I give in and turn around and with a smile, I accept.

***

We have played four rounds in a row. Anna drank an entire pot of chamomile tea by herself before retreating to bed. Stewart, to my amazement, is a fabulous chess player. I wonder who he plays with normally because Anna doesn't seem to have any interest in the game whatsoever. But he's very good.

We end up tying in the end, calling it quits after looking at the clock and deciding four rounds was enough for one night.

"Tomorrow's another day," Stewart chimes. "And another day is another opportunity to learn and be better," he smirks.

Where does he even come up with these sayings?

Something tells me Stewart missed his calling to become a poet or maybe even a pastor. Part of me feels like I'm a teenager again, wanting so badly to make a funny remark and roll my eyes, but I don't. Stewart strikes me as wise. He never speaks unless it's something important or interesting— he's not one for idle conversation. He's polite and intuitive. For someone as lost as I am, I welcome his wisdom and try to grasp it through my fingers tightly before it flies away with my past and everything else I've lost.

For some reason, inexplicable in the face of my new vagabond life, I feel myself let go. My fists are beginning to unclench. I can feel my jaw relax. My hardened exterior is of no use with these kind souls. I don't need to be the tough one here like I was in my office and with my friends. I don't need to compete here.

As crazy as it sounds, I feel like I might even be starting to trust them.

43

ELISABETH

After helping me stagger back to my bed and tucking me in, my mother strokes my hair lovingly with tears running down her face. We haven't talked since before I got sick, but I can tell she wants to, sitting on my bed, looking down, avoiding my gaze.

She explains quietly, "We need to be very careful and we cannot, under any circumstances, tell your father".

She seems afraid—for me or for her, I'm not sure.

She tells me we will get a pregnancy test in the morning to find out for sure. She tells me not to worry, that we need to pretend that everything is fine. She stands up and quietly tells me to try to get some sleep and that she will make up an excuse in the morning to explain my absence at school until we figure all this out.

Not sure how to react appropriately or what to say in this situation, I just nod slightly, tears falling down my cheeks as the weight of my new reality begins to settle around me. I still haven't told her about that drunken night, about the rape, or about Ethan.

Rape—there it is.

The word I've been trying to avoid, the word I've been afraid of thinking. I feel confused, hurt, and betrayed. I feel hot shame that my mom now looks at me with those sad eyes, with disappointment in her daughter for giving up her virginity so easily.

I know my mom already suspects Ethan is the father, but she doesn't know how it happened.

We haven't talked about it, but she must assume it's him. She doesn't get angry at me like I expect her to. She doesn't yell at me or pester me with questions. She just kisses me on the forehead and slowly closes my bedroom door behind her as she tiptoes back to her room to slide back into bed next to my snoring father.

There will be time to tell her what's happened. Later. If I choose to.

***

It's not long before the sun makes its way in through the curtains temporarily blinding me. I haven't been able to shut my eyes since my mom left the room. Flashbacks haunt me every time I close them. Ethan's large hands pinning me down, his rough chin scraping my bare back, the pain between my legs, and now this. A baby?

Why is this happening to me?

I can't take care of a baby! Panic has haunted me all night long, making it hard to breathe.

Why do I have to be constantly in pain and torturing myself while Ethan gets off scot-free?

I need to confront him. I won't let him get away with this. He's ruined my life forever! He said I was his queen—that he loved me! When in reality, he's been treating me like the mud on the bottom of his shoe.

I cry even harder as I imagine Ethan's sweet face, his clear blue eyes. How could that kind soul be capable of something so evil? I guess it's true what they say, it's usually someone close to you, someone you don't suspect, someone you trust.

Well, I will never trust anyone or let anyone hurt me like this ever again.

From this point on, I will be on high alert and never let my guard down again.

***

After breakfast, my mom and I go quietly about our normal routines so that my father doesn't suspect anything. As usual, at 7:30, I pretend to leave for school, but instead, I walk straight into the backyard and wait for him to leave for work. Once he leaves, my mother meets me on the front step. We don't exchange any words as we get in the car and begin the hour-long drive to Saint John. On the way, it occurs to me that my mother is embarrassed that someone in our village might see us buying a pregnancy test, which is why we're driving so far to get one.

I never considered how all of this might affect her. I was so caught up in my own version of hell that I didn't see that my mom was living through her own right next to me.

One daughter missing and the other knocked up.

Shame courses through me and I get angry at this situation and the injustice of it all. This wasn't because I couldn't keep my legs closed or even because of my choice of outfit. This wasn't something I wanted or even asked for.

Hell, I didn't even know it happened until last night.

It had been my first time having sex and I never even got to enjoy it. Instead, my first time fantasies have been replaced by torment and a permanent feeling of nausea as I keep getting stronger and more vivid flashbacks. I'm sure I'll be chasing these nightmares away for the rest of my life, whether I'm awake or asleep.

Instead of making love, I got raped by the man I loved.

All I got was pain, and now this—a baby.

216

We park in front of the store and my mother tells me to wait in the car while she gets out a twenty-dollar bill from her wallet to go buy a test. I register that my mom has planned ahead and decided it would be best not to use her bank card.

She comes back minutes later with a translucent, grey plastic bag with two pregnancy tests inside it. She hurries towards the car looking left and right like she stole them, like a criminal. Why are we the ones trying to cover this up when I'm the one who's been victimized here? I shouldn't be hiding in the shadows! I haven't done anything wrong!

We get home with plenty of time to take the tests. I drink water until my bladder hurts. My body is ready to take the test but my mind isn't ready to accept the truth. When I can't hold it in any more, I use the first test, and then the second. I sit on the toilet bowl, waiting, head down, not willing to risk looking up.

Alone in the room, my head is spinning with questions. According to my calculations, I'm about six weeks pregnant. I still can't believe I never noticed I'd missed my period last month. My mother stands still on the other side of the door, patiently waiting with me in her own prison. This might be the first time I don't see her managing her anxiety by cleaning. That tells me just how serious this is.

When the time is up. I wait another minute, trying to enjoy the blissful ignorance a little while longer although I know I'm kidding myself. I'm in no rush to see just how screwed I am. My mother on the other hand, unable to wait any longer, knocks quickly on the bathroom door. She must have been counting down the time in her head to know exactly when the tests would be ready.

Before I look at the tests, I rush to open the door, deciding at the last minute that I can't do this alone. I need my mom with me. We stare at each other and then both of our gazes make their way to the corner of the sink, where both tests are lying side by side, just as we are standing, in solidarity. We know that whatever happens, it will be our secret—ours alone.

With my brows knit close together, I hold up both of the tests. At first the results are unclear to me, but my mother's open mouth silent cry is enough to tell me that both are positive. That's when I understand the significance of the faint pink lines—two pink lines for pregnant.

Both tests are identical.

A wave of overwhelming force crashes into me at the realization of this development. I am indeed pregnant and doomed for life.

44

ELISABETH

All day, I torment myself thinking about what's next and what I need to do. Do I tell Ethan that I know what he did, or not? Do I stay with him, or not? How can I ever forgive him? Do I keep the baby, or not?

Hundreds of questions, but no clear answers.

While yesterday, I was constantly warm and my skin was dry, today I'm freezing and my skin is oily. Now I understand the scenes in movies when pregnant actresses look over at each other knowingly and say, "Hormones."

I get it now. They're terrible and unpredictable—they are evil.

If my hormones are going crazy, what does this mean for the life of the baby growing inside me? Will how it was conceived affect its personality? Will my anger and rejection of it be felt through my womb? This baby isn't even fully formed yet and all it's ever known is hate and anger. What kind of life will that be?

I consider my options, but my Anglican background is ingrained in me so deeply that abortion is the furthest thing from my mind. It's not the baby's fault it was ill-conceived. I cannot get rid of this baby, no matter what. It's a living thing. It's a person and it's growing inside of me. I'm responsible for it now, even if it wasn't planned.

My hands haven't stopped shaking since I took the tests from the bathroom sink and wrapped them in a towel to hide under my bed. I don't want my father to find out. He once said that if either my sister or I sinned terribly or brought shame down on our family, we would no longer have a family. We would have to leave immediately. I've never thought of what I could do to shame my family or my father that badly—until now.

What if Fran had done something sinful like this in my father's eyes? Is that why she's gone? Maybe she's not missing at all, but exiled.

Right away, I let that thought go. Fran was a fun girl, but she was a respectful girl. She followed the rules when they mattered. She worked hard. Fran was the smarter one. Still, what happened to me had nothing to do with wit or hard work. Maybe something similar happened to her too.

Whenever I would complain about having to go home right after school to play chess, Fran would somehow turn it around and make it fun—a competition between us. Of course, she was unbeatable, the champion of chess in our house. She would even beat our father often. She was his rising star. She could do no wrong in his eyes. Fran even learned German and spoke it almost fluently. My father was so proud of her. It took everything for me to shine in her shadow.

Before Fran went missing, my father used to take each one of us out on father-daughter dates, individually. He always took Fran to his golf club. She was gorgeous and I think my father liked the attention he got whenever she was with him.

Fran, the tall, pretty blond daughter, got a lot of attention.

Those guys were dirty old men and my father warned us never to approach them without him present. That didn't mean he didn't like the response he got when Fran was around. Everyone likes to feel popular once in a while.

No, Fran would never escape my father's eyes.

She was his pride and joy. She was flawless in his eyes, honest and kind. She had an appetite for knowledge. She was the first-born—the one with all the promise and she lived up to it. Up until she disappeared and broke their hearts.

My father hasn't been the same ever since. He's been drinking more and more. He's less patient and angrier. Try as I may, I never seem to be good enough—a consolation prize. I've never been able to measure up to Fran in his eyes.

I'm so grateful for my mother's help and discretion so far. At least I know I can count on her.

Right now, she's the only one I can trust.

***

As I sit on the edge of my bed, wrapped up in a knitted sweater, shivering from head to toe, I feel the pregnancy tests ever present under my bed, like in the story of *The Princess and the Pea*. Their very meaning so intense, I feel like they are burning a hole through my mattress and reaching out to me. Like the gates of hell opening up below me, just waiting to swallow me whole.

My mother may try to cleanse the house, clean every single surface as I'm sure she is cleaning the bathroom right now while I sit in my dark room. But she cannot cleanse the evil sin I have committed and the trouble I now face.

No amount of scrubbing can make me new again.

She won't be able to sweep me up like the dirt on the floor. She will pretend for my father, that she still loves me. She will carry on as though nothing has changed, but as this baby grows and my belly begins to swell, she will change. She will not be able to keep her eyes from my bulging belly. She will never be able to love my child. She will pray for this situation to be fixed—for this inconvenience to go away. She will ask for mercy from God to free us from this, beg Him to make me clean again.

My mother forgot an important detail though—you can't clean rape.

My soul will forever be dirty, always be dark.

45

CLAIRE

In the morning, Stewart and I head over to the shop early. We start off the same way as yesterday and I can tell this guy loves routine. Breakfast, lunch, and dinner, always at the same times. He's a stickler for a schedule. It keeps him grounded, he reasons. He thrives on it. I wonder if he suffers from anxiety like me, or just has a need for order. I like order. I like rules. I inherited that from my mother.

It helps that we seem to be on the same page. It's like a game of who can speak the least. We haven't worked together long, but there's already a natural flow to how we work. As though we can anticipate each other's movements. We seem to process things the same way which makes me believe that he and I will get along well.

Stewart has just finished teaching me how to measure twice and cut once on his Miter saw. We're building new shelves for the cold room in the basement so Anna can store her preserves for the winter.

As we're cutting the pine sheet, I notice in the distance a dust cloud and the faint silhouette of an old run down forest green Honda Civic approaching quickly. Those cars last forever it seems.

The car speeds down the gravel driveway and stops abruptly just two feet from the house. We make our way over to it. Stewart, concern on his face, hurries to the car and opens the driver's door. A few words are exchanged too quietly for me to hear. The driver is slightly hidden by a glare from the cloudy day, reflecting back my own distorted silhouette at a distance in the car's front window. Stewart's arm is holding the door open as he leans into the car to talk to whoever was in such a big hurry to get here.

The ground moves under my feet. An earthquake? No, just my heart beating so loudly it feels like I might fall over.

It's happening. They've found me.

Who's in the car? Is it Inspector Riley? Ethan?

I shouldn't stand here in full sight. I start to turn to make a run for it when the driver steps out. One leg at time, a woman carefully steps out of the car, helped by Stewart. A strand of brown hair obscures most of her face but not fast enough. I spot a large bruise, black and blue, maybe three inches in diameter visible around her right eye. She also has a large gash on her cheek that appears to have been made with something sharp, most likely by keys or a knife. The cut is crusty with rusty blood under her left cheek bone and will probably require stitches.

The woman's face is as white as a ghost. Her front teeth are crooked and so is the thin bridge of her nose. I'd guess that it's been broken several times in the past and has healed on its own before being reset. Even under the black eye, I can tell she has dark circles under her eyes similar to mine, so I can safely assume that she hasn't slept in a while.

Her coat has a large hole under the armpit where the puffy white down has started to fall out. I can see that one of her bootlaces isn't tied. She must have left in a haste.

The woman appears to be slightly younger than Stewart, but there is a familiarity to her features, something about the shape of her mouth. Their comfort together makes me believe that she must be a relative of his, possibly even a younger sister.

The woman barely acknowledges my presence or ignores me on purpose, which is fine by me. The fewer people who know I'm here, the better.

Stewart doesn't even glance back at me as he escorts her up the stairs and into the house. After several moments, he reappears, his face red. I can't tell if it's out of sadness or anger—maybe it's both. Stewart has been nothing but calm and collected since I've met him. This is new territory for me. I'm not sure if I should say anything or stay out of his way.

My father used to be a quiet man just like Stewart. He always kept his emotions at bay until Fran left. I think his peace left the same day she did. Before Fran left, my father never would have considered hitting my mother or me. After my sister disappeared, every time my father would get upset, he would always turn aggressive.

The first time my father hit me, it was square across the face. It was the day I told him I was three months pregnant. I'd waited until the end of the summer before telling him, my belly not yet showing. I felt I couldn't hide it from him much longer—someone else might tell him. I wasn't sure how he would react to the news. But I had wanted him to find out directly from me.

My mom had begged me not to tell him. Urged me to wait, just in case. *Just in case what?* I had asked her, but she had stayed silent. She never did tell me why. I ended up finding out what she'd meant too late, on my own.

I thought he would disown me like he always threatened to do if ever I committed an unforgivable sin or embarrassed him and the family. But after that flash of anger, he subsided. It was like something inside him broke. His eyes were vacant for a moment, lost in thought. It was as though he wasn't even there. Only a shell of my father remained.

I didn't know how to react. I couldn't hit him back. I mean, he's my father! It was terrifying. My cheek, red-hot under my touch, my shaking hand patting it gently where my father had hit me, my eyes wide as saucers. I couldn't believe he'd actually hit me. He'd never done that before. I don't think he even knew he was going to.

He was just raging and I got too close.

When his eyes regained focus, I braced myself for the scolding of a lifetime. Instead of more angry words and more abuse, he did the complete unexpected. He fell to his knees before me, his face buried in his large hands, sobbing. He murmured something in German. I only caught bits and pieces.

I was stunned. Here was my father, kneeling at my feet, begging for forgiveness. Not from me, but from God.

When my father finally stood, he didn't meet my eyes. He simply turned around, walked upstairs to his room, and shut the door with a soft click. We never spoke about it again, but I wonder what he was really praying for at my feet.

Was he praying the same thing my mother was praying for? That I be cleansed of my sin? That I be forgiven?

I think he prayed I would lose the baby, because on a cold, miserable September day, less than a week later, I did.

46

ELISABETH

When I accuse Ethan publicly about the rape, he denies it. Of course, he does. Who would admit to that kind of allegation?

Perhaps I could have kept this sensitive conversation for a better time, but heck, my hormones were all over the place. Besides, why should I give his feelings any consideration when he clearly hadn't considered mine? I couldn't keep on pretending that everything was fine between us. I couldn't be normal and happy like I had been before.

Those first few days and weeks after the party, all I'd had were doubts and jumbled memories. But now—now I have proof. Proof of what I've been suspecting all along. Proof of what he's done.

I can't hold it in anymore. I'm bursting at the seams. I can't wait for a better day, like perhaps a few weeks after graduation, when things would have cooled off a little bit. And when maybe, I could have asked him to come for a walk and discussed things peacefully. When we could have come up with a plan together.

I swallow painfully, a hard ball building in my throat as I find myself coming to terms with the fact that there will never be a "we" again. Ethan and I will never be together again. Parts of me still ache for him. As twisted as this is, I still loved him.

No more hesitation, this has to happen now. He has royally screwed up my life and I'm mad. Really mad! Seeing red kind of mad.

He never considered the consequences of his actions and he's been lying to my face. I'm so sick of pretending everything is perfect, that nothing has changed, because everything has.

I'm tired of the charade—the game is up. I know now.

At any other time, I might have been more in control, more prepared. I might have cared what other people thought, but not today. Today I'm fuming, bordering on irrational. The hormones and emotions are right on the surface. I feel justified and entitled. It's time for the truth to come out, even if it's graduation day.

Forced to wear flats because of my swollen feet, the June heat's side effect to my pregnancy, I storm into the school and spot Ethan by the white robes. He's standing there in a small group with Rebecca and his favourite side-kick, Rob.

I feel more alone than ever.

A wave of betrayal courses through me watching them all having an enjoyable chat, laughing together. They are completely unaware of the storm forming in my mind, the picture perfect glass shattering in my eyes as I now know the truth and have a baby growing in my belly. My eyes have been set on them from way down the hall. I've zoned-out every other noise but for his voice. All I can see is the back of his head. That dark, thick hair. I can see every single strand—hyperaware.

When I finally reach him, I don't wait patiently to be acknowledged. I don't wait for my turn to talk. I put a hand on Ethan's shoulder and spin him around forcefully to face me. I grab him by the arm and tighten my grip around his bicep, pressing my nails hard into his flesh, hard enough to leave a mark, but a mark so small it won't even last the week.

Nothing compared to the permanent mark he's left on me.

"Hey! What the hell? Babe? What's going on?" He's trying to get away, trying to pull his arm loose. To wiggle out of my grasp like I tried to all those nights ago, but I'm not letting go.

I have the advantage now.

I'm not looking back, only forward. I know that if I'm going to accuse him of this and break up with him, I can't look into his eyes, or I know I'll fail. I know I'll be a coward and that my heart will win out. That despite all my instincts, I will forgive him.

Twisting under my grip, Ethan cries out, "Ow, babe, that really hurts! What are you doing?" His voice is getting louder as I pull him. "Where are we going? Why are you so mad?"

I stop in my tracks, never reaching the stairwell I was gunning for. I forget all about secrecy, about trying to keep this quiet and just between us.

Why am I so mad? Did he really just ask me that? Rage is building inside of me, my blood hot.

I don't stutter. I don't cry. I force myself to focus right on his eyes, wide like saucers, when I shout, "Why am I mad?" I barely recognize my own voice. A voice so strong, it barely resembles any sound I've ever heard coming out of my own mouth. It's fueled by an unknown source of strength deep within me.

"You raped me, you asshole! And then, you lied about it!" My voice echoing through the halls has attracted a large crowd.

A hundred eyes are on us now, the graduating class in their white gowns, an ironic symbol of purity, of new beginnings. In their heels and ugly square hats, they are all taking in the drama unfolding between us, barely capable of containing their excitement at the breaking up of the most popular couple in the school.

"What?" Ethan practically chokes the word as he stumbles backwards, short of breath suddenly.

He's acting and he's terrible at it, I tell myself. It's just more lies. This makes me even angrier and helps me finish what I've come here to do.

I'd taken another pregnancy test this morning which fuels my anger now as I pull out the wrapped up test from my back pocket and hold it up to his face.

"Proof, Ethan! Proof that you raped me. At your pre-graduation party when I was passed out in your bed." A collective gasp is heard through the corridor as many of the girls slap their hands to their mouths in shock.

Ethan, speechless, seems dumbfounded at the positive pregnancy test. He's acting like a lost puppy trying to find his tail—completely lost. Thinking he's wasting time until he comes up with any sort of a defense to save his own ass, I finish what I've come to say. This is even harder for me to declare than announcing to the whole school that I'm pregnant by a rapist, but I push on anyway.

"And now, I'm dumping you! I don't date losers who rape their girlfriends when they're passed out and get them pregnant. I don't date lying assholes. Thank you for ruining my life. We're done."

I turn away from Ethan and all the other students and start making my way down the hallway. I hear heavy footsteps running after me and Rob yelling my name, begging me to wait, but I don't even turn around.

I don't look back as I push through the steel doors and quickly find my way down the stairs and out of the school, skipping the long-awaited graduation ceremony, suddenly not in the mood for celebrations at all. Let them go on without me.

Finally, my face is hit with the warm, humid June air. I exhale loudly, keeping the tears in check. *A new start*, I think to myself as I gently rub the tiny bulge of my belly.

With every step, I walk further and further away from my past, from the school, and from Ethan and the life I thought I had wanted.

47

ELISABETH

I've managed to wear loose clothing all summer to cover my growing belly. Thankfully, I was able to wear cute flowy bikini cover-ups at the beach so my father didn't get suspicious. Until last week that is.

September is the month our family always picks apples to make a year's worth of apple pies, crumble and apple sauce, an old favourite of mine. Only, this year, the sweet smell of the boiling sugar and flaky dough made my stomach turn. It didn't take my dad long to notice I'd left my pie slice untouched.

I felt a wave of nausea hit and barely made it to the bathroom, my father on my heels. Concern immediately turned into understanding and then to rage. He started screaming in my face, right there in the bathroom, the toilet bowl still full. I barely had time to get up off my knees when I felt the sting of his hand on my cheek.

My father and I haven't spoken all week about the incident or about my 'situation,' as my mother puts it. I think all of us want to just hide it under a rug and forget the pregnancy ever happened. We all want to be a perfect, normal family again, but we can't. Too much brokenness has seeped into the walls of our house. The dirt is consuming us alive—this shame, this secret, too big to ever conceal or clean up.

I don't know if my father has been forgiven by God for striking his child—his pregnant child.

And I don't care.

All that matters to me is for him to ask for my forgiveness, but, of course, he hasn't apologized to me yet and probably never will. I know he thinks very little of me now, yet here I am, still in his house. He hasn't kicked me out, and to my utmost surprise, hasn't disowned me.

Idle threats, it seems.

This doesn't stop me from staying angry with him. I may well still be here, only two feet away from him, sitting across from him at the kitchen table, but he has yet to acknowledge my presence. He's choosing passive-aggressiveness instead of physical aggressiveness, but this feels worse somehow.

Like torture.

I can't stand his silent treatment any longer, feeling the now familiar rise of anger bubbling to the surface. I stand up from my chair too quickly, ready to confront him, demand an apology, but instead I hit the table with my small belly bump. I'm not yet used to the growing swell. My quick motion lifts the entire table several inches off the floor before it falls back down hard onto the linoleum flooring. My father's cereal splatters all over his pressed, grey work pants, and milk drips to the floor.

The room is eerily quiet as we all take in the scene.

I'm about to speak when suddenly I feel a strange wave of weakness and an urgent need to grip tightly to the table. Nausea rushes through me as quickly as a train from *Ground Central* and I'm hit with a sudden pain in my back.

I rush up the stairs to the bathroom, my wobbly legs barely supporting my extra weight, followed by the angry, threatening voice of my father.

Something about "you get back here right this instant or there will be hell to pay!", but I can't be bothered with him right now.

I'm not one hundred percent sure yet, but I believe I'm indeed starting to pay for it. Someone up there is definitely siding with my father these days.

I'm sick into the toilet and gripped by intense cramps. The pain in my abdomen resembles my period cramps, but this is way stronger. I sit on the toilet just in time to see deep red blood coming out of me.

Panicking, I cry out to my mother, still downstairs, forced to listen to my father's angry outburst over his ruined work pants. She doesn't hear me right away. I can picture her, like a magnet to the dirt, her knees on the floor, cleaning up the soggy cereal and sticky milk, unable to help herself. Her own way of fixing a situation out of her control.

I yell for her again as a clot of pink-red tissue comes out of me and makes a tiny splashing noise in the toilet bowl as it hits the water. Just like that, I know that I've lost the baby. I'm immediately filled with a deep sorrow and grief for a life I never got to know.

I'm still staring down between my legs, tears running down my cheeks, when my mother walks into the bathroom and falls on the ground in front me, sobbing loudly and emitting ugly wails, but not from relief.

As I embrace my weeping mother, I spot my father in the slight crack of the open bathroom door, his look downcast and unreadable.

48

CLAIRE

Stewart doesn't speak for several moments, busying himself with odd tasks in no particular order. He's definitely bothered by the recent events. I can tell the woman's unannounced visit and her physical state has upset him. Yet, I'm not sure how to comfort him. Or if I even should. I've only known him for two days. I decide to respect his silence and not pry into his personal life, like he's stayed out of mine. Respect for respect.

After about an hour of working in silence, the woman appears in the doorway of the garage, her gaze down. Our busy hands grow still as we stare at her, waiting for her to speak. When she peers up, it's my face she looks at. Curiosity gets the better of her, lines of it displayed across her forehead as we lock eyes for a moment.

There's a flash of something in her eyes and then it's gone.

What was that? Who is she? Does she know who I am? Does she recognize me or something?

I do quick math and realize that by now, it's highly likely that I've been classified as a missing person. But that would be local news in New Brunswick. Certainly, it wouldn't have reached Nova Scotia yet, right?

Although due to my possible connection to Sandra's murder, the police might have sped up the process and extended the reach of the missing person report. I guess it's possible that my face is plastered over newspapers here too.

After a moment, the shock of seeing me there evaporates. She composes herself and looks over at Stewart with tears in her eyes. He rushes over to her and hugs her tightly for a minute. He inspects her cheek, which has been stitched up neatly and kisses her forehead. A few hushed words are spoken between them, their voices growing louder, angrier. Then the woman's face contorts as she whispers one last thing, silencing him immediately.

Reluctantly, Stewart walks her back to the old Honda, dusty from the road, and opens the door for her. No words or glances are exchanged as he helps to settle her in the car and buckles her in. Standing next to the car Stewart hunches over, his shoulders heavy like a defeated dog who's disappointed his owner. I can only imagine the puppy eyes behind his thick-rimmed glasses.

As she turns the car around and leaves, Stewart looks on until she's all the way back on the main road before walking passed me and into the house. After a few uncertain moments, I follow him in. Anna is clearing the table of rust-coloured rags, alcohol swabs, needles, and a sewing kit. She dumps ice cubes out of a damp cloth and into the sink before rinsing out two empty cups of tea.

The air is thick—somber.

I consider walking straight to my room so they can speak in private, but Stewart motions for me to sit down. I hesitate for a moment, but my legs are killing me so I welcome the break. He hesitates, looking over to Anna for reassurance before talking.

"That was Mary, my younger sister." That explains the resemblance. I'd been right to assume the age difference.

Not bothering with formalities or courtesy, I ask point blank, "Who did that to her? Her husband?"

Stewart fixes his eyes on me, half impressed at my correct guess, half pissed off at my bluntness.

"As a matter of fact, yes, her husband, Mike Andrews." The name is spoken carefully, like bad food at a dinner party that you can't wait to spit out, but are trying to keep it together and pretend you like it.

"Why doesn't she leave him?" I ask, not sure why I'm suddenly in the middle of this very private family situation.

"They have a boy together. She would never leave, even though their son is older now and in his thirties." At this, he glances up briefly, his gaze questioning, but I don't move from my seat, don't offer any reaction to what he's guessing. He's thinking his nephew is about the same age as me and he's absolutely right.

"So? If he's thirty, he's got a job, right? Doesn't live at home anymore?" I ask, not following.

Stewart and Anna glance at each other and she nods for him to continue as she stands up to put the kettle on the stove for her second or third cup of tea of the day. I can't help but wonder how boring her days must be. How she must find drama like bloody sisters-in-law and foster kids exciting. What does she do to fill her days now that she's not fostering?

She takes in runaways like me, for one. Cleans up wounds on the side. Cooks damn good meals and cleans the entire house every day.

Being a housewife is not my cup of tea. I was made for business, for strategy. For analyzing, for asking questions and finding solutions. I would go stir-crazy spending all my time in a house, never leaving it.

Sensing I wasn't satisfied with his answers, Stewart stands slowly, and with a slight tilt of his head, he motions for me to follow him in the living room.

We step onto the old, grey, shaggy carpet, which looks like it hasn't been replaced in at least fifty years and we make our way to a bookshelf on the far side of the room.

Stewart is silent as he stops and stares at the books and pictures on the shelves, lost in thought. Following his cue, I begin to scan each book title, searching for an indication as to why he's brought me there. I'm beginning to lose patience when, out of the corner of my eye, an old sepia picture of a large family catches my attention. An elderly couple is seated on an antique sofa, surrounded by what must be their own children and their spouses, as well as their grandchildren.

Not sure why the picture sticks out to me, I make my way closer until I'm right in front of it. Although I'm quite tall, I need to strain my neck to see properly.

Noticing this, Stewart doesn't hesitate to grab the framed picture that's peaked my interested. He takes it right off the shelf and puts it into my hands for a closer look.

He explains everyone's place in the family, starting with his parents sitting on the couch. His older brother Gerry, his wife Stella, and their daughters, Isabelle and Grace, standing behind them. Stewart and Anna with no kids, followed by Stewart's younger sister Mary, her husband Mike, and there, between them, a young boy.

I blink a couple of times to make sure I'm seeing this correctly.

It's him—younger, but most definitely him.

49

CLAIRE

What the hell? In my shock at seeing a familiar face in this stranger's home, I almost drop the picture frame to the floor, feeling dizzy, and my mind spinning.

This is getting weird.

How can Stewart and Anna, these strangers I've just met, who live so far from my childhood home, have a picture of someone I know in their living room? Coincidence? I'm starting to think not so much.

I swallow hard, my throat is dry.

Suddenly I become extremely aware that I desperately need a drink, preferably with alcohol in it. It's been a whole week since my life was turned upside down, my past rushing towards me like a freight train, ready to knock me off my feet. It's a good thing I'm quick on my feet and have good balance.

Still, I immediately start to wonder if it was really stupid of me to pick a number off a random ad and put my safety in these strangers' hands. I have to consider the possibility that Anna and Stewart aren't strangers at all but that they know exactly who I am. Because, here in this living room, next to people I don't know, I'm face to face with a picture of a young boy I recognize.

A young boy whose best friend raped me.

I stare at the photograph of Rob in awe. He looked so much like Ethan when he was younger.

Noticing my sudden interest in the picture, Stewart continues the family history as though there's been no awkward silence. Of course, I'm only half listening, but I do catch on to something. Stewart mentions that the young boy in the picture, Mary's son, is named Tony Andrews.

This makes no sense. Why would Tony look identical to Rob? Was I wrong in thinking it was Rob? Was there a twin brother?

Surely his own uncle would know his real name. Stewart goes on to explain that Tony was a little troublemaker. That he took after his father in that way. Tony broke every rule and couldn't make friends easily. He explained how he got into fights at school.

This description of the boy in the picture is so different from the boy I knew, Ethan's best friend. The quiet, pleasant, and loyal friend. It makes me think that perhaps this isn't Rob after all.

Then, a sudden realization hits me. For the life of me, I don't have any memories of Rob in grade nine. I can only really remember him as of grade ten. I first saw him and Ethan talking near their lockers down the hall from me, before we started dating. I remember seeing the two of them throwing around a football, laughing easily. Best pals.

I turn to Stewart, abruptly interrupting his thoughts, and ask him if Tony transferred during his high school years to another school?

'As a matter of fact, he did.' He eyes me curiously. 'Now, how could you possibly know that?' he adds with a nervous laugh.

Suddenly, I feel hot all over.

It doesn't make any sense.

I need to think. I need to be alone.

I excuse myself and retreat to the safety of my new room. Once inside, I turn the lock silently. Is there no one I can trust anymore?

Grateful for the time alone to think, I sit on the bed and go through the stored files of memory in my mind. How can Tony be Rob? I guess if I can be both Elisabeth and Claire, he can be two people as well. Did I really think I was the only person out there with a secret? I lie down on the bed, my arms supporting my head, staring up at the slow rhythmic movement of the ceiling fan, getting lost in memory.

Sitting alone in the dark used to calm me when I was younger, but ever since Ethan's party, I prefer to leave a small light on at night. I try never to let myself be engulfed in total darkness again. I need to know what's going on around me to feel safe. That's one of the main reasons why I can never really fall into a deep sleep. For a long time, I always slept with one eye open, my ears on high alert, ready to jump up at a moment's notice. No wonder I suffer from insomnia and chronic headaches.

Just like that, as if the simple fact of thinking about it can bring one about, I definitely feel a headache coming on now. Like a songbird responding to its mate, my headaches and my thoughts are forever connected. Nausea and black spots blur my vision so I turn my head on the frilly old-fashioned pillow. I briefly shut my eyes, my breathing heavy, and force myself to calm down.

Think.

There must be a reason I'm here. Something I need to find out. Something that will connect my past with my present situation. Someone is framing me for murder. Someone who knows my true identity, someone who hates me.

This whole week, since seeing the chessboard and the displaced queen pawn, I've been assuming Ethan was after me. He and I always used to play chess after school, supervised by my father, of course. Ethan was always so competitive. Even though I had been the one to teach him how to play, he relentlessly tried to convince me that he was the chess champion.

The clue I'd found in my apartment of the chess game and the drawing of a crown pointed to our special connection. I was sure he was seeking revenge on me for ruining his reputation, for exposing him to the entire school. He definitely has reason to be angry with me. Yet, I can't picture him being a murderer.

Then again, I never pictured him as a rapist either.

There aren't many people who know my past life. Rebecca is the only one I've remained close to, who knows my real name. A creeping thought courses through me. I can trust her, right?

I'm not sure I can trust anyone anymore.

***

With my eyes closed, my palm resting on my forehead, willing the headache to stay at bay, I keep replaying the conversation upstairs. Mary's battered face, her quiet demeanor, the way she shifted her eyes downwards. Where had I seen that look before? Why did she seem so familiar to me? What was it about the lingering stare she'd given me before she left?

Had she recognized me?

I slowly rise from my lying position and place both feet on the ground. I make my way over to the tiny closet to retrieve my gym bag where I'm hoping I will find something to cure my headache. As I roll my head backwards and rub my sore neck with my hand, I spot something at the back of the closet.

Unfortunately, the ceiling light doesn't quite illuminate the bottom corner of the closet enough and so it's difficult to decipher what I'm seeing. I kneel down closer, careful to turn my body so that the faint light isn't obscured completely. I squint now, trying to see it better. Close enough to the floor that I smell the dust mites in the carpet, I finally see what it was that caught my eye.

I stifle a cry in my throat. My blood runs cold.

There, at the bottom of the closet of my rented room, in black permanent marker are the words 'Rob Johnson + Elisabeth Smith = true love forever' with a big heart circling both our names and a tiny drawing of a crown next to my name.

A cold chill sweeps over my arms as I quickly crawl out of the closet and stand several feet from the words, bewildered, as though being too close to them might make me fall into the closet, trapping me forever.

I was right! Rob and Tony are the same person! What does this mean? Why would Rob have been in here?

Stewart and Anna used to foster children who were going through hard times. Maybe they helped Mary and Mike when Rob, or rather, Tony, was acting out in his teens.

I take a closer look at the crown drawing over my name. It's identical to the tattoo on my back. How would Rob know about that? I've never shown it to him. I got it late in the summer before senior year. He wouldn't have seen it unless he spotted it by chance when I'd worn a bathing suit.

Sure, Ethan might have mentioned we got tattoos, but there's no way Rob could know exactly how it looked, unless he'd seen it himself. Yet, here I was staring at an exact replica of my tattoo.

Come to think of it, this drawing was also identical to the drawing left in my apartment earlier this week. I had assumed it had been Ethan, because no one else knew what my tattoo looked like but him.

How close were Rob and Ethan? I wonder. How much did they share? Best pals.

I examine the inscription again. Had Rob had feelings for me this entire time and never said a word out of loyalty to Ethan?

I remember the way Rob had gaped at me at Ethan's party that night and I'm hit with a flashback so vivid, I backup right into the corner of the bed and fall to the floor with a hard thud. Rob—his hesitation at Ethan's party, his downcast look. The same as Mary's today. His mother—Tony's mother.

At that moment, there's not a doubt in my mind that Rob is Tony and that Tony is Mary's son.

The resemblance is uncanny.

Now that I know Tony is Mary's son, it also means that his father is Mike—the same asshole who beat up Mary. Did Tony also acquire some of Mike's aggressive nature towards women? It's entirely possible.

Stewart had even mentioned that Tony used to get into a lot of trouble and start fights at school. When I knew him as Rob, he was so different, so calm. Perhaps he was on his best behaviour because he'd finally felt accepted by Ethan. Maybe being around Ethan had made Tony a better person.

Or maybe not.

If Tony—Rob—had been in love with me, if he'd stuck around Ethan just to be near me, then maybe he wasn't so innocent after all.

Didn't Rob wear one of Ethan's shirts that night at the party? Didn't Ethan mention he'd been stuck cleaning up downstairs until the early morning?

Rob and Ethan had always looked so similar. It might be why they became friends in the first place. People are often attracted to others who look like them. One guy wearing a striped shirt sees another dude in a striped shirt and suddenly, they're best friends. That's how guys work.

I remember Ethan's denial and how completely confused he'd been as I accused him of raping me. As I stare at the words in the closet, like a dirty little secret trying it's best to remain in the shadows, I feel bile rise up my throat.

I struggle to swallow it down.

Putting the pieces together after all these years in the dark, my memory of that night was a scattered puzzle full of missing pieces I couldn't place. Now it's unfolding at a rapid speed, a perfect picture in my mind. That odd voice, the intensity, the rape, the denials, the guilt-ridden face. It hadn't been Ethan after all!

Rob had been the one to sneak into Ethan's bedroom that night. He'd known I'd be there, passed out. He saw his opportunity to finally have what Ethan had. Me.

When I'd resisted, he'd taken it anyway, his father's impulsiveness and abusive nature coursing through his veins as well. It had been Rob's baby I'd carried, Rob's baby I'd lost.

Ethan had been telling the truth the whole time!

A familiar anger greets me like an old, faithful friend, an old deep need for revenge and justice.

Welcome back, Elisabeth, it taunts.

50

CLAIRE

Grabbing my scattered belongings, I hastily throw them into my gym back and I race up the steps, determined and fired up. I almost knock over frail Anna standing by the stove, preparations for tonight's dinner well underway.

I mumble an apology and ask for Stewart. She tells me he's returned to the shop, eying my gym bag slung over my shoulder as she did my first day here.

'Going somewhere?' she asks me curiously, genuine concern spread over her face.

'I'm not sure yet. I just need to get some fresh air for a little while.' I do my best to appear put together and focus on pacing my breath.

As I wander back in to the living room for a last glance at the photograph that set all of this in motion, I spot the chessboard in the corner of the room, the same one Stewart and I played on that evening. Putting the rest of the story together, I ask Anna to confirm my suspicions.

"You know Mary's son, Tony? Did he ever stay here with you and Stewart?"

Anna hesitates a moment, uneasy with my aggressive tone and the urgency of my sudden interrogation. Desperation is seeping out of my skin and she can almost see it glowing red. She seems unsure if she should tell me or not.

We haven't exactly had much time to chat since I've been here, but then she nods slowly.

"Yes, there was one time. He stayed in the bedroom you're in now. Mary and Mike had gotten into a big fight and she had considered leaving him. Tony was going to school somewhere far away, but she pulled him out of school for a while and he and Mary stayed with us." She pauses and continues, "Tony was a great help to Stewart, helping out in the shop and all. Such a strapping young boy. He was a hard worker and had so much talent. Stewart had just injured his leg back then and Tony was young, strong, and good with his hands. Lord knows that boy needed something to distract him. He was constantly getting into trouble at school here, so they sent him away until Mary had decided to leave. She needed our help to watch him for a bit until she sorted it out with the lawyers and found a new place to live, but of course, she never did leave. Stewart and I had experience with teenagers who act out, so we kept him busy around here. Straightened him out," she adds with a proud smile.

I stare at her blankly.

How can I tell this kind woman that her nephew, the boy she thinks she straightened out, is the same boy who raped me and got me pregnant? I glance at the chessboard again and ask her if they'd also taught Tony how to play chess during his stay with them.

"But of course! There's not much for entertainment around here, darling." Anna laughs softly. "He was always so smart, that Tony. He picked it up really quickly. Like his mind was hungry for it and, pretty soon, he was beating us all."

So there it was. All the pieces laid out in front of me. All the walls breaking down, uncovering the ugly truths.

"One last thing," I ask hesitantly, something gnawing at me. "What's Tony's last name again?"

"Andrews. Why?" Confusion crosses Anna's face as mine contorts in horror. I bolt out the door and run as fast as I can to the shop.

Tony Andrews.

That's Jess's new boyfriend's name. The one I spotted her kissing in the dark in front of the bar. The same guy Jess wanted me to meet that night.

If I'm right, and if Rob Johnson is truly Tony Andrews, then Jess is in grave danger. I need to warn her somehow. I have to get to her before he does—before he kills her like he killed Sandra.

51

CLAIRE

My heart is beating so fast, I feel like it will explode out of my chest. I burst through the front door and rush down the steps, two at a time. I almost twist my ankle as I run towards the shop, feeling the old running muscles scream in pain from the lack of use. My mind is racing along with my legs. My head slightly inclines forward, trying to get there before the rest of me does.

I almost run right into Stewart as I keep up the speed when I enter his shop. He's bent over a workbench fixing some saws for a wood project he wanted to start this afternoon.

Looking up, he notices my face right away and his eyes tell me he knows something bad has happened.

"What's wrong? Is Anna ok? What did you do?" he questions, reproachful. He drops everything in that instant and starts making his way towards the house, limping as quickly as he can. His tone is accusing but in my current mood I'm not interested in a fight. I need to cooperate. Still, the thought that he would even suggest that I would hurt his wife stings. I've come to really care about this old couple as though they were my own grandparents, but who could blame him for thinking that?

Of course, he would think that. Of course, he would be wary of the strange woman staying at his house. Who knows what sorts of people he's had living here in the past.

In between breaths, I quickly reassure him that all is fine at the house and with Anna but that something has come up and I need to leave immediately. Stewart hesitates a moment as he glances towards the house and his shop, adrenaline coursing through him from his earlier fright.

I can see the gears turning as he's weighing his options. I follow closely behind as he begins to walk back towards the shop.

"Well, I have some things to do here, but I can drive you to town in an hour or so." He motions to his worktable, filled with tools and debris as an explanation.

"No!" I almost yell back, my voice breaking, panic rising in my throat.

I don't know how to reach Jess to warn her.

I left my cell phone behind. I don't know her phone number to call her from here. I haven't memorized a single phone number since high school—since Ethan's. I haven't seen the need for it until now. I don't know if Jess is safe or not. I've been so isolated from society, living in the small town of Salt Springs for almost a week, I don't know if anything has happened to her.

I know that if I step out of the comfort and security of this secluded place, I'll be putting myself at risk. But when my mind flashes to Jess, my own safety becomes the least of my concerns now.

My friend needs me.

As Claire, I've always kept my friends at arm's length, never wanting to trust anyone again. Never wanting to let anyone close enough to get hurt again.

It doesn't mean I don't care about my friends. Although I tend to put up walls and be short with them, I still care.

I just can't trust anymore.

I learned a long time ago never to trust anyone because anyone can betray you if you allow them to come close enough to know you. I had taken precautions to make sure that it would never happen again—not as Claire.

Now, years later, my friend needs me. It doesn't really matter if I can trust her or not, because I'm the only one who can save her.

There's no way in hell I'm going to wait around for an hour until Stewart finishes his work. I'm already losing my mind worrying about what might be happening to Jess. I need to see her in person to make sure she's OK. I hug myself against the chill and realize I'm still wearing the coat Stewart lent me the other day.

He's watching me curiously, trying to figure out what it is I'm not disclosing. He notices my gym bag flung over my shoulder and understanding crosses over his face.

"Ah, I see. You're leaving now, with or without my help, and you're not coming back," he guesses as understanding plasters his face. I detect a tone of disappointment in his words, like he knows that there's nothing he can say or do to change my mind.

"It's not like that!" I start to protest. "I love it here!" As the words come out of my mouth, I realize just how much I have enjoyed being here, and how much it hurts to leave.

"I just need to take care of something," I declare more urgently than I mean to, my face apologetic.

Stewart seems to grasp the severity of my situation.

"What do you need?" he asks.

He must think I need money. That's why he's offered me a job to help him out in the first place.

He thinks I'm just some poor maladjusted young woman down on her luck. Maybe he's right, but money? I have enough of that.

For now, anyway.

That's when it occurs to me, my way out—Stewart's truck.

It's just been sitting out in the driveway since the first night he picked me up. With a fresh new headlight, it's a great truck. Drivable, or at least legal. Stewart's been trying to sell it for years. He'd mentioned wanting to get rid of it the other night while we were playing chess. No one would buy it. He had said he was asking $3,500 for it. Looking at the large piece of rust now, I find myself scrutinizing its safety and durability.

Would it do the job? Who am I kidding? This isn't a rational business decision where I can worry about the proper assessment or spend time debating. This is my only chance. I need this truck.

I need a way to get to Jess, and fast.

"Your truck. I need it," I demand, never taking my eyes off of it, I add, "I'll buy it off of you. I'll give you $3,000 cash right now, plus the rent I owe you, and you can pretend I was never here." I turn my head to face him. "Do we have a deal?"

Stewart searches my face, contemplating his options. He doesn't let me stew for long. He extends his hand and agrees, "Deal."

A sad smile crosses his face, but I'm not sure if it's because of me leaving or because of selling his beloved truck.

Men can be so attached to their cars and trucks, it can be just like losing a close friend, and no matter how many times that friend has let them down, or left them on the side of the road in the cold without a working heater. They have a soft spot for those old pieces of metal that hold so many cherished memories.

I grab the envelope from my bag and count the money before handing the bundle over to Stewart. He reaches for a set of keys on a hook in the shop and hands them to me, dropping them in my open palm.

I mumble a thank you, too stressed-out to pronounce my words accurately, and hurry to the old truck.

I sit down and take a few seconds to familiarize myself with the old dashboard, choosing to ignore missing switch covers and the wear on the steering wheel. I place my gym back on the passenger seat, not trusting the cab floor to stay intact much longer.

I fasten the seat belt and think about where I need to go. The drive should take about five hours. I should be able to find Jess at work at the Saint John Police Force before she goes home or meets up with Tony for the weekend.

I shudder at the thought of entering the police station willingly, knowing my face is probably plastered everywhere in their system. I imagine "Wanted" or "Missing" posters with my name spilled across every desk. It might be my last time walking into the station as a free woman.

I surely won't be walking out of there freely.

Jess might not even want to be associated with me. Who knows how she reacted when she first heard the news of my disappearance or the fact that I am a suspect.

The thought occurs to me that I might be able to find the number for the station in a phone book, but sitting in the truck now, I can't waste time running back to the house and flipping through hundreds of pages. Even if I found her number, what if I only got her answering machine?

Thoughts of my old life begin to filter in.

Do any of my friends even know what's happening with me? I wonder if Inspector Riley has gotten anywhere in his investigation. I fully expect my apartment to be monitored, so I know I can't go there. I need to reach Jess somehow. I don't have much time to waste. I hope that my new hair colour will help make me less recognizable, just long enough to check on Jess and tell her I'm ok before I disappear again.

I'm getting ready to leave when I remember that I'm still wearing the jacket Stewart lent me and I begin to remove it, when he appears at the rolled-down driver side window, arms leaning on it.

"Keep it." He waves away my protest and I thank him. As I begin pulling way, he slaps the open window base and offers, "Good luck, Claire."

I register it too late to stop and ask him how he knows my real name.

How long has he known? I'd rather not find out.

The point is, he knew but never called the cops. In that moment, I see him in my rear-view mirror, small and surrounded by a cloud of dust. I wish I could have known him better. I wish I could have stayed there, in this safe place, just a little bit longer.

I push away the tears, willing myself to remain focused, eyes ahead. I press on the accelerator and refuse to look back again at the man who gave me shelter, a chance, and an escape vehicle. The man who treated me better than anyone has in all my years as an adult. I promise myself that one day I will come back and thank him.

One day, but not now.

Now I have to stick to the plan. I need to find Jess and warn her about Tony, if he hasn't gotten to her first.

52

TONY

When I finally get to my mom's house, all the lights are off. The house is cloaked in darkness and I hesitate for a moment. I park the truck behind the house so that if my father decides to reappear tonight, I'll have an advantage. I need the element of surprise on my side.

He can't know I'm here protecting her. He doesn't know it yet, but he's hit my mom for the last time.

I find my mom at the kitchen table, sipping cold tea, alone in the dark, cold room. The wood stove barely has any embers left in it. It's only September, but out here in the country, with flat fields and sparse trees to break the harsh winds, older houses like ours weren't built strong enough to withstand the elements without heat.

You can hear the wind whistling through more cracks than I've been able to keep up with. Every time I show up here, I'm fixing one thing after another. The drafts are frustrating and it's a constant fight to keep the fire going long enough to actually heat the small space.

I approach my mom carefully, aware of how much I resemble my dad now that I'm in my thirties.

I don't want to scare her.

I attempt to turn on the light only to realize the electricity has been shut off, again. This must have been what set off my father.

It's always the same argument, the same cycle that starts the fights, the reason my mom called me over in the first place—money, the poison of our day. No matter what's going on, whether or not I live here, they never seem to have enough of it.

Even though my father works two jobs, they're always tight on cash. My mom used to have a job working as a secretary at a car dealership down the road. She lost her job several years back because my father had beaten her face so bad she had to call in sick for a whole week just for the swelling in her eyes to come down. Eventually, her boss lost his patience and let her go without a severance package. Since then, she hasn't seen the point of seeking other work as the beatings only increased with the loss of income. She's stuck in the middle of a vicious cycle.

I restrain my anger as I assess the damage he's done to her this time. I'm stuck between hatred for my father and admiration for the strength of my mother, for surviving his abuse. I carefully take a seat next to her and she doesn't even flinch.

She hasn't moved since I walked in, unaffected by my presence. This is how she pulls through these things. Her mind wonders into a different place where she can pretend she lives a different life. My father has finally done it, he's driven my poor mom to madness.

Up close, she looks so different than the last time I saw her. *She's barely even recognizable*, I think in disgust, as I stare at my mom.

She's so thin, her clothes hang loose on her fragile frame. Her hair has begun to fall out, even at the young age of fifty-five.

My mom's once full, pink cheeks are now sunken and hollow, one of her eye sockets punched in. She's barely a shadow of the woman she once was, when she had something to live for.

There were years when my father was more careful, more restrained in his beatings. He used to think more deliberately about how hard and where he would hit her. *Just to send her a message, shake her up a little,* he used to tell me.

He's always been so entitled—an arrogant son-of-a-bitch if you ask me. He always said it was his duty as the husband to teach his wife to respect him. He felt it was his responsibility to put her back in line whenever she did something that didn't please him. He justified it by stating he was only doing his duty as the man of the house.

When my mom was working, my father used to complain that he didn't like her working in a predominantly male environment. He was always the jealous type, but he's never seemed to appreciate my mother, not even when I was little. All my memories of my father are of him being loud, angry, and frightening. When I grew up to be as tall as he was, I tried to stop him. I'd often stand between him and my mom and try to protect her. Sick of how he treated us, I'd stare square into his eyes and shove him away as hard as I could, but it was useless. If anything, I usually just ended up making him angrier.

Unfortunately, I was just as thin and as weak as my mom. We only had enough money for healthy meals once a week. The rest of the time, we survived on rice and beans. We tried growing our own fruits and vegetables in the summertime, but the damn rabbits usually cleaned out most of it before we'd even think of harvesting, so we were left with mostly potatoes.

I fucking hate potatoes.

Examining my mom's pale frame, I hesitantly lay my hand over top of hers, inching closer and closer slowly as not to frighten her, as though she's a wild animal I'm trying to domesticate. Only she's not the one who's wild—I am. When she's like this, I could do anything to her. It's scary how she has no concept of her surroundings.

It's as though she really, truly isn't here.

There's no telling how long she can remain in this state of disassociation. It can be hours before she snaps back to reality, and when she does, she will cower away from me and scream insults. She will try to scratch my eyes out because I look just like my father. She will fight for her life like the prey that she has become. She's forgotten how strong she once was.

It makes me so sad to see her like this. Knowing there's nothing I can do, I get up and gather some wood to start a fire in the woodstove. I grab an old blanket from the couch where it appears my mom slept last night and wrap it around her shoulders in an attempt to keep her warm.

This seems to startle her and I immediately bring my hands up, shielding my face instinctively. She never means to hit me, but I know she's usually terrified when she comes out of her episodes.

"Tony? Is that you? Why are you here, baby?" she asks, confused. Her eyes are glazed, and I wonder if she's taken her pills again.

"Mom, you called me last night and I came right over." I speak slowly, articulating every word carefully.

"Did I? I don't remember." There is a faint pain in her voice as her throat catches.

"You said dad had hurt you again." I sit down next to her. Her eyes tear up as she begs me not to tell anyone.

She's gaining more and more awareness as she studies me, not avoiding my eyes as she normally does.

"I can't live like this anymore, Tony. I'm scared." She lets out silent tears.

It kills me to see her like this. You're never supposed to see your parents cry. Kids aren't supposed to protect their mothers from their fathers.

"I know, Mom, we need a plan." I stare at her intently, trying to see if she's finally done for good. If she's finally ready to change her fate—to do something about it, to stop it once and for all.

She's often said this, but nothing ever changed. I was beginning to lose hope. But this time, something is different. She knows I'm old enough to do some real damage and she trusts me completely. It seems like all my training over the last few years has finally paid off. People have stopped doubting every word that comes out of my mouth and are starting to put their faith in me, their lives in my hands.

Little by little, I'm changing my reputation by making people believe I've changed who I am.

I try not to let this go to my head as I still have much work to do, with Claire, for example. I need to take care of Claire before I can take care of my father.

I need time to plan.

I urge my mom to go see Aunt Anna to get fixed up while I work on getting the electricity back. I tell her to hurry as we don't know when my father will be back on. She agrees and rushes out the door.

I wave at her as she drives away—not that she bothers to look back.

***

While she's gone, I go downstairs to the basement to my old bedroom and find the main breaker panel with a flashlight. I can tell the breaker has tripped. It must be getting weak. With a comforting humming sound, the power comes back on as I flip the switch.

I feed the fire until the house begins to feel cozy for when she returns. I take a peek at the contents of the fridge, but find nothing more than beer cans and an old ketchup bottle. The only food in the fridge has layers of mold growing on it.

I will need to go to town and buy some food for her, strengthen her from the inside out.

Not wanting to be gone too long, I hop in my truck and run over to the corner store to stock up on some fruits and vegetables. I grab a fresh loaf of bread, milk, butter, and eggs. The only meat they have are cold cuts and bacon. I grab a pack of each and toss them in the cart. I pay cash, having learned long ago never to use a card when you're trying to remain anonymous or hidden.

As I walk out of the store, something grabs my attention. I notice a folded up newspaper on a bench in front of the store. There's a picture on the cover with the words "Missing Woman" on the front. The picture is folded in half so that all I can see are the eyes of the woman, but even before I reach over and unfold it, I know it's her. I'd recognize Elisabeth's eyes anywhere. Those eyes still haunt me every night when I close my eyes.

The same eyes I fell in love with so many years ago.

She's made the front cover of a local newspaper here in Nova Scotia. Her disappearance is now big news. The police mention that they are very eager to find her, that she may be in danger, and that she is wanted for questioning. I tuck the soggy newspaper under my arm as I climb into my truck and drive back to the house.

When the items are safely stored away in the fridge, I grab the broom and begin sweeping up large cobwebs my mom can't reach at her height. Thinking about the picture in the newspaper on the kitchen table, I start feeling nostalgic. I begin to doubt my motives.

Maybe I should call the whole thing off.

Besides, since my mom called me last night, I've lost track of Claire altogether. Who knows where that old truck drove her to? Was he a local? A secret contact? With no way of knowing, I feel my hope dwindling. She could be anywhere by now. I'll have to start my search for her all over again.

She's obviously decided to hide somewhere and stay low.

***

A few hours later, my mom comes back. The cut on her cheek has been stitched up, but she's still as pale as a ghost. I ask her if she's OK, and she claims she feels fine. I get her settled down at the kitchen table while I make her a sandwich and boil some water to make her some hot tea.

She hasn't spoken much since her return and hasn't seemed to notice the sudden light, warmth, or food that has magically appeared. She doesn't thank me for it either, but I've long stopped expecting it from either parent.

When she does speak, it's not about the house or the assault.

Instead, it's about something I never expected her to say in a thousand years. She tells me Uncle Stewart and Aunt Anna have someone staying with them. She mentions that at first she thought it was another foster kid, but then she remembered they didn't do that anymore.

When she asked Aunt Anna about the new girl, Aunt Anna had shrugged and avoided the question, which seemed odd to her. Aunt Anna usually enjoys gossip and talking about the kids under her care. Her foster kids have always been a favourite subject of hers, but not today.

My mom claims she had taken notice of the girl on her way out. She's convinced the girl seemed too old to be in the foster system, but that she had a haunted expression—the girl's eyes told a story of a hard life.

Suddenly, my mom pauses, staring at the newspaper I've forgotten to throw out, which is still sprawled on the kitchen table in front of her.

"That's her!" she exclaims, startling me as she grabs hold of the newspaper, clutching it like it could fly away at any moment. "I can't believe it! That's the woman I saw at Aunt Anna's house! I swear, she looks just like this missing woman! Except, she has brown hair instead of blond, cut shorter with bangs. I'm sure this is her!"

Agitated now, I do my best to calm my mom down. I tell her I believe her and that I will go and visit Uncle Stewart and Aunt Anna in a little while to get the story straight. I suggest she have a nap and even help her lie down on the couch.

When her breathing is even, I finally give in to the adrenaline building up inside me and run to the truck with only one thought.

I must find her, and when I do, I must kill her for what she did.

PART THREE

53

CLAIRE

I drive a little too fast, the only sound is coming from the tires on the road. The radio is turned off, but my mind is racing loudly. I go over everything from this last week and everything from my past. I push back the tears that often accompany my anxiety and try hard not to focus on what might be happening back home.

What if Jess is hurt?

What if it's my fault? I could never forgive myself.

And Rob, of all people! The silent guy, in the background all this time, is now suddenly in the foreground of my mind taking up residence like a new tenant. Ethan is also floating around in my brain and pulling at my heart.

Ethan.

He's been an innocent victim this whole time! What have I done?

I humiliated him in front of the entire school. I ruined his life. Tears begin to blur my vision as I remember that day, so long ago. Graduation day.

How angry I'd been at him! How justified I'd felt! I'd thrown it all in his face, everything we had shared together. I'd accused him of the worst possible thing. Not only had I been wrong about what really happened, but I had lost him, and my only chance at love.

It had never made sense that Ethan had been the one to hurt me all those years ago, it hadn't felt right.

My gut had told me something wasn't right, but who could have blamed me? How could I not think it was him when all the facts pointed to him?

Sadness and guilt soon turn to bitterness and anger at the loss of years. Ethan and I could have been happy together. I grieve my lonely life built on the fear of never letting anyone get close to me again.

I am so angry at Rob for what he did all those years ago and what he's started now. I'm also mad at myself for not checking the facts more closely, for being weak, and believing Ethan could have done this to me when my gut always told me he hadn't.

"Always listen to your gut", my mother says, but I had been blinded by my emotions and influenced by anger.

I couldn't see clearly back then. Maybe it was the hormones, or the memory lapses from that night, or even the deep need I'd felt to defend and protect myself. I've pushed everyone away. Not just Ethan, but all my friends. All because of Rob.

I notice the time on the dash and press harder on the gas petal. If I focus and keep a steady speed, I have a good chance of reaching Jess at work to warn her before anything happens to her.

Stewart's jacket clings to me like armor, giving me confidence. It will give me a slight advantage of camouflage from the dozens of cops in her office. I'm hoping I can encounter as few people as possible before I speak directly with Jess so as not to blow my cover.

About three hours into the drive, I notice a black truck following three cars behind me.

It reminds me of the truck I saw a few days ago.

Could it be Rob following me? Did he know I was in Salt Springs? Did Stewart tell Mary who I really was? If Rob's mom lives there and I was staying with his aunt and uncle, he might have found out and followed me up here.

How am I going to lose him now?

With my heart beating fast, I grip the wheel tighter, my palms sweaty. Every second glance at the road, I peer at the rearview mirror and see the black truck, advancing rapidly towards me. It's swerving between lanes, gaining speed, and so do I.

I haven't seen Rob face to face since graduation. Except, of course, for Monday night when I saw his silhouette, but that barely counts. I had no idea it was him at the time.

Has he changed? Why is he following me? If that's even him. Why is he doing this? Why would he kill Sandra?

A few moments later, I get stuck between two vehicles and can't change lanes. I consider going on the shoulder for a moment. The truck is near me but in my blind spot. I crane my neck to see the driver, expecting to see Rob, but find a hot-headed teenager with a ball cap and a cigarette between his lips, music cranked up loud, passenger window down, yelling across to me. Even with the windows up, I can hear his weak pick-up lines.

I sigh in relief and refocus on the road ahead.

***

I reach Jess's station about ten minutes before it closes for the night. Thankful I made it in time, I grab a parking spot on the side of the one story brick building next to some graffiti drawings, surely meant to represent those who works inside the building.

Happy with my timing and that the old truck hasn't let me down, I make sure to pull Stewart's coat around me.

The light outside is quickly dimming as fall approaches winter's time schedule. I truly hate the month of September—so many years ago I lost my baby during this cold, miserable month when everything else dies.

I get out of the truck slowly, as though I'm just another civilian, not a potential murder suspect. Keeping my head down, throwing the hood up over my head, I pretend to be enthralled with something in my pocket as I search the deserted street. I play with my coat's zipper while walking through the front door to avoid the security cameras.

At the front reception desk, I scan the room to get my bearings and notice only three men and one woman working silently in individual cubicles, but there's no sign of Jess anywhere.

I spot a folded newspaper on a table, presumably the employee lunch table. I only see the eyes, but I know they're mine. I suck in my breath and do my best to maintain a normal appearance. I need to get out of here quickly, but I still haven't seen Jess.

I need to see her and warn her. Maybe she's in the back, or on break. Did she take the day off? I gather up my courage, casually remove my hood and smile politely at the receptionist, not wanting to draw attention to myself. The blond receptionist seems to be in her early fifties, with wrinkles around her eyes and long, fake, pink nails.

I ask her if Jess is in today, but all I get is a blank stare.

"Jess Levac?" she asks, an Acadian accent in her speech.

"Yeah, is she here?" I repeat, straining my neck over her head to try and find Jess.

"Humm, are you a friend of hers?" she asks me suspiciously, and the concern for my friend turns into concern for myself.

Still, I nod, half ready to make a run for it, thinking she's recognized my face from the newspaper.

"Oh hun," she begins as she rests her palm on her chest and pouts her lips. "Haven't you heard?" she asks me, her big doe eyes tearing up instantly.

No! No! No!

Alarm bells go off in my head. This can't be happening. Not again! Not Jess. I stare at her, begging to hear what's happened, but too afraid to ask.

"Jess had an accident," she hesitates, gathering her strength. "She was mugged, it seems. Just the other day. She's in the hospital, poor thing," she says, grabbing a handful of tissues and blowing her nose profusely.

"Oh my God! Is she OK?" I ask, seriously doubtful about the mugging theory.

"Well, she's alive, if that's what you mean, but the poor thing was badly hurt. I heard she's in an induced coma until her body begins to heal." A coma. Oh, poor Jess!

Rob went for her brain, the piece of shit. Had Jess found out something? Instead of killing her, he'd made her suffer and kept her alive, although barely. A message for me. A warning, to show me just how far he will go. He won't stop, not until he has me.

Well, bastard, here I am. I'm ready. Your move.

54

CLAIRE

I leave the station, the receptionist behind the counter dabbing runny mascara from her eyes and bolt to the truck with only one thought: I need to go find Jess at the hospital.

I need to see her.

I start the engine. It takes me all of ten minutes to get to the hospital grounds.

Apartments and small shops surround the hospital. I'm driving so fast that I almost don't see them, sitting by the window in the warmth of a local café. Both of them are holding comically large cups of coffee, heads bent over, talking in confidence.

"What the hell?" I bluster out loud, almost slamming the truck right into a blue Jeep in my distraction.

Rebecca and Emma are sitting in a café across from the hospital, deep in conversation. How do they even know each other? Emma is crying. Her puffy, red cheeks can be easily seen from the street.

Thankful for the excruciatingly long traffic light, I get a good look at the scene unfolding before me. What does this mean? What is Rebecca doing talking with Emma? They've never met. They don't know about each other. I've been so careful about keeping my past life and friends from when I was Elisabeth separate from my life now as Claire.

This makes no sense.

As the light turns green and the car behind me beeps for me to drive on, I'm left puzzled at this new development. Then a thought occurs to me.

Could Rebecca, my oldest and best friend, be behind all this? Could she be in on it with Rob somehow? She used to have a huge crush on him back in high school. Has she been planning this with him all this time?

As my mind races through possibilities, I think back to Monday—the day everything began.

Had Rebecca actually been 'stopping by' to chat, or had she come to check my plans? Had she come to make sure I was working late and wouldn't have an alibi? How else would Rob have found out my new name, my new job, my new apartment? How else would Rob know about Sandra?

But where does Emma fit in?

How do Rebecca and Emma know each other? From what I saw through the window, they seemed like close friends. This wasn't a first meeting. Somehow Rebecca had learned about my friendship with Emma.

Emma must have told Rebecca about Jess and her access to secure police files. And this could be how Rob found Jess and began charming her in order to gain access to my files.

My blood is boiling now. I've been betrayed by so many people, I don't know who to trust anymore. Jess is an innocent victim in this sick game.

It only takes me another few minutes to drive into the underground parking lot. I back up the truck into a spot near the exit. I quickly jump out, and I leave my gym bag behind.

I won't need it to visit Jess. Forgetting about wearing my hood this time, preoccupied by the thought of getting to Jess, I don't realize what's happening until it's too late.

I'm half way to the hospital entrance when I smell something familiar. Before I can fully register it, my head is yanked back in one quick movement. With no time to react, I stumble backwards awkwardly in hot pain, my butt hitting the cold floor so hard I wonder if I've broken my tailbone. I let out a yell that echoes deep against the concrete walls of the parking lot. My mouth is my best weapon right now, and I keep screaming, hoping someone will come down to the parking lot at this very moment and help me. But to my dismay, the parking lot is deserted.

For the first time in a long time, I cannot run away.

I'm being dragged by my hair and I'm helpless. Road rash burns my skin as I wiggle, trying to get away. Not ready to give up, I feel a surge of foreign strength explode through me. I swing a hand up and connect with flesh. Warm blood runs down my arm as I dig my fingernails so deep inside my attacker's forearm, he has no choice but to release my hair. I have just enough time to spin around, palms to the ground, and push myself up before a strong fist connects with my nose.

I'm blinded momentarily as my nose explodes with pain and starts to bleed profusely down the front of my coat. Great, now I definitely can't return this coat to Stewart. Another person involved in my bad decisions.

A punch in the stomach wakes me of the daze from the first hit. All my adrenaline kicks in and I decide to use the only thing I know I'm good at, running.

My legs are the strongest parts of my body.

I charge straight towards my attacker, shoving him hard. His feet lift slightly off the ground and he loses his balance, stumbling backwards, just long enough for me to run past him back to the truck.

I struggle for a moment to find my keys in the pocket of my coat, my vision slightly blurry from the earlier hit to the face. My nose throbs painfully, and I breathe through my mouth. I finally manage to get the driver's side door open, but he pushes me down on the seat, face first.

No! Not again!

There's no mistaking the forceful way he's push me down. To humiliate, to own me. My terror at the unfolding scene is mixed with white hot pain and a surging anger that I'm, once again, in the hands of the same attacker. There is no way in hell I will let him win this time! But with all his weight pinning me to the seat, I'm left fighting for breath, struggling to get enough air in through my broken nose.

I can't remember what I did to injure my head, but blood drips down my forehead and I do my best to blink it away.

Not wasting any time, I kick with my legs, trying to hit some part of him in the hopes of injuring him enough so that he will loosen his grip on me or get off me. He lifts my shirt, exposing my back, my tattoo exposed to the cold and to him. I feel extremely vulnerable.

I don't wait to find out what comes next. I twist underneath him like a worm in a bird's beak, fighting for my life, until I feel the cold of steel press against my bare back.

55

CLAIRE

I stop moving immediately. There's nothing quite like the barrel of a loaded gun shoved against your skin to make you stop what you're doing. *This is where it ends*, I think to myself.

He's won.

I've been defeated. I'm hurt. I'm bleeding.

He's got me pinned so tightly against the seat, I can barely move my arms. His voice is like ice, cold and lifeless, as he finally addresses me.

"Game over, my queen," he states with disgust in his voice.

Rob. So it is him doing all this.

His voice hasn't changed. It's exactly the same as it was back then on that night. It's always been him.

I'm about to give up and accept my fate when I notice a small screwdriver wedged under my gym bag. The bag must have fallen to the floor of the truck during our struggle. The screwdriver's blue handle is almost unnoticeable. If not for the underground parking light reflecting slightly off the metal of the screwdriver, I would have missed it entirely.

I remember the day when Stewart and I fixed the headlight on the truck with that screwdriver. He'd shown me how to fix the light bulb and had thrown the tool back in the truck for the next time he was in a jam, he'd said.

Little did Stewart know that this small tool would become my weapon of choice against his own nephew.

Careful not to move my back in the slightest, the gun still pressed hard against my back, I'm counting on Rob's vision being compromised by the shadows in the truck and the doorframe. As I inch my fingers as far as I can reach, I hear a phone ring. For a moment, the cell's ring is the only noise in the parking lot.

"Hello," Rob answers, curt and confident, nothing like the Rob I used to know.

As the caller speaks, I take advantage of Rob's momentarily lack of attention and shift a little closer to the base of the truck, until I feel the rubbery grip of the screwdriver and firmly grab hold.

"Yeah, boss. I have her," he answers, sounding dignified and proud of himself.

Boss? He's working for someone, but who?

I can almost imagine the smirk Rob must be wearing on his face. Acting so self-righteous and triumphant.

With the screwdriver tightly wrapped inside my left palm, power and confidence return, and I have the strength I need to do what comes next. He might pull the trigger, out of shock, but at least this way, I'll have my dignity back. I'll always remember that I tried to free myself. This time, I'm not going down without a fight. This time, I have the advantage and I'm armed.

I don't wait for him to end his conversation—the element of surprise on my side. With all my force, breathless as I am with my nose compromised, I twist my torso as quick as I can and without hesitation, I shove the screwdriver directly into Rob's gut.

I feel the narrow blade penetrate through layers of fabric and flesh until it hits softer parts and he lets out a loud yell.

The next moments are a blur.

He drops the phone and pulls the trigger. I feel a sharp burning pain in my shoulder. He's leaning over my back now, holding the screwdriver in place, his hands covered in blood.

Pain rips through me and I start seeing spots—I've been shot.

From my position, I can tell that Rob is still alive. I see the gun laying on the passenger seat and I ponder ending his life and my misery right now. But I'm not a murderer. I squirm out from under him until I'm sitting in the passenger seat, watching his face turn white. I kick the gun to the ground and send it to the other side of the parking garage. If I'm going to get answers about why he's trying to kill me, it will be now.

"Why are you doing this, Rob? Or should I call you Tony, you asshole?" I grit through my teeth.

A trickle of blood falls from his mouth as tears run down his cheeks. Barely a whisper, his voice raspy I hear him say so quietly, "I'm sorry. I'm so sorry, Elisabeth."

Sorry? Why the sudden remorse?

Then I remember the words written in Stewart and Anna's basement closet. Rob used to love me. Has this all been done out of jealousy? But then, I remember, he's not working alone. Who exactly was that on the phone? I begin to panic and scan frantically around me. Is there someone else down here, someone else looking for me? Before I can ask, he speaks again.

"I wanted you for myself. We could have been happy, but then...the baby...You killed our baby!" he cries with tears falling down his cheeks.

Confused, I respond angrily, "I did not kill MY baby. It was never OURS to begin with. You raped me and if that wasn't painful enough, I lost the baby!" I'm crying now, allowing myself to speak the words I've held in for all these years. "You're a rapist, Rob, and a murderer!" At this, his eyes shoot up with a pained expression.

"I never meant to hurt you, Elisabeth. I just wanted you to love me like I loved you." He winces as he presses on his wound, trying to stop the bleeding.

"Love?" I yell. "That's what you do to people you love? You're sick!" In a fury, I kick at him, making him slide out of the truck and stumble to the floor. I quickly edge myself over to the driver's side, pulling myself up with my good arm, using the steering wheel. As I pull the door closed, I hear him mention Ethan's name, and stop short.

"What about Ethan?" I ask him, my breath uneven. "I lost him too because of you." I yell through tears as he lies there squirming on the concrete floor.

I see him lifting his shirt and twisting, which at first sight I take as him wanting to check his wound. But then he twists even more to show me his back, until I see what he's trying to show me—a king's crown tattoo. The same one Ethan got with me all those years ago. Rob got the same tattoo, but hid it all these years.

He really was crazy. Did he think he could take Ethan's place? Sure, they looked alike, but to actually become him? He's sick. I recoil and sneer at him. I fight the urge to kick him again.

"What did you do to Ethan?" I demand, but all I get is his silence.

Was this all a game to him? Playing with our lives? Moving pieces on a chess board? Him being the king and me the queen?

280

Fed up, I almost spit at him. "Well, I'm done playing your game. You just lost." I look down at him one more time and hiss "Check mate, you bastard! I hope you rot in hell!"

Just then, a steel door bangs further down the parking lot and two armed security guards come running towards us.

"Hey, you there! Stop!" they scream at me, weapons drawn. They must have heard the gun shot. They think I'm the one who fired the gun.

I shut the door quickly and in the mirror I see Rob lying motionless on the floor, a pool of blood underneath him. A tear rolls down my cheek, but I swipe it away fast. I will not shed another tear for that monster.

Good riddance, I think.

Without waiting another second, I put the car in drive and peel out of the parking lot getting back on the road, not looking back. I know I've been seen now.

It's just a matter of time before cop cars begin tailing me. I just need to get away from this place. Rob might be dead, but who knows who else is after me? I never found out who he was speaking to on the phone. Someone else was calling the shots. Someone who managed to convince Rob to kill someone he loved. What kind of psycho would do that?

If Rob is working for someone else, they might be even worse than him.

56

CLAIRE

My left arm is on fire. I let go of the steering wheel for a moment to feel the bullet hole in my left shoulder. I feel a hole at the entry point and another in the back.

Good.

That means most likely the bullet isn't jammed in my shoulder. Adrenaline is pumping through me, making me lose a lot of blood. I blink away the nausea that accompanies the pain of the wound.

It takes a few minutes for me to realize I could be in a lot of trouble here. I need urgent medical attention. I don't know how long I have. I've been bleeding quite a bit, and I need to get it under control. I make a rushed decision to stop on the side of the road, the street is dark and slick with light rain beginning to fall.

I inch the coat off me to better assess my shoulder. The bullet left a dime-size hole, making my arm limp and useless. I can't lift it more than a few inches before a radiating pain shoots through my whole body.

I feel around the truck with my free hand. My gym bag is still on the floor by the passenger seat. Underneath it I see some scattered menstrual pads. They must have fallen out of my bag at some point.

I grab a few of them and rip open the plastic wrapping with my teeth.

I wrap one over the wound and another on the back. I find a t-shirt in my bag and tie it over the pads, tightening it as much as I can muster with only one hand and my mouth.

I know that I need stiches, maybe even a blood transfusion, and soon, but going back to the hospital is out of the question. They would recognize me there instantly. Plus, I've just possibly killed a man.

I can't go back there. All would be lost.

This entire week of running towards freedom would have been a waste. At least I know now that Jess can heal in peace. Rob won't be around to hurt her any longer. If she makes it, that is.

With the rain growing heavier, it sounds like a hundred shards of glass are hitting the windshield all at once. My wipers are on the fastest setting—intense, quick and steady, like my heartbeat. Their rhythm keeps me focused. I could make the four-hour drive back to Salt Springs and get Anna to stitch me up like she did for Rob's mom.

The blood drains from my face. Oh no. Rob's mom.

She doesn't know that I might have just killed her son. No, I can't go back there either. I ease my way back on the road and take another quick peek into my gym bag. I don't have much money left. I won't survive out there with a wound like this and no cash.

I make a sharp U-turn and head towards Crown Street. It's time to go to my apartment and face the music. I need money and my phone, but I have no idea who I'll run into while I'm there. Still, I've got no other options right now. I'm counting on everyone being called to the hospital, giving me a few minutes alone in my apartment to gather some supplies before disappearing again.

I park the truck at the far end of the parking lot, where there are no overhead lights. I slide slowly out of the truck, trying hard not to aggravate my oozing and aching shoulder. The blood is showing through the pads which are doing their best to hold on. The truck is high off the ground, and when my feet hit the pavement, a painful vibration shoots from my shoulder through my entire body, making me bite my lower lip as I stifle a cry.

I glance around quickly but the parking lot is empty. It's around dinnertime for most people, pre-drinking time for others going out on a Friday night. Bed time for little ones—babies.

Why did Rob think I'd killed my baby? Who had told him that? Was he that messed up that he thought everyone in his life was a criminal? Did he assume I did it because suddenly I wasn't pregnant anymore? Why would that be the first thing he would think?

So many girls at our school had been rumored to have gotten abortions. I guess it could have been a possibility, but that thought had never even crossed my mind. If Rob had truly known me, he would have known that abortion had never been an option. Sure, the pregnancy had been forced and violent, but that wasn't the baby's fault. The baby had been an innocent victim and deserved nothing but love and a fair chance at life.

Sadly, I hadn't even been able to provide that.

An unsuitable uterus was the explanation I'd later been given for my fertility issues. I was in my late twenties when I finally gathered up the courage to talk to a doctor about my miscarriage. I knew they were common, but I wanted to know if there was a reason for mine.

I was careful to leave out the story of the conception, not wanting to drag up that part of my past once again.

Still, feeling that little life grow inside of me all those years ago, only to lose it so early, created an emptiness in my heart that I'd been unable to fill. Even though the whole thing had been traumatic, I've always wanted kids. I wanted to find out why I had lost the baby.

Had it been stress, willpower, or prayer from my parents? Or something else? As it turned out, the results concluded that I would never be able to conceive a baby naturally.

It's too bad that my one and only pregnancy ever was such a disaster. An unfortunate end to an unfortunate beginning. The poor thing never had a chance. I guess we had that in common.

Lost in thought it takes me a moment to realize I'm standing at the base of my apartment building. It feels strange being here after being away for a week. This week has felt like months. The familiar building now seems like a large fortress, standing strong and tall in the dark. Will I be able to get in? This small obstacle, nothing compared to what I've just overcome, leaves me weak in the knees.

I should be feeling strong. I just fought for my life and made it out alive. Still, all I'm left with is cold rain dripping down my hair onto my face and blood seeping out of my shirt. I shiver as I notice I've forgotten to put on my coat. I might have won the fight, but I'm not unharmed, not untouched.

Even after the wounds heal, I will always have these scars to remind me of this day, this fight.

As I climb into the elevator, I dream of a warm shower, to be cleansed from my past, the blood and my pain. But I won't have time for that.

When the elevator dings, I hesitantly peer out and carefully make my way down the empty corridor towards my apartment door. The quick movement of the elevator seems to have thrown me a bit off balance.

Surprised to see no one waiting for me with handcuffs, ready to whisk me away to the nearest police station, I begin to relax a little. My feet are heavy, my muscles are tight, and my head is pounding. All the adrenaline I had to get me here seems to have suddenly vanished. The closer to my door, the worst the pain gets.

Unsure if I'll survive the bullet wound, I consider lying down on my bed, imagining it waiting for me inside my apartment—my final resting place. I don't even think I care because I finally got justice and that's enough for me.

I can feel myself becoming sleepy and dizzy. I lean on the hall wall for support to keep me moving forward, leaving a trail of blood on the wall as I drag myself towards my door.

My nose has finally stopped bleeding, but it's definitely broken and will need to be broken once more to be set properly. I try not to think about that as I dig in my pockets for my keys and unlock the door. I push the door open, and the hair on the back of my neck rises in shock.

I'm not alone.

Ethan is sitting on a chair in the middle of my living room, duct tape over his mouth, and his body wrapped up in a thick rope. A gun points at his head.

57

CLAIRE

"Ethan!" I cry, half in relief that he's still alive and half in confusion as to why he's in my living room.

What the hell is going on? What is he doing here?

I'm so confused. I snap out of my grogginess. This is a never-ending, terrible journey. It takes everything for me not to rush over to Ethan right away. I almost don't notice the blond chick in high heels and tights, wearing bright red lipstick holding the gun to Ethan's head. She's wearing a snug hoodie and sunglasses indoors, in the dark.

"Hi, sis," she grins, not bothering to glance in my direction.

Dumbfounded, I take a step back, fighting the urge to run right out through the open door and back down to the safety of the truck. But I can't leave Ethan—not now.

Fran?

A part of me, tugging at my heart strings, wants to go over to her, hug her, and cry in her arms. However, my gut warns me not to. Perhaps it's the way she said "Hi, sis," or the fact that she's holding a gun to Ethan's head that makes me rethink that.

"What the hell is going on here?" I ask with more strength than I feel.

I am physically weakened by my injuries and a week on the run with little sleep. I'm also emotionally drained.

I just killed an old friend, and now my ex-boyfriend, the one my friend betrayed to get to me, is sitting in front of me after all these years.

Ethan, the only guy I've ever truly loved, is tied up in my apartment with a gun to his head. The lights are dimmed low, but I would recognize his face anywhere. His thick brown hair is exactly the same, save for a little bit of a receding hairline. No greys yet. He's aged well.

His mouth is taped shut, but his eyes are speaking volumes. He's utterly terrified.

In his mind, he's screwed. In his mind, his ex-girlfriend and her sister have conspired to make him pay for a crime he's been denying he committed for most of his adult life. A crime, I know now, he didn't commit.

His only mistake was to love me.

The last time I laid eyes on Ethan, I was screaming at him and breaking his heart. His eyes then, full of confusion, are the same ones he wears now.

Back then, that expression had fueled my anger, made me feel more entitled to lash out at him, but now, it makes me cringe with guilt. He didn't deserve my scorn then and certainly doesn't deserve to be in the middle of this mess now. He's just a pawn. Just like Sandra—caught up in the middle of a game too complicated and serious for him to understand, with my sister as the keeper of the rules.

I turn my focus on her and assess the situation.

I make peace with the fact that my long gone missing sister is actually alive and well and that she's standing in front of me right now.

She has that look of revenge and anger I saw in myself years ago. Something about her stance and the determination on her face tells me she's completely convinced of her motives that led her here—that she's dead serious about her threat on Ethan's life.

"What's going on here is payback," she replies, finally staring directly at me, never lowering her weapon.

"Payback? For what?" I'm genuinely confused. "Look, Fran, why don't we sit down and talk? I haven't seen you in forever. I thought you were dead!" I risk stepping further into the room. "Where have you been all these years?" I try and change the subject, change her focus, get her distracted and talking as I get closer to Ethan.

Ethan's eyes are pleading for me to stop moving.

He's so scared. Ethan's always been terrified of dying. He grew up without faith of any kind and never knew what would happen to him whenever his time came. We used to talk about the best and worst ways to die. I feel like "by bullet to the head" would have been on his list for worst.

Almost at arm's length now, Fran swings her arm sharply so that the gun is now pointing directly into my chest, almost touching it. I flinch, unable to hide my shock at the situation.

She takes in the blood on my face and the makeshift bandage job on my left shoulder for a moment and begins to laugh.

"What the hell happened to you? This is how you come to a fight? Already bruised and bleeding? You could have at least pretended to be strong! Come on, what the hell is this? You're not a really good fighter are you?" she scoffs, her voice full of hatred.

"You're just making it too easy for me. I was hoping to win this honorably, but now it will just look bad." She does a "tsk" sound through her teeth and cocks her head slightly.

She stares down at me, her high heels making her several inches taller than me, her posture intimidating. Her eyes land on my wrist, where the charm necklace still shines, wrapped twice around it.

"Thought you didn't believe in luck," she smirks. "So predictable! I knew you'd never take it off. It was easy to find you". She cocks her head, "Good job with the hair change though. I'll give you that."

As I listen, trying to make sense of all this, an image slowly takes shape. Fran is the "boss" Rob was speaking with earlier.

"How did you find me?" I ask her, wanting to hear her side of the story.

"I've been searching for you for years, and then I bumped into someone else who'd been looking for you, too. You know Tony Andrews, right? I believe he's the one who gave you that bullet hole." She presses the gun in my shoulder as she speaks, making me wince in pain.

"He was looking like a lost puppy, standing in front of our parents' house one evening, trying to catch you there, when I drove by as I often did, just to check in on things," she says coyly. "He was easy enough to manipulate. He was so in love with you as a teenager and still is now. He would do anything to find you." She laughs. "He knew he couldn't have you though, not with Ethan still alive. Luckily, I was there to fill the void." Her smile is evil, conniving.

She slowly walks behind me and uses the barrel of the gun to lift my shirt until my back is exposed.

I don't dare move an inch.

With a laugh she adds, "When Tony told me about your tattoo, I almost didn't believe him. It was his idea to draw it at your apartment and on Sandra's body. I gave him some leash and he ran with it." She laughs, proud of herself.

"So, you and Rob? I mean, Tony? You're together? Or were," I question, with shame on my face.

"Oh, Tony's still alive sweetheart. You see, I was the one on the phone with him when you pulled your little stunt. When you drove off, those security guards that were chasing you found him lying unconscious and took him to the emergency room. Conveniently, it wasn't too far away." She acts triumphant and this infuriates me. "Did you know you can survive up to five hours with a gut injury? That's what one of the guys told me when they found his phone on the ground," she mentions smugly.

Fran—always the smarter one.

Always one step ahead.

I can't believe this. Tony's going to live. I'm both relieved and terrified about this news.

"Okay, but how did Tony find me then?" I ask.

"It wasn't hard, really. We knew you'd screw up sooner or later. It just meant we had to wait a long time. Even years, if necessary. But you know me—I'm good at being patient," she winks.

"Remember, I taught you how to pace your run? I was always better at it than you," she continues, readjusting her stance to stand even taller.

"That's what makes me a winner. You've always wanted immediate results—ever so impulsive, so emotional. Although you do a good job at pretending to be in control." She scrunches her face with a look of pity. "Tony saw the conference you were in for work and recognized you instantly. It was a piece of cake from there."

That conference, welcoming new students to the university. The one Phil had forced me to speak at. The only time I'd allowed any media exposure, Tony had seen it. He'd been watching me at work for weeks, trying to get an idea of my schedule.

Fran goes on to explain Tony's part and her own regarding the attacks on Sandra and Jess.

After Sandra left the office, Tony had followed her and lured her to a park near my apartment, where he'd then knocked her head so hard with a large rock that she'd died almost instantly. He'd then drawn a crown in black marker on her back to resemble my tattoo.

He'd killed her to get my attention, knowing her position close to me at work and the markings would lead the investigation my way. He'd been tailing me while Fran arranged the assault on Jess.

As though she's reading my thoughts, Fran continues, "Jess knew too much. She'd been putting it all together. At first, we'd thought her access to police records would be useful, but she outsmarted us. She'd found the file that inspector had on you. She even called your ditsy friend, Emma, to tell her," Fran adds with another "tsk" of her tongue. "Naturally, I just couldn't help myself. I don't like to lose, so I followed her and bashed her head in."

I look down, disgusted at her actions.

How can I be related to this monster? None of this makes any sense. It still doesn't explain why Fran needed to find me. Why is she so bitter towards me? I don't understand what I've done to make her hate me so much.

"Why were you trying to find me?" I ask.

After a beat, she finally answers. "To teach you a lesson," she explains evenly, matter of fact. "Bad girls need to be punished," she adds.

"What did I ever do to you? What did I do that was so bad?" I plead with her now. The unknown driving me crazy. I'm exhausted and none of this is making any sense.

"You were born!" she screams, revulsion distorts her face in an ugly sneer.

When I don't answer, she continues her explanation.

She walks around the room now, gun still pointed directly at my chest. I move around so that I'm always facing her and inch closer and closer to Ethan's side. She might be holding the gun and Ethan might be tied up, but he's not useless. We're still two against one. Ethan might be the only hope I have of getting out of this alive.

"Ever since you were born, you've been the favourite." She pauses, and I realize all these years she's been carrying this hatred. How could she think I was the favourite?

She was always the favourite, not me. She's got it all wrong.

"You were always the privileged one, the untainted one. Perfect little Elisabeth." She paces around with a touch of mania in her speech, her stare far away, as though remembering another life.

"No matter what you did, you were never punished. You were supposed to be the one to walk in my shadow! Not the other way around!" She's screaming at me now, pointing at her own chest with the gun and then waving it around to accentuate her speech as she adds, "Mom and Dad always used your good behaviour as an example for how I should be. Why couldn't I be more like you, they'd ask me, but I've never been like you. Never been the good girl who listens."

She stops pacing suddenly, her tone barely a whisper. "But I learned quickly and I did what they asked. I played the good girl for them. It was going well enough, until one damned day when I told Mom I was pregnant and didn't know who the father was. Dad overheard, and that was the end of that. He threw me out! Said he didn't want to hear my name ever again. It was as though I'd never been born at all!" She cries, with tears filling her eyes.

Now everything is beginning to make sense.

Fran is jealous of the freedom I'd had with my parents. Of all the times I should have been punished but wasn't.

When I think of it now, Fran did take a lot of the blame for our misbehaviours. I assumed it was just part of her role as big sister, but I never did appreciate the slack I got being the second child.

My parents were definitely strict with me, but they were also more lenient than they had been with her. When I got pregnant in high school, they never kicked me out and never disowned me. Perhaps this was why. They'd already lost one daughter, and they didn't want to repeat the same mistake again.

"I didn't want any of that, Fran," I point out. "It's not my fault they disowned you, that you got pregnant."

"No. It's not, but they never treated us the same, did they? When you got pregnant, they didn't exile you to the streets all alone, pregnant and broke." The jealousy and bitterness fall out of her mouth like spit. Envy marks her face.

"They gave you the royal treatment. Mom bought you new clothes, took you to the clinic, and was in on your little secret. She even calmed Dad down for you. She never did any of that for me! All she did was promise to keep in touch, but she never did. After a while, she stopped contacting me. She always made me chase after her. I had to leave anonymous calls and take late night drives around the house just to catch a glimpse of her. She's never even met her granddaughter."

Her ignorance of the reality of my pregnancy makes me laugh. Our dad had been so furious when he found out about my pregnancy. I could try to explain this to her, maybe make her see she wasn't the only one, but I decide against it.

I try a new tactic and change the focus. Somehow, I think she needs to feel like this story is unique to her, that she is special because of it.

I shake my head in disagreement and tell her, "Dad was a mess when you left. He took up drinking and lost his job. He was miserable. I'm sure they'd take you back if you wanted to." I try my best to sound hopeful, knowing that after this there's no chance of her ever going home.

"You ignorant bitch! You think I want to go back to that place, that prison? Where I had to pretend every day of my life that I was perfect? To be like you? Queen Elisabeth." She laughs and turns her nose up at Ethan.

"You two are pathetic! The king and queen! One's tied up and scared shitless, while the other is limping and bleeding. What a pair you two make."

I'm growing impatient. Not yet seeing a way out of this, I try and buy more time—that's when I spot it.

On the sofa is my cell phone lying where I threw it on Monday night.

Pretending to walk closer to Ethan, I go sit on the sofa and slip the phone in my pocket, afraid to turn it on. The noise of the welcome ring might let Fran know what's going on. I try to distract her and keep her talking as I fiddle with my phone. I carefully turn it on, muffling the speaker with my palm, and fumble to dial 911 by feel while hiding the phone behind my back.

"You said you were pregnant. What happened to the baby, Fran?" I say her name like when we were younger, partly in disbelief that I'm actually talking to her, and partly because I'm trying to remind her that I'm a person.

Her sister.

I try to keep her talking and it seems to work.

"I had it," she replies defiantly. "A girl by the way. She's seventeen now. Almost the same age you were when you killed your baby," she says with a satisfied smile.

She already thinks she's won this argument.

She stops talking as though she's proved her point. Well, that didn't go as planned. I thought she'd talk for a lot longer. I realize then that I'll need to stretch this out myself, and in order to do that, I'm going to have to be honest, for once. My phone on, I'm hoping I've reached an emergency coordinator and that I'm speaking loudly enough so that they can hear me.

"Fran, look, you've got it all wrong. Why don't you let Ethan and I go so we can talk about this without guns."

"No way, sis, you won't get off that easy," she spits back.

"I didn't kill my baby, Fran. I lost it. I had an early-term miscarriage." I don't dare meet Ethan's eyes when I admit the next part. "I know now that it wasn't Ethan who raped me that night, but Rob, or Tony Andrews, whatever his real name is." I pause here, praying that whoever is on the other side of the line is listening intently enough to pick up the name and do a search.

"He'd been copying Ethan for months. He had a huge crush on me and wanted me all for himself. No one knew what he'd done. Not even Ethan." I pause to swallow. "Rob snuck into the room after I'd passed out and pretended to be Ethan. Then he raped me and got me pregnant. But a few months after I confronted Ethan at school on graduation day, I lost the baby. That's when I moved out and made a new life for myself."

There it was.

A little truth package all tied up with a neat bow—my story, my shame, and my truth.

I glance over at Ethan now. Continuing to rip off the Band-Aid. I might as well get this over with.

"Ethan, I know I can't undo or unsay what I accused you of all those years ago. It was a confusing time. Until today, I had nothing but blurry, dark memories of that night. You guys looked so much alike." I explain. "Did you know Rob even has the same king's crown tattoo you have and wears the same cologne you used to wear?" He shakes his head ever so slightly. "Anyways, I'm so sorry for all the pain I've caused you. You were the only guy I ever loved. I really messed everything up." My voice shaky, I wipe away a tear.

I've never been more honest in my entire life.

Ethan can't speak, but I know he's heard every word. His eyes are glued to mine as I look at him. He blinks twice—I love you—our secret code. As it turns out, it's all I need to find enough strength to get through this next part.

"Enough with the lovey-dovey load of crap! I've had enough of this. God, you two are like Romeo and Juliet. Barf! Makes me want to kill the both of you right here and now." After a slight pause, she continues, with more anger in her voice. "Which is exactly what I'm going to do."

She inches closer to where I'm standing. "This is one game that I'm going to win. One time where you won't be able to get your way. I've got you cornered just where I want you. Tony made sure I'd have the final say. You see, that's what I like about him. So loyal. So motivated to serve. He does everything for me. Hell, he's killed for me. Now if that's not love, then I don't know what is." Sneering down at Ethan, she adds, "What's this loser ever done for you?" She's waving her gun at us, but we don't flinch.

She's too caught up in her high and mighty speech to hear the slight creak of my front door opening.

I hadn't closed it all the way when I first entered the room and now cops are trickling in. They must have had some police officers on standby near the apartment building in case I came back. They've come for me, but they are prepared regardless. It doesn't take them long to assess the situation.

They hear just enough to know that I was set up.

"Ethan treated me like a queen," I stress, full of confidence now that our rescue has arrived.

Fran must sense the change in my voice, the way my back straightens. I catch her peering over my shoulder at the large glass windows reflecting the interior of my apartment like a perfect mirror image, the night so dark outside. She spots the cops, and straightaway, spins around quickly, just as I tackle Ethan to the floor.

My instincts kick in and I pull him and the chair he's tied to behind the large sofa. Fran lets out four shots, all missing the cops and earns three shots in return, taking her down. Lying on the floor next to Ethan, my eyes squeeze shut.

I know what's happened even though my eyes are still closed.

My sister is dead—it's over.

58

CLAIRE

When I finally open my eyes, Inspector Riley is standing at my feet, a grim expression on his face. He extends his hand to help me stand, and together we steady Ethan and untie him.

Ethan is shaky, but otherwise unharmed.

He is standing and alive, which he probably didn't imagine he'd be when he had a gun pointed at his head. Pretty soon, my small apartment is crowded with people in uniform. While Ethan is in a corner of the living room being checked over by a paramedic, I stand in the kitchen, leaning on the island, talking with Inspector Riley as another paramedic removes my makeshift bandages and cleans my wounds.

"Lovely to finally meet you in person, Miss Martel," he says with the hint of a smile. "You're a difficult woman to track down. You look a little different than the picture I was given."

As it turns out, Inspector Riley isn't old and fat like I'd first imagined he'd be, but rather, he's quite handsome and stylish. "I'm sorry about your sister. We had no choice. She was shooting at the police officers." He nods curtly and so do I.

"You just did what you had to do," I say in response.

"Just like you did," he offers in explanation of my disappearance.

"I'm sorry I ran off. I could see the signs were all pointing to me. I didn't want to be caught up in it and get blamed for something I didn't do," I explain.

"Like Ethan?" he points out, glancing briefly at the man I had vowed to spend my life with. "I think you two have quite a bit of catching up to do." I nod slowly, eying him suspiciously.

How does he know all this?

Catching my hesitation, he explains. "When you went missing, I reached out to your office at the university and someone there told me you'd had a friend visit you at work on Monday, the day Sandra was murdered. I got hold of Rebecca and after much prodding, she told me a little about your history with Ethan. She's a loyal friend, that one."

I feel my eyes watering, thinking about how frightened Rebecca must have been while I was missing, and how angry I'd been towards her just hours before.

"What about Tony?" I ask. "Is he going to live?" I finally remember that I left him bleeding to death in the parking lot of the hospital.

"Appears that way." He stares at what seems to be an interesting spot on the floor now, suddenly uncomfortable. "Can't say he didn't deserve it. He's been in and out of prison for years. Violated his parole. The security guards at the hospital already tipped us that Tony Andrews has a long list of sexual assaults, and of course, there's the fact that he is going to be charged for the murder of your assistant Sandra." He pauses here out of respect.

"When you called 911, we recorded the conversation between you and Fran and sent an alert to the police officers on stake-out tonight so that we could get someone here as fast as possible. We didn't know how long we had before things turned ugly. If I may say so, Miss Martel, you were lucky tonight." For the first time in a long time, I have to agree.

I had been lucky. I'd almost died twice in one day.

"I have many questions for you, but for now, I'll be content if you allow our paramedics to take you to the hospital to get you checked-up. You suffered quite an injury." His smile is kind and honest.

"I think it's more my pride that's been hurt," I answer with a smile. "I always thought I was smart enough to disappear, but I guess you can't run away from everything. With time, the truth always seems to come out."

EPILOGUE

TWO WEEKS LATER
CLAIRE

Sandra's funeral was held in a small chapel last week, attended by many of the university's higher ups, her family, her boyfriend Matt, and our team in the communications department. I finally made it back to work this week with the promise of taking it easy. My shoulder is still sore, but it's healing at a steady pace.

It feels good to be back in a routine.

I've been looking forward to beginning this new chapter of my life. It's been nice driving my own car again. I'd missed it. Stewart's truck just didn't cut it. The transmission broke just a few days after I got back. I'm still grateful the old truck got me where I needed to be.

At work, everything is out in the open now. No one judges me for being a rape survivor. As it turns out, I'm the only one. It's inspired me to start a support group on campus to help other survivors and exchange stories. Who knows, it might help someone.

Fran's funeral was yesterday.

I couldn't bring myself to go, but my parents went. I had thought of her as dead for most of my adult life, so it would have felt strange to attend. That and the fact that she hated me and threatened to kill me just two weeks ago.

Fran's daughter was at the funeral. Mom said she looks so much like Fran did at that age. I would have liked to meet her, but I'm afraid it would have brought back too many painful memories.

I'm trying to focus on the future now.

Being seventeen years old, Francesca (named after Fran), would need to find either a permanent home or a foster family to live with until she turned eighteen in April. My parents and I were offered the parental rights, being her immediate surviving relatives, but neither of us felt right about it. Luckily, I knew some wonderful foster parents not too far away. I might go pay them a visit again. I still need to give Stewart his coat back once I get it back from the dry cleaner.

Inspector Riley called me before Fran's funeral and said they'd found security footage of Tony's attack on me in the parking garage. It appears that they will be ruling my actions as self-defense, therefore taking me off the hook.

Jess is recovering amazingly.

She woke up a week after the attack, surprisingly with no long-term brain damage. It's a real miracle. Rebecca, Emma, Val and I have gone to visit her almost every day.

I found out that Rebecca and Emma had met years ago when Emma did the make-up for Rebecca's sister's wedding party. They had remained great friends, but hadn't known they had me in common until they'd both had a friend who'd gone missing on the same day.

Now that everyone knows the truth, the real me, I'm back to calling myself Elisabeth Smith—my real name.

Ethan and I have met a couple of times since the incident. The spark is still there. We're taking things very slowly. We have a lot of years to catch up on, but I can tell in his eyes, he still feels the same way about me as I feel about him.

Who knows? Maybe this will be my happily forever after story, but somehow, I doubt it. Even if he wasn't the one who hurt me, I can't shake the negative feelings his face brings up for me. I wonder if we'll be able to stay friends.

For now, I've got a lot of work to do on myself.

A lot of healing.

Since that day, I've been able to sleep better than I have in years. Having all the missing pieces put together has helped me to finally get closure. The demons are at peace and leaving me alone. Now that I know the truth, I can finally move on.

Fran is gone, but I know where she is. She is where she's always wanted to be—free and at the sea. As for me, I'm feeling lighter these days. I don't have to carry the shame of my past with me everywhere I go, dragging me down. I can run as lightly as a deer.

I can finally be free.

*****

ACKNOWLEDGMENTS

The birth of this story started about two-years prior to publication, when my sister-in-law, Sarah, wanted to practice writing. We began writing a story together, taking turns adding one section at a time. As the story grew, it began to take shape in my mind. Sarah and I never got to finish our story, but I asked her if I could take the general idea and turn it into a novel.

The story has changed quite a bit since then, but I do owe Sarah a lot of thanks for helping me get inspired to write it in the first place.

Claire's character is inspired by the real stories of too many friends. The shame and trauma caused by someone trusted taking advantage is something that should never happen in the first place. To the women who share a similar story to Claire's, you are not victims—you are warriors.

I would like to thank my incredibly patient and loving husband, John, for listening to my ideas along the way, for believing in me, for the many cups of tea you made me, and for pushing me to see this book come to life. I wouldn't have gotten here without you.

For their support, advice, and encouragement throughout the entire writing and editing process, thank you to my parents, André and Danielle, for their continued guidance and weekly babysitting to allow writing time. Your excitement for this book and continued support has kept me going when I wasn't sure I could.

Thank you to my wonderfully insightful and hardworking sister, Karine, for all your magical editorial work and your constant encouragement.

Thank you to my daughter, Melissa, who inspired the infertility and adoption parts of this story. You are so loved.

I am also unbelievably grateful to my talented and dedicated beta readers, John Young, Danielle Landry, André Landry, Karine Landry, Melanie Mackay, Lori Forstinger, Anne Landry, and Laura Porc for helping me tie up the loose ends and giving me your opinions on various elements of the story.

A special thank you to author and friend, Natalie Banks, for cheering me on, reading my first draft, and providing support along the way. Thank you for teaching me so much.

Thank you to author Sheena Kamal for your early advice on novel writing and publication.

Thank you, Sherry Torchinsky, my exceptional editor, for revising and polishing my manuscript, and making it what it is today.

For their professional insights, thank you to the two Ottawa police officers I interviewed and consulted spontaneously during their lunch at Tim Hortons—needless to say that any legal or investigation errors are entirely of my own making.

Thank you to each and every one of my friends and family for being my biggest cheerleaders.

All the booksellers, librarians, bookstagrammers, and social media friends who encouraged me along the way, and who kept me accountable to get to the finish line. You are too numerous to mention here but I know I could not possibly do this without you.

And, of course, to my readers. Without you, none of these pages would live beyond my computer screen. Thank you for believing in me and supporting my work and for your lovely messages on my website, Facebook, and Instagram.

ABOUT THE AUTHOR

Michelle Young is the author of two poetry books, *Salt & Light* (2017) and *Without Fear* (2019). She received an Honours BA major in psychology, and a minor in communications from the University of Ottawa in 2009. Young lives in Ottawa, Canada with her husband and daughter. Your Move is her debut novel.

If you enjoyed this book, please make sure to leave a review and follow Michelle Young on Facebook, Instagram and Goodreads.

Facebook.com/michelleyoungauthor

Instagram @michelleyoungauthor

www.michelleyoungauthor.com

Made in the
USA
Middletown, DE